trust

NEW YORK TIMES BESTSELLING AUTHOR

KYLIE SCOTT

Trust / Kylie Scott – 1st ed.
Library of Congress Cataloging-in-Publication Data
ISBN-13: 978-1546768098 | ISBN-10: 1546768092

"THE MOST
COMMON FORM
OF DESPAIR
IS NOT BEING
WHO YOU ARE."

– Soren Kierkegaard

playlist

"(Don't Fear) The Reaper" – Blue Oyster Cult

"Bad Habit" – The Kooks

"I Wanna Be Sedated" – Ramones

"Girls" – The 1975

"Get It On" – T. Rex

"Liability" – Lorde

"Heart of Glass" – Blondie

"Teen Idle" – Marina and the Diamonds

"What Is and What Should Never Be" – Led Zeppelin

"Adore" – Amy Shark

"Because the Night" – Patti Smith

"Tear in My Heart" – Twenty One Pilots

chapter
one

"Don't forget the corn chips!" yelled Georgia, hanging out of her car window.

"Got it."

"And hot salsa, Edie. None of that mild crap, you coward."

I flipped her off and kept walking, watching the ground.

Rain had turned every pothole in the Drop Stop's parking lot into a mini-swamp. We were finally out of a drought, so yay for rain. Bottle caps and cigarette stubs were floating like tiny boats on murky waters. The Northern California wind made waves, blurring the yellow light reflecting off the Open sign. Everything else was dark. Things were quiet in Auburn around midnight. Georgia and I were forced to drive across town to meet our movie marathon snacking needs. Watching all eight Harry Potter films in a row being our contribution as citizens of the Endurance Capital of the world.

"Oh, Oreos!"

As if I'd forget the Oreos, I said to myself, entering the shitty little store.

What you're most likely to drop at the Drop Stop are your standards. And I had. It had been my black yoga pants, a sports bra, and a baggy old blue T-shirt versus Georgia's satin unicorn-print slip. In the jammies most likely to be mistaken for normal clothing competition, I was the clear winner. I don't think it occurred to either of us to actually bother getting dressed. Too much effort for summer break.

Inside, the fluorescent lights were dazzling, the air-conditioning cold enough to give me goose bumps. But there it was. An aisle's worth of every bad food choice you could possibly make and as my ass could testify, I'd made them all. Happily and repeatedly.

I grabbed a plastic shopping basket and got busy.

There were only a couple of other customers. A tall guy in a black hoodie and some other kid, talking in low voices, over by the beer fridge. I highly doubted either one of them was of legal age to be drinking. One of the local college students manned the shop counter, identifiable by the textbook he'd chosen to hide behind. Note to self: Study like crazy all through senior year if you want an offer from Berkeley.

Hershey bars, Reese's Pieces, Oreos, Gummy Bears, Milk Duds, Skittles, Twinkies, Doritos, and a jar of salsa. The bottle proclaimed it to be hotter than hell; there was even a demon dancing on the side. It all went into the basket, each and every major processed food group represented. Still, there was a little room left and it'd be silly not to go all in since we'd driven to the other side of town. Why, it'd take a good ten to fifteen minutes at least just to get back to Georgia's parents' place. Sustenance for the journey alone would be required.

A tube of Pringles for good luck and prosperity, and we were done.

I dumped my basket on the counter, making college boy jump. Guess he'd been seriously engrossed in his studies. Startled brown eyes gawked at me from behind wire-rimmed glasses.

Shit, he was cute.

Immediately, I turned away, only to be facing an entire stand of titty magazines. Wow. I sincerely hoped a percentage of sales went toward helping women with lower-back problems. Some of those breasts were scarily big. Nothing much could be seen through the filthy window, but it might have started raining again. So wearing flip-flops had probably been a mistake.

Beep, beep, beep went the sales register, adding up my purchases. Excellent. Cute clerk guy and I were ignoring each other. No further eye contact was made. This was the best of all possible outcomes. Human interactions in general were a trial, but attractive people were far and away the worst. They unnerved me. I always started sweating and turning red, my brain an empty, useless place.

All of my loot got shoved into a thin white plastic bag, guaranteed to tear halfway across the parking lot.

Never mind. I'd hold it against my front, stretch the bottom of my T-shirt out to bolster it or something. Easier than asking him to double-bag it.

I shoved the money in his vague direction, mumbled thank you, and got moving. Mission accomplished.

Except a scrawny guy entering the store was in an even bigger hurry than me. We collided and I lost, my flip-flops sliding out from under me, thanks to the wet floor. I stumbled back into the shelving before dropping, hitting the cold, hard ground. The plastic bag broke and shit went everywhere. *Fother mucker.*

"Awesome," I muttered sarcastically. Followed up fast with a sarcastic, "I'm fine. No problem."

How embarrassing. Not that anyone was paying me any attention. Must have caught a metal edge on the way down because I had a scratch on my waist. It stung like a bitch, both it and my bruised ass.

College boy gasped. Fair enough. I'd be pissed too if some fat chick in pajamas started throwing her stuff everywhere. But the douche canoe who'd sent me reeling slammed his hand onto the counter, snarling something, as college boy stuttered, "P-please. D-d-don't."

I froze, realizing this wasn't about me crashing into the shelf.

Not even a little bit.

College boy fumbled with the register, panic written all over his face. This was wrong. All of it. Time slowed as the kid punched register buttons, tears flowing down his face because it wouldn't open for some reason. Skinny guy was shouting and waving something in the air like he'd lost his mind.

Suddenly the drawer flew open with a discordant little jingle.

College boy grabbed a wad of cash, shoving it into a plastic bag as the skinny guy slammed a hand down on the counter again, full of frustration and anger. Then the scream of a police siren split the air and I heard tires screech. I watched in horror as a battered car careened out of the parking lot, knocking over a garbage can and spilling trash across the pavement. A cop car followed it over the curb as another came to a halt in front of the store, lights blazing.

The man at the counter spun toward the parking lot, yelling something indecipherable as he twitched, his eyes messed up, pupils swollen and huge. Red patches—sores —covered his face, and his teeth were nothing more than rotting stumps. Then I saw the gun in his hand and my heart stopped.

There was a gun. A *gun*. This was happening, right here. Right now.

Red and blue lights flashed through the filthy windows and I sat stunned, my eyes wide, nothing computing. It was all moving so fast. I saw the instant the gunman realized he'd been left behind, because his whole body jerked. The gun wavered and then he turned on the college guy.

For one second they stood frozen, one shaking in terror as the other pointed his weapon. Then a loud cracking noise filled the air. College boy fell. It looked like someone had thrown a bucket of crimson paint across the rack of cigarettes.

The sound of sirens grew louder as more cars surrounded the building.

"You bitch!" the man screamed, even louder than the siren and the ringing in my ears. "*Joanna, you fucking bitch!* You weren't supposed to leave! *Get back here!*"

I couldn't breathe. Throat shut tight, I stayed cowering on the floor.

He turned back to the mess of blood behind the counter and swore long and hard.

"Put down the weapon," said a woman's voice through a loudspeaker. "Put it down slowly and come out with your hands in the air where we can see them."

Heavy, mud-splattered brown boots smacked against the floor, coming at me. *Oh, no.* I had to reason with him, talk him down somehow. But my brain remained stalled, my body shaking. He might've been skinny, but he easily dragged me to my feet, the grip on my arm strong enough to break me in two.

"Get up." A hand fisted painfully in my hair, the hot muzzle of the gun shoved beneath my chin. "Get to the door."

Step by shuffling step we moved forward as he used me as a human shield. I almost tripped on my Pringles, the tube rolling beneath my foot, messing with my balance. His grip tore at my long blond hair, ripping a chunk free. Tears of agony flowed down my cheeks.

"We can end this without any more violence," said the policewoman, voice crackling. "Let her go."

The headlights were blinding, lighting up the rain. I could make out the shadow of a head, one of the cops half-crouched behind a car door, arms extended with a gun in hand. Georgia was out there somewhere. God, I hoped she was safe.

"We've got both exits covered. Let her go and put down the weapon," she repeated. "We can still end this peacefully."

Pain tore at my scalp again as he pulled my hair, shoving the gun into my mouth. My teeth chinked against the hard metal, the muzzle scratching the roof of my mouth. The stink of gunpowder filled my head.

I was going to die, here, tonight, in the Drop Stop in my fucking pajamas. This was it. Out in the parking lot, someone screamed.

"I'll kill her!" he yelled, foul breath hot against the side of my face, holding the door ajar with his body.

"Don't." The cop sounded panicky now. "Don't. Let's talk."

The gunman didn't respond. Instead, the hand that had been in my hair grabbed the store door handle, pulling it closed. Next he locked it, dirty fingers pushing the deadbolt home. No escape. Not with the gun in my mouth, trembling just like his hand. All of the things I'd never do if he pulled the trigger filled my mind. I'd never get to go home again, never say good-bye to Mom, never become a teacher.

"Back up," he said. "Move!"

The gun pressed deeper, making me gag. I dry-heaved. It did no good. Slowly, I put one foot back, then another, panting as we took baby steps. Racks full of magazines filled the front glass wall; nothing could be seen of us below chest height. Above that line, the world was red, white, and blue. It looked like some messed-up disco, colors flashing between the posters advertising drinks and other stuff. In the distance, I could hear the blare of a fire engine getting closer.

Then he pulled the gun from my mouth, pushing me to the floor. I lay there, sucking in air, trying to keep calm, to make myself small, invisible. High above me chrome flashed, his arm swung in a mighty arc, and *bam*. The pistol's butt slammed into me, pain exploding inside my skull.

"Stupid whore," he muttered. "Stay there."

Then nothing.

He did nothing else. For now.

Honestly, I couldn't have moved if I tried. When I was eight, I'd broken my arm falling off the top bunk at camp. That had sucked. This, however, was on a whole different level. Agony crashed through me in waves, flowing through me from my head to my toes, turning my mind to mush. Staying aware of him wasn't easy between the hurt and the blood flowing from my forehead, dripping in my eye. I peered out from behind my hair, the world a blur.

No movement, no noise at all. I tensed at the sound

of footsteps, but they were moving away from me this time. I breathed as shallow as I could, crying silently.

Everything turned to shadows as he switched off the overhead lighting. There was still enough light coming in from outside to see, though. Guess the policewoman had run out of things to say. The rain on the roof was the only sound.

"Don't shoot," said a male voice. Muffled footsteps. "We've got our hands up. You're Chris, right?"

"Who the fuck are you?" spat the gunman.

"Dillon Cole's little brother, John," said the same voice.

"Dillon..."

"Yeah." Footsteps moved closer, toward the front of the store. "Remember me, Chris? You came around to see Dillon a few times at our house. You two used to hang together, back in school. You were both on the football team, right? I'm his brother."

"Dillon." The gunman rocked on his feet, voice slurred. "Yeah. How the fuck is he?"

"Good, real good. Keeping busy."

"Shit. Great. Dillon." The muddy boots moved back, both coming into view. I could see bits and pieces, my face mostly shielded from view by my hair. The gunman leaned against the blood-spattered counter. "What are you doing here, ah..."

"John," he repeated his name. One of the guys who'd been standing by the beer fridge. It had to be. "Just re-upping. You know how it goes."

"I know, I know," said Chris. "I was just...I was picking up supplies too."

"Right." John, the guy in the hoodie, sounded friendly, relaxed. Probably drugged to the gills like Chris, our friendly neighborhood psycho. I didn't know how else you could be calm at a time like this. "You should try the back door."

"Yeah," slurred Chris. Straight away, he headed for the door in question, disappearing out of sight with a wave of the gun in our general direction. "None of you three fucking move."

It was so quiet. The click of the lock on the back door and the slamming of the same door a second later came through clear as day. Chris swore bitterly, striding back to the counter. "No good."

"Damn," said John.

"Not a bad idea, though...you know. Shit. Forgot this was open." Out of the topmost corner of my eye I could see Chris reaching over the counter, pulling cash out of the register. "You need any?"

"Twenty never hurts, right?"

"Right," laughed Chris, handing a couple of bills over. "Go around and grab me some cigarettes, would you?"

"Sure. What do you smoke?"

Chris huffed out a breath. "Marlboro."

"No worries," said John, moving around behind the counter. "Man. What a mess."

Squelching noises came from back there, the kind you get when a rubber-soled shoe meets something wet.

My stomach turned, bile burning the back of my throat. I swallowed it down, trying once again to calm my breathing, trying to stay still.

"What's your problem?" asked Chris.

"Slippery back here," said John. "Never been great with blood."

"Pussy." Chris giggled like a lunatic. "You've gone gray, man. You going to puke?"

A grunt. "Go easy, I'm still in high school. I got a few years to get hard like you. Mind if I grab a pack?"

"Sure, kid. Help yourself."

"Thanks."

I stayed still, taking it all in. And wasn't it beautiful that John and his hero Chris the meth-head could spend this quality time together? Fucking hell.

Chris cleared his throat. "Who's your friend? Grab some for him too."

"Ah, that's Isaac," said John. "A friend from school. He's on the football team."

"No shit?" said Chris. "What position?"

"Receiver," came a quieter, less assured voice.

"I was fullback, Dillon was quarterback," said Chris proudly. "Those were the days."

Isaac mumbled something agreeable-sounding. A match flared and the acrid scent of tobacco smoke drifted through the air.

"Want me to get us something to drink?" asked John, like he was helping to host a damn party.

"Mm."

Squelch, squelch, came the footsteps toward me. Faded green Converse, the soles stained red with blood. I stayed still, sprawled on the ground, blood puddled around my face. At least the cool floor eased the ache in my head a little. A very little.

Chris's friend, John, stopped beside me, watching for a moment. Without a word, he about-faced, leaving a trail of bloody shoe prints behind him.

"Better not go past the door," he muttered.

"No," said Chris, giggling again. "That'd be bad."

Bottles clinked against one another. Outside I could hear car doors slamming and lots of different voices. The flashing red, white, and blue were brighter than before, as if a whole squadron of cars had joined in with the light show. *Please, God, let one of them do something constructive to get me out of here.* I'd go to church; I'd do anything. I was only seventeen, still a virgin, for fuck's sake. And while I knew I'd probably never make prom queen, I'd at least like to live long enough to attend the damn thing.

"Nice," said John. "They've got Corona."

More noises. The pop of beer bottles being opened as the boys settled in to celebrate the whole hostage situation. I couldn't see the other kid, Isaac, just Chris the tweaker and John. They were sitting on the ground with their backs to the counter, hanging out. It was ridiculous. And they might've known each other, but I don't think John did drugs. At least, not seriously. His shoulder-length hair wasn't patchy and greasy like Chris's. Scruff covered his jaw, framed his mouth. But his lean, angular face didn't have the same sores or emaciated appearance.

"What's your name?" he asked when he caught me looking.

I licked my lips, trying to summon up some moisture. "Edie."

"Eddie?"

"No. Ee dee."

A nod. "Eee-dee allowed to have a drink too, Chris?"

"Whatever," the guy mumbled, staring off at nothing.

John rose, carefully approaching me like I held the gun. You'd have thought the meth-head would be the bigger concern. Then the nutter—John, that is—winked at me. Not a come-on kind of wink, but a play-along sort of thing.

Huh. I'd read him all wrong. He wasn't trying to be like Chris. He was trying to *manage* him.

"Sit up," he said quietly, crouching down at my side.

God, it hurt. Moving, thinking, breathing, everything. I set myself right, leaning back against the edge of a shelf. Gray fuzz filled my vision, the world tilting this way and that. He popped the cap on another Corona, putting it into my hand, closing my fingers tight around the cold, wet bottle. The way he touched me might have been the only thing that didn't hurt.

"Drink up, Edie," he said. "We're being social, right, Chris?"

Chris huffed out a laugh. "Sure. Social."

"That's right," said John. "It's all good."

I only just stopped myself from snorting.

"Maybe hold it to your head," he said, a little quieter. "Okay?"

"Yeah."

Beer had never been my thing. Georgia and I were prone to liberating the occasional bottle from her mom's wine collection. All of it cheap and nasty crap. It wasn't much like she'd notice, let alone care. The beer slid down my sore throat, joining the churning and nausea going on in my belly. I willed it to stay put, taking deep breaths, swallowing it back down.

John nodded.

I nodded back, still alive and all that. "Thanks."

His eyes were intense, gaze heavy. In a pretty-boy contest, he'd have beaten the now-dead cute clerk guy easily. What a screwed-up thought. Who knew whose blood would wind up decorating the walls next?

"What school you from?" John asked.

"Greenhaven."

"Poor little rich girl," said Chris, words slurred. "Bitches, all of them."

I kept my mouth shut.

"Dillon always liked the Green girls." John joined Chris back over by the counter.

"Liked fucking them."

"That too," said John with a false smile. "Said it was easier, going with a Green girl. They couldn't hassle him at school. Less maintenance."

Chris chuckled.

"What do you think, Edie, want to go out sometime?"

asked John. He couldn't be serious. The boy had to be crazy.

"Sure," I said, keeping the WTF off my face.

"What do you want with *her*?" Chris scratched at this chin, lips set in a sneer.

"I like blondes." John just smiled. "And Edie here seems cool with drinking stolen beers. My kind of girl."

Chris shook his head.

No words were safe, so I sipped my drink.

Drawing back his arm, Chris let his empty bottle fly, glass smashing against the rear wall. My shoulders jumped, the sound was so startlingly loud.

"Another?" asked John, calm as can be. Like he saw this kind of thing every day. Maybe he did.

"You." Chris jerked his chin at the silent friend.

"I'll get some more," said Isaac, voice shaking.

"Wish I hadn't left my stash in the car," said John. "Be good to pay you back, Chris."

Chris coughed out a laugh. "'nother time."

With a nod, John smiled.

A sudden obscenely loud trilling broke the silence, making my breath hitch. It was the phone. Just the phone. At this rate, I'd die of a heart attack long before the head wound could do its damage.

"Don't answer it," said Chris, body snapping to attention, glaring at all of us. As if we'd dare.

The ringing stopped, a moment later starting up once more.

"Bastards!" Chris struggled to his feet, keeping low as

he took aim. Crack went the gun, again and again. It took him three tries, but he finally managed to score a hit. At least, the ringing stopped. "I'm just...just going to wait. Joanna, she'll come back. She'll have a plan. She's always got a plan. Probably have to ram a window or something, I don't know."

Isaac returned, handing out more beers.

"Cool," said John, lighting up another cigarette and exhaling a ring of smoke.

"You can go then." Chris smiled, flashing a mouthful of black and broken teeth. "We just have to wait."

John licked his lips. "You didn't want to get rid of Edie now?"

Frown in place, Chris turned his head. "Why the fuck would I do that?"

"Like you said, useless Green girl. We don't need her," said John, voice smooth, compelling. "Bet you she'll panic and mess things up, make shit difficult for you. Might as well send her out, right?"

"Wrong!" Faster than I'd thought possible, Chris grabbed the younger boy. "What the fuck you playing at? You think I'm stupid?"

"No, no. Wha—"

"Shut your fucking mouth," Chris snarled, his fingers tightening around the gun. "She's the only real hostage I've got. You think the cops would give a shit if I killed your drugged-up ass right now?"

"I won't panic," I said, not stopping to think. "I prom-ise."

Face lined, gaze angry and a little confused, Chris turned my way.

"We just have to wait for Joanna," I continued, my breath coming fast. "Thank you...thanks for the beer."

Slowly, Chris eased back, the fury falling from his face. "That's right. We just have to wait for Joanna."

I didn't risk looking directly at John, to thank him for trying to help, to see if he was all right. Eyes down and mouth shut, that was safest.

"Won't be long now," Chris mumbled as if to himself. "It'll all be over."

chapter
two

I don't know how long I sat there sipping beer. Long enough for my head to stop bleeding, if not to stop aching. The whole County Sheriff's Office must have been out there by now, given the bright slivers of light shining in, the hum of a crowd.

A while back, Chris had started scratching, opening up sores. His trembling had also gotten worse. Calm as can be, John kept talking, telling stories he'd heard from his brother, asking after people they had in common. Empty beer bottles collected around us and his voice went on and on, husky and low. Probably on account of all of the smoking. The friend, Isaac, didn't utter another peep.

"Chris, son," said a man over a megaphone. "It's Sheriff Albertson here. I've had a talk with Joanna—I know this was all an accident."

"Jo?" Chris scrambled over to the front glass wall on his hands and knees, still gripping the gun. He peeked out from behind the safety of the magazine stands.

"Why don't we talk this over, just you and me?"

"No!" cried the tweaker, pulling at his short hair. "She's not...I can't see her."

John said nothing. His eyes were glued on Chris.

I couldn't stop the shaking, first in my arms, then my legs. *Please, please, please. Somebody get me out of here.*

"Get up." Chris rose to a stoop, standing over me. "Move, you fat bitch! Time to show these fuckers that I'm serious."

"N-no. Please."

He knocked the almost-empty beer bottle out of my hand, sending it spinning across the floor. Again he went for my hair, dragging me up to my feet. A cry caught in my throat, chunks of hair tearing out. I grasped for his hand, trying to ease the grip he had on me, the way he ripped at my scalp.

"Hurry up," he said, and the flat of his hand smacked against my face.

Blood dribbled from my nose, putting the taste of copper on my tongue. The right side of my face was throbbing. He shoved me toward the door, the gun pressed hard against my spine.

"Open it."

I squinted, staring out into the night. It was hard to see much. There was a lot of light, so many people out there, watching. No one doing a goddamn thing to help. All of me shook, tears, blood, and snot dripping down my face. My hands fumbled over the deadbolt, fingers numb. Then I flicked the lock, pushing the door outward. I held it open with one hand.

Chris's arm came around me, his hold like a lover's. Give or take the gun shoved under my chin.

"I want Joanna!" he said, yelling the words loud in my ear.

"Chris—" the sheriff started in his nice, calm voice.

"Now. Bring her out."

"She's not here, Chris. That's going to take a little time."

Behind me, Chris swore. "No. You get her here now."

"If I bring her out here, you need to do something for me. Why don't you let the girl go?"

Chris's response was less than happy. I was sickened by the rancid smell of him, and the sound of him breathing hard and muttering to himself echoed in my head, through my hollow bones.

"You're not listening to me. I'm in charge...*I* am. You need to see that."

"Chris—"

"Shut up! I didn't want to have to do this!" he shouted. "This is your fault."

I swayed, and pee ran down the inside of my legs, beyond my control. It puddled in my flip-flops.

"Hold on. Okay," rushed the sheriff. "I'm making the call right now. Let's keep calm."

Wonder if my mom was out there? I hoped not.

Something seemed to move in the shadows beside us. I couldn't see. All of the lights were blinding, intensifying the pounding in my face and the pressure of the gun. Chris tightened his hold on my ponytail. Finger on the trigger and still hiding behind me, he pointed the gun out in the direction of the sheriff's voice.

"You bring Jo here," he said. "And her car, too."

"Okay. Whatever you want, Chris."

"I've got three. And I will blow their fucking heads off, one by one, if you—"

John hit us from side on. Chris came down hard on my back as I struck the ground. The heavy shop door swung shut. A knee dug into my spine and Chris's weight lifted as he tried to rise. But another body, Isaac, joined in, arms punching and legs kicking, fighting for control. We were all tangled up, in each other's way. They might have been aiming for Chris, but I caught more than my fair share of punches. John's tackle had knocked Chris forward, however, and I was no longer pinned completely beneath him. Sheer terror drove my muscles. I struggled to get free, squirming and pushing out from under Chris's writhing hips and legs. Just above me, Isaac was desperately clutching at Chris's waving arm, trying to get the gun off him.

Meanwhile, John rained punches down on Chris's face, turning it to a bloody pulp. The pistol went off, the sound deafening. Someone screamed in pain, and blood painted the air for the second time this evening. Chris's weight shifted at the shot, and for a split second there was space for me to squirm out from under him. Free at last, I scrambled onto my knees. Isaac had both hands on the gun, twisting it in Chris's grip. *Bang, bang, bang!* After the last retort, Isaac stumbled back, wrenching the weapon free from Chris. Thank God. It clattered against the floor, landing right in front of me. Without hesitation, I grabbed it, scooting back on my ass until I could go no farther. Blood—I don't know whose—was misting up my right eye. But I could see well enough for this. Finger tight on the trigger. Barrel pointed straight at Chris's chest. *Click. Click. Click.* Nothing happened.

Oh shit. No ammo.

The door flew open and police crowded in with guns and bulletproof vests. Bright light blazed in from outside. Two of them wrestled John off of Chris.

It was strange. People's mouths moved, yet it sounded like we were all underwater. Every noise seemed muted, delayed. One cop crouched down beside me, hands sliding over mine, clicking on the safety before prying my finger off the trigger. At first, I didn't want to let it go. It might be out of bullets, but I could use it as a blunt weapon if necessary. Hammer the asshole's head in even. But the cop's hands were stronger than mine. Eventually, he won, giving the gun to someone else, who took it away. There was so much light, so much movement happening all around.

"Is it over?" I asked, taking it all in through one eye. The other was swollen, eyelid glued shut with dried blood.

Whatever the guy beside me said, I couldn't hear.

Man, the Drop Stop was a mess. Way worse than usual.

Chris lay still on the ground, his face like ground beef. Barely recognizable. Two officers stood beside John, who had blood dripping from his fists and a long, ugly gash high on his upper arm. Isaac lay crumpled on the floor, still. Gaze blank, he stared at the ceiling. His chest was dark, something soaking into the pale gray material of his shirt. I kept watching, but he didn't move. Not once.

Emergency medical technicians were the next to rush through the door, bringing their bags of equipment. They wouldn't have let them in if it wasn't safe, I guess.

It was over. I shut my one good eye and rested my head back against the milk fridge.

chapter
three

I walked out of there on my own two feet. Mostly.

An EMT gripped my elbows, carefully steering me toward one of the ambulances. They'd been pissy when I refused the stretcher. Chris was taken away strapped down on one, raging incoherently. Isaac and the clerk behind the counter got body bags. Meanwhile, the cops were still talking to John.

I huddled beneath a blanket, face turned away from the crowd of spectators gathered behind the police line. Media and other assorted curious douches surrounded the place.

"Edie." Mom was crying, her face red and worn. Her eyes widened, horrified at the sight of me.

The front of my shirt was covered in the red stuff, both dried and new. I pulled the blanket tighter around me. "It's not all mine."

Mom was not appeased.

"Here we go," said Bill the EMT, directing me to sit on the back step of the ambulance.

Every last bit of energy was gone. My arms felt ready to fall off, my head hanging down. Bill got busy, gently but efficiently tending to my face. The rest was really just bruises. His partner climbed into the back, handing him bandages, etcetera.

Lots of cop cars. Some uniforms were rushing back and forth between the parking lot and the Drop Stop, while others simply stood around. Bill answered Mom's questions in a gruff, no-nonsense voice. Repeatedly saying we'd be heading to the hospital soon, and the doctors there would tell her more about my condition. Mom kept asking him stuff regardless of his unchanging answers.

It was all just background noise. None of it seemed real. My friend Georgia hovered nearby. Her parents had arrived too, their faces pale and weary. Probably relieved as all hell it wasn't Georgia sitting in the back of an ambulance covered in blood, face all busted up.

Two Johns were being ushered toward a police cruiser, their hands cuffed in front of them. I blinked repeatedly, concentrated. Slowly he blurred back into one.

What the hell was going on? I tried to get up

"Edie." Bill put a hand up to stop me. "Hey, kid. Where are you going?"

"I need to talk to them."

"I'm sure one of the detectives will want to talk to you at the hospital."

"No." I slowly stood. Whoa, nothing felt good. Not that I'd thought it would. But if it weren't for Bill's hold on me, my poor bruised ass would probably have hit the ground. Again. "I need to talk to them now."

"What you need to do is let me patch you up."

"No. Now."

Bill sighed. Then he helped.

"Stop," I said, voice horribly weak, even to my own still-ringing ears. "What are you doing? Why did you cuff him?"

The cop pushing John into the back of the cruiser frowned, closing the door. "Stay back please, miss."

"He didn't do anything."

A man in a rumpled gray suit stepped forward, giving me a professional smile. "Miss Millen? Can I call you Edie?"

"Get him out of there," I demanded, swaying on my feet. Not good. "He helped me. He saved my life. Christ's sake, his friend just died!"

His smile turned to condescending. "Edie, I'm afraid it's not that simple."

"What?" I wanted to scream in frustration. But honestly, I didn't have it in me. Wondered if they'd wait to continue this conversation after I had a brief nap. "Why are you doing this? I don't understand what you're doing."

The cop opened his mouth, doubtless to continue on with more of the same. Except John tapped on the inside of the car window. He didn't smile, didn't frown; he just looked at me. Blood speckled his face and stained the fresh white bandage around his upper arm. His light-brown shoulder-length hair hung around his face. There were clumps in it too. Out of the five people who'd been in the store, only he and I were left. Besides Chris, of course.

The car engine rumbled to life.

The tapping stopped, and John pressed a bruised and bloodstained palm up to the door window. Maybe it was his way of waving good-bye or signaling glad-you're-okay. But with the gray-metal handcuffs looped around his wrist, the gesture just made him look lost and alone. His expression didn't change, haunted eyes looking out from a pale, shell-shocked face. Nothing about this was okay. While I was shrugging off the attentions of Mom and Georgia and the nice ambulance officer, John was being carted off in the back of a police car.

We held each other's gaze as the vehicle slowly moved forward, more police clearing a way out through the crowd. Cameras and reporters pressed in like a frenzied mob. Once the cruiser was gone, they trained their lenses my way. I turned my blanket into a Jedi-style cape, hiding my face from view.

"Come on, tough girl," said Bill, ushering me away with a firm hand. "They'll be taking him to the hospital to get patched up. Same place you need to go."

The man in the gray suit said nothing, but he didn't look happy. Made two of us.

chapter
four

Turned out the man in the suit was one Detective
Taylor. He, along with a Detective Garcia, ques-
tioned me at the hospital Sunday afternoon. It was
as soon as the doctors and Mom would allow. My story
never changed, no matter how many ways they came at it
or how many times they made me repeat the sequence of
events that took place Saturday night. Eventually they
were satisfied. The good news was that because everything had happened in plain sight, Chris had pled guilty,
which meant I wouldn't have to appear in court as a witness or anything. Suited me just fine. If I went the rest of
my life without ever seeing Chris again, that would still be
too soon.

An unsmiling Detective Taylor confirmed that John
had been released after questioning. That was welcome
news. I kept replaying the haunting picture of John in my
head, alone and injured, as the police drove him away. At
least things had been made okay since then. Chris was
behind bars and John was free. That made me feel better.

Still not great, but better. Pain meds and careful movement were what the doctored ordered. It was hard to stay still, though, when my head worried that every tall figure walking into the room might be Chris. Shaking and imagining all sorts of crazy shit seemed to be my new normal.

When Georgia came in, she cried all over me. It wasn't pretty and it also wasn't comfortable what with my cracked ribs, cuts, and bruises. But it was great to see her.

"I told them we were only there by random fate or whatever," she said, wiping at her cheeks with the palms of her hands.

"You gave interviews in your unicorn satin pajamas?"

She nodded. "I looked like a total lunatic."

It hurt, but I couldn't help but try to laugh. Stabbing pain, so much fun.

"God, Edie. I'm so sorry."

"For what? None of this is your fault." I grimaced, trying to get more comfortable among my mountain of hospital pillows.

"But—"

"Don't. Seriously."

A heavy sigh.

Looks-wise, Georgia and I were total opposites. She had short dark hair, her body petite. Perfect for the acting career she'd been dreaming of since birth. Our shared sense of bad humor, love of Sephora, and taste in books bound us tight. We'd be friends forever, Georgia and I.

"Your TV debut and your hair is a mess and you don't even have any makeup on," I teased. "Catastrophe."

Hands slapping her cheeks, she fake-gasped. "Can you believe it?"

"Such bad timing."

"Yeah." With a small frown, she sobered. "What the hell went on in there? I've never been so scared in my life. But you were actually stuck inside there with those people."

"It was just the one, that meth-head Chris."

"Are you sure? They led that other kid away in cuffs; I saw them."

I shook my head, vision wavering and pain stabbing at my brain. Concussions sucked. Careful, they'd said. I needed to be more careful. Groan. "No, John did know the guy, but he tried to help. He actually handed out beers and cigarettes to everyone."

"What?" Her nose wrinkled in disbelief.

"It's true. I drank beer at gunpoint." My attempt at a smile hurt. It twisted into a grimace. That hurt too. "He was trying to keep the asshole calm. It worked...for a while."

"But he definitely knew the robber?"

"Yeah." Everything had started to hurt. Guess the good stuff was wearing off. "At first I thought they were like best buddies or something. But then he winked at me, and I realized he was just trying to get us all out of there alive." It was hurting just to talk. I closed my eyes against the pain starting up inside my head. Tiny little people with tiny little pickaxes mining my frontal lobe. God only knew what they were after. "John's brother and Chris were friends or something."

"Holy shit. Still, the cops must have had their reasons for hauling him out of there like that," she pressed, curious, needing to know. Georgia always asked too many questions, used too many words. "Don't you think? I mean..."

I tuned her out, keeping my eyes shut, trying to calm the pain. Just breathing hurt.

Mom had returned from getting coffee or whatever. She mumbled something and the chair Georgia had been slumped in shifted. I heard footsteps and a request for a nurse out in the hallway. Hoped they brought the good drugs.

"More flowers," said Mom the next day with an almost painfully cheerful smile. It's a wonder her face didn't hurt worse than mine. Her determination to remain upbeat was strong.

"The place smells like a funeral parlor." I sniffed.

"Don't say that." Carefully, she moved a couple of vases in order to fit the arrangement on the hospital windowsill. "There. It's from all the students at your school."

I coughed out an attempt at a laugh. Yep, ribs still hurt like hell. "Yeah, right."

In lieu of a response, she picked up her cell phone and settled back into the comfy corner chair.

"You don't have to stay," I said. "I know you've got

other things to do."

Her brows snapped together. "I'm not leaving you here on your own, honey."

"Nothing's going to happen."

No response.

Oh, well. If Mom was determined to play guard dog, there wasn't much I could do. She might even have a point. There was a big media storm happening over the whole thing. The standoff had taken long enough for some press to get there. Georgia had said there was even actual footage of Isaac getting shot making the rounds on the internet. *Bastards.* One overly enthusiastic reporter had already tried to sneak in and grab an exclusive. Like I had anything to say or was even remotely worth photographing. Mom hadn't been keen on the idea of me talking to the media, but left the final decision up to me. It was a big N-O on my front.

In my dreams, my teeth still clacked against the muzzle of a gun as I stood in a stinking puddle of urine and blood. To relive the holdup again, to tell the story—the thought alone made me want to puke. With stitches holding part of my forehead and right eyebrow together, along with all the swelling and bruising, Frankenstein's Bride would have been jealous. Why the hell would I want anyone other than the police taking my picture for evidence?

"I take it you're still pushing to go home this afternoon?" asked Mom.

"Yes."

She sighed. "Your injuries aren't nothing, honey."

"Please," I begged. "You heard what the doctor said: my concussion is improving and there's nothing they can do about the cracked ribs. And I'd rest better at home—I know I would. It'd be so much quieter and I'd be in my own bed."

Eyes narrowed on me, she sighed in defeat. "You promise me you'll rest and follow the doctor's orders?"

"Absolutely."

"I'm serious, Edie."

I gave her my best sweet and innocent: eyes wide, small hopeful smile. Then with a finger I drew a line across my upper chest. "Cross my heart and hope to die."

"Stop talking about death."

"Sorry."

With a final look of disapproval, she gave up the fight.

I'm pretty sure Mom was as keen to get out of the hospital as me, to get back to some kind of normalcy. Mom and I were a team. I even looked a lot like her. Tall and blond, but with boobs, belly, and butt, not to mention my lovely thunder thighs. Mom's been on a diet almost every day of her life. *Combatant* would be the most accurate word to describe her relationship with food. Always denying herself, taking a crumb when she wants a full piece of cake. Maybe, for her, slipping into a small size made it all worthwhile. I don't know. Either way, I didn't want to live like that. Though right then, I was just glad to be alive in general.

We got home without incident. I wasn't at the level of notoriety that the hospital had journalists camped outside it or anything. The living room couch had never felt so good. I slumped back into it. Home was everything.

Home was safe.

"That boy the police took away," started Mom, "how did you know he was innocent?"

"He tried to save my life."

"According to the detectives, he's been detained on suspicion of dealing drugs before," she said. "Among other things."

I shook my head, immediately regretting moving. Again. Talk about never learning. "Ouch. You're as judgy as Georgia. Doesn't matter what he's done before. There was only one psycho criminal there that night and it wasn't him. Heck, Mom, if it wasn't for John and Isaac, you'd be standing beside my coffin."

Mom's lips tightened in disapproval at my words, but she stopped bugging me about the topic.

Tired and bored, I sagged back against the pillows with the remote in my hand, flipping through channels. Normally I could channel-surf the day away without too many complaints. But today was different. Everything on TV seemed far off and trivial. An old black-and-white film, people arguing politics, a documentary on frogs, and some woman selling a face cream guaranteed to help you recapture your youthful glow. The model she was slapping it on looked about fourteen.

Then there was a music video featuring a girl shaking

her ass in front of the camera like it was double-jointed. Her ass, not the camera. A replay of a college basketball game came next, and then there was Georgia.

Georgia?

She sat on a white lounge wearing a scary amount of makeup, her short, dark hair all teased up. It barely even looked like her. If they hadn't kept stopping to flash pictures of her and me together, at camp, a selfie at the movies, and another goofing around in her room, I never would have bothered to look. *Oh fuck no.* She'd even given them the one of us sitting by her pool last summer with me in a bikini. It was a cool retro style and I loved it, but still. That photo had no business being on the TV without my permission.

"...she acts tough, but Edie is actually really sensitive and easily hurt," she said.

"You must be very worried about her." The interviewer, a middle-aged man with cool hair, shook his head sadly.

"Yes, I am." Her voice dripped with syrupy concern. "I don't know how she's going to get over this."

"I understand your friend confided in you about what happened inside the store?"

Georgia looked down at her hands, clasped in her lap. "Yes."

"And about eighteen-year-old local John Cole's involvement in the events?"

"He definitely knew the robber; Edie told me."

"There've been rumors Mr. Cole has a history dealing

drugs in the area."

She squared her shoulders. "I don't know about that. But apparently he was stealing beers and cigarettes inside the store. Like they were having a party. He was winking at Edie and everything. It seems really wrong to me that the police let him go."

The interviewer frowned thoughtfully.

"I just, I don't want him hurting her anymore," she said, voice rising. "He's out there somewhere, doing who knows what."

"You're a good friend," said the man. "Georgia Schwartz, everybody. Best friend of hostage victim Edie Millen. Thank you very much, Georgia."

"Thank you." She even managed to squeeze out a tear. All of those drama classes her parents put her through were really paying off.

Cool-hair man started talking about an upcoming local dog show and I switched the TV off. The rage inside me grew, wanting out, pushing at my sore ribs. Yet I just stared at the blank screen in stunned silence. How many people would see this? How much similar shit was already out there? People showing pictures of me, saying my name, talking about what happened like they had a clue. Talking about John. God, I wanted to hurl.

Mom was quiet.

"Georgia hasn't tried to visit again?" I asked. "Hasn't called?"

Her mouth opened, eyes softening as if she might try and peddle some excuse. But in the end, she didn't. "No, she hasn't."

"No," I agreed, closing my eyes. "She didn't say anything about doing this, talking to them."

"Are you okay?"

"I'm fine."

"You sure?"

"I told her that stuff in private, Mom. I trusted her."

Mom shifted in her seat, a little line between her brows. "She said she was concerned about you."

"So she goes and gives some interviews?" My headache was back, better than ever. "No, she had to know I didn't want this, not that she bothered to ask. And she doesn't even know what she's talking about. God, John's going to think I believe that crap."

Nothing from Mom.

"How could she have done this?"

Even if I'd wanted to cry, I couldn't. It might be cathartic, a release. But the wall between me and my feelings allowed only the worst of the worst to get out. Terror and angst and all of their friends were just waiting to party hard in my head. Best to keep on aiming for numb Who knew? Eventually, it might work.

A day later when Georgia finally did call, I didn't answer. I tried not to miss her, but it was hard. Next she texted me and I ignored those messages too; after reading them, of course. It was all such bullshit. Any media outlet who'd give her the time of day, she'd talked to, sharing her insights on me and the situation. Giving them pictures of us together and all sorts of personal information I'd entrusted her with. True or not, she'd already said it all. There was nothing left for me to say.

chapter
five

Generally, at home, things were better. People left me alone. Mostly. We had to call the cops on some overzealous reporters sneaking through our garden and loitering out front. I dropped all of my social media accounts and sure as hell didn't answer the phone. But at least there were no doctors or nurses constantly checking on my condition. Though I did miss the good pain meds.

After a few days of me assuring Mom of my well-being, she went back to work. Mom managed the front desk at a resort near the lake. Over a year ago when I turned sixteen, she started doing the night shift. It paid better, apparently. Though I think she also liked it being quieter. Given the new circumstances, she offered to change over to working during the day so I wouldn't be in the house at night on my own. But I told her it was fine.

At home, I could eat what I wanted, or I could freak out for no reason. Generally no one was around to judge. Just in case, I avoided TV and the internet unless Mom and I were doing our Sunday TV-series together time. Last year we'd watched *Nashville*; this year it was *The 100*. I honestly didn't miss social media, given what a cluster-fuck it had turned into. I lacked the care and the energy to deal with it. Besides, who needed it? I had my bed, perfectly positioned beneath my bedroom window for staring up at the sky. When I couldn't sleep, or didn't want to sleep, there were stars to count and a moon to stare at. Bet it was quiet on the moon. Peaceful with no people. The one downside to the situation was my focus had been shot to shit. Pun intended. I couldn't seem to concentrate on reading. My books sat on their shelves, staring at me accusingly. Every single damn time I tried to read, the words would blur and my mind would wander. Surely it was enough that my best friend had betrayed me, without my books deserting me as well? It sucked.

All of the pictures of Georgia had been taken down and thrown away. Years of friendship, gone. I felt angry and bereft, completely and utterly alone. Loving someone sucked.

Interestingly enough, it turned out that I now mostly used my phone to hang up on anyone who called. Easily done, since there was no one I actually wanted to talk to. If someone stopped by to visit, I feigned sleep or didn't answer the door. Mom found some therapist for me to talk to, and I found excuses not to go. With me barely managing to keep my shit together as is, a therapist might drag up all sorts of horrible truths.

Gradually, my bruises faded to yellow and green.

Man, did my ribs take their sweet time healing; in the meantime, any kind of movement hurt. Turned out little could be done for cracked ribs; you just had to wait while they healed. An ugly pink line dissected my right eyebrow, reaching another couple of inches up toward my hairline. Courtesy of Chris pistol-whipping me.

Despite doing my best to ignore the world, time passed. School was looming, God help me. The new school year would start again in a couple of weeks. In life, unless you're willing to run away and live in the woods and risk being eaten by bears, some things just were unavoidable.

chapter
six

"Edie, hurry up," called Mom.

"Just a minute," I yelled back, doing up the zip on my gray school skirt. Yay for uniforms. *Not.*

Toothpaste on and I cleaned my teeth, working the brush back and forth with great zeal. A little concealer and a lot of foundation hid the remaining bruises along with the shadows under my eyes. I'd tied my hair back in a low ponytail, leaving a bit at the front to sort of sweep over my forehead and tuck behind my ear. If this style didn't cover the scar, I'd cut myself some bangs. Lack of sunlight during the last while had left me sickly pale, but whatever. I'd done my best to look presentable.

"Edie, you're going to be late!"

I paused in the process of giving my molars a scrub to bellow my reply. Froth from the toothpaste slid into the back of my throat and my gag reflex kicked in. Just that easy, my heartbeat hammered, sweat breaking out all over my body. God, it was just like that night, having the gun in my mouth.

I coughed into the sink, spitting out the toothpaste. My breakfast of coffee and Pop-Tart followed straight after, stomach heaving. Going, going, gone.

Dammit, my ribs hurt. Not good.

I turned on the cold tap, washing out the sink, sipping a little water to wash the taste of acid from my mouth. So gross. The bathroom stank of sick. A slow breath in, then out. Everything was okay. I wasn't at the Drop Stop gagging on the barrel of a gun. No one stood behind me; no one was even in sight. It was just a random accident involving too much toothpaste, for heaven's sake.

"Calm down, you idiot," I told myself. "You're fine."

"Edie—" Mom appeared in the doorway, then stopped cold. "What's wrong?"

I swallowed hard. "Nothing."

Worry lined her face. I hated that.

"Seriously," I said. Mouth rinse was what I needed; I'd give the toothbrush a pass for now. I swished the minty goodness around with my tongue, then spat it out "All ready."

"Are you sure? You look a little pale."

"I'm fine."

"Do you want me to drive you?"

"No. I'm fine." I squeezed past her, a fake smile on my face. "See you this afternoon."

She followed me out, eyes boring holes into my back. "Your hair looks lovely," she said.

"Thanks, Mom." I gave my ponytail a nervous tug. *Ouch.* My scalp still hadn't fully healed from Chris taking a chunk out of it. At least it wasn't anything visible, like the scar above my eye. "Bye."

We lived in a one-story wooden bungalow on a quiet street. Lots of trees. It was nice. I gave Mom a wave as I climbed into my sensible eight-year-old white hatchback, inherited from my grandma. Edith, my namesake, lived in Arizona and was apparently going through a late-life crisis. There could be no other reason for her suddenly requiring a sexy sports car. It worked out well for me, though, so whatever made her happy.

Grandma also footed the bill for me to attend private school. I think the "My granddaughter is on the Honor Roll at Green" bumper sticker probably cost her almost as much as the sports car she stuck it on. Once upon a time, she'd been a teacher. She strongly disapproved of girls and boys being in the same classroom. Apparently our raging hormones wouldn't allow for learning and all would be perversion and anarchy. From what I saw, the gay students at same-gender schools were doing fine. They weren't having sex on the cafeteria tables, at any rate.

Eyes on the road, my focus straight ahead. I couldn't afford any distractions. Ridiculous, how a random person on the sidewalk could spook my stupid nerves. Any cop with a gun could be Chris; my overactive imagination swapped them out with scary efficiency.

I drove extra slow, but it did no good. The bell hadn't rung, I wasn't late, and swarms of girls in gray uniforms filled the hallways. Never mind. Crowds were good for hiding in. This might work out even better.

Head down and bag on my back, I made for my locker. So much noise and people pushing. But I could handle it. Deep breaths, calm thoughts, and all that crap.

My hands were wet with sweat as I entered my locker combination and opened the door. The material under my arms was damp. Eventually I'd have to deal with Georgia, and frankly, she could kiss my ass. Her betrayal stung as fresh today as it had when it happened.

"Hey, Willy," came a noxious voice from behind me. I didn't turn around, didn't need to. Kara Lamont. "I hear somebody tried to take your freedom."

Free Willy, as per the movie, was apparently the only whale Kara knew about. Original and well educated didn't describe the girl. I finished grabbing my English notebook, taking my time. A crowd had gathered, more than her usual posse. I could hear them all whispering and giggling, feet impatiently shifting, eager for action. There were always a few ready to see an uncool student get served her daily recommended dose of humiliation

But this level of curiosity went well beyond that. Awesome. The Drop Stop had made me famous, unfortunately.

"Is your face really all fucked up?" she inquired, voice full of glee. "Poor you, Willy. Though I guess it's not like anyone wanted to look at you anyway."

A wave of laughter swept through the crowd. People just loved a good spectacle. Kara sucked up the attention, standing taller, smiling wider. I knew her opinion shouldn't matter, and yet it always had. Despite my best efforts, the bitch featured heavily on the recording in my head of every rotten thing ever said to me. Every insult, every put-down—it had all been saved up there for posterity.

But this time felt different, somehow. Kara's voice sounded far off, as if she were struggling just to be heard.

"You must have made a great human shield," she continued. "You're as wide as the ass end on a truck and I bet with the amount of fat you're packing, you could probably even stop a bullet."

More laughter and even a few gasps of outrage and surprise. Amazing really. Anyone who'd been in school for more than an hour should have realized Kara was nothing but a bully. Still, the whole robbery thing had given her some new material. After several years of hearing the same insults day in and day out, it was actually kind of refreshing. Sometimes I wondered if this was the pinnacle of her existence. If in twenty years she'd look back on these days and think they were the best of her life. When she'd been able to torment people without any real repercussions because we were just kids. No consequences, not really. Like what happened in these halls didn't matter at all.

I wish I *were* a killer whale. I'd bite Kara's head off and use it for a beach ball. God knows, it was already full of air.

Instead, I said nothing. It only excited her to see the

little people fighting back against her reign of terror. Ignoring her and heading straight to class was what I needed to do. But when I turned around, there were more people watching than I'd imagined. Fifty, sixty maybe, jamming up the hallway. Hell, even Georgia was hiding back there, waiting to see what happened.

Kara stood front and center, her smile huge, delighted by the attention. What the hell was her problem? She was rich, thin, and popular, everything I wasn't, and still she had to pull this shit.

Normally in this situation, I would be able to feel my heart punching hard in my chest, hot embarrassment burning my cheeks. There was nothing. My heartbeat stayed firm, my breath slow. The titter of the assembled crowd felt as detached and irrelevant as crickets chirping on a summer night.

Kara looked smaller than I remembered her. Lightweight. Chris would have found it easy to throw her around. To stick a gun between those sharp white pretty teeth.

"Move your hair, Free Willy," she ordered, stepping toward me with her hand outstretched. "Let's see."

Like hell she'd be touching me. I'd been touched against my will enough for one lifetime, and by someone a lot scarier than Kara. My thumb curled beneath my fingers and I swung hard and fast, lashing out. *Bam*, my fist smacked into Kara's face. The crack of the bone, the sound of her nose breaking, was amazing. Pain tore up my arm, my thumb throbbing in agony. Dammit, it hurt.

Kara was crying and carrying on. Her screams filled the hallway, blood gushing down the front of her uniform. People were running everywhere, putting as much distance as possible between themselves and this mess. Even Kara's gal pals had deserted her, the cowards. I stood alone, leaning against the lockers, cradling my hand. Totally worth the possible broken bone.

Not the return to school I'd imagined, however. Mom would not be impressed.

"Holy shit," whispered Georgia, slowly stepping up beside me. "Edie, are you all right?"

"I'm fine," I said tiredly.

Her mouth opened, then closed. She looked so lost.

I don't know. Maybe I should have forgiven her regarding the media blitz and shit talk about John. Neither of us were rolling in money and they'd probably offered her a sum for selling me out. Or at least, I sincerely hope they had. Georgia was here on a scholarship. She had big dreams. All of those interviews were just a step toward her making contacts in the entertainment industry—getting her one step closer to becoming an actress. Her texts had explained all of this and more. From a certain point of view, it was perfectly understandable. But that didn't mean I had to like or accept it. Life was too short for fair-weather friends, and she'd broken my heart.

"You should go to class," I said. "You don't want to be late."

She took a step back. "Okay. See you later."

I nodded, letting her go for good.

chapter seven

"Hey, kid."

"Hey, Bill." I sat on a stretcher in emergency care, swinging my legs back and forth. Mostly trying not to fixate on the all-too-familiar sounds and smells. Hurling on the floor would be bad. "What are you doing here?"

"Just getting a cut checked out, home-renovating accident." The EMT from the night at the Drop Stop smiled. "The kitchen sink attacked me."

"And I thought your job was dangerous."

He just smiled some more. "How you doing?"

"Fine."

"Why are you here?" he asked, leaning against the opposite wall. He looked to be about forty, fit, with a shaved head. Hot if you were into middle-aged people. Bet my mom would like him.

"Dislocated my thumb." I showed him my bandaged hand.

"How the hell did you do that?" he asked, crossing his

arms, getting comfortable.

"I punched a girl at school."

A frown darkened his face. "Did she deserve it?"

"Oh, yeah. Big time. She'd been bullying me for years."

He shook his head. "Picking on other people, putting them down to make yourself feel big, is bullshit behavior at any age, frankly."

"I couldn't agree more."

"Give me your left," he said, holding out his hand.

He held up his palm like a stop sign. "Let's see that punch. Hit me."

I punched hard into his hand with my left. There was a loud slapping sound.

"Okay, there's the problem," he said. "Good news is that you're rotating the fist and punching through the target. You're a natural. Bad news is that thumb."

Gently, he rolled my fingers over, then stretched my good thumb out along the bottom against my palm.

"Like that," he said. "Thumb on the outside backing up your fingers, okay?"

"Okay."

"You want to hit with those two bad boys right there," he said, tapping my front two knuckles. "Anything else will just get you back here again with a dislocation or fracture. Got it?"

"Got it. Thanks."

"I didn't show you that."

"Of course not." I smiled. "Say, you single? Like girls?"

"I'm a little old for you."

"I was thinking more of my mom."

"Ha." He laughed. "I'm seeing someone. Sorry, kid."

Couldn't blame me for trying. "Good to see you again, Bill."

With a shake of his head, he took off. There was a job I couldn't do, being an EMT. Imagine picking people up, trying to put them back together long enough to get them to a doctor. The things he must have seen. Why, even that night, at the Drop Stop...and there was a thought leading nowhere good. My stomach tumbled queasily in agreement.

I needed out of this place. The sights and smells, they were all too reminiscent of that night. Thankfully, Mom had finished talking to the doctor and was heading my way.

"Come on," she said, marching straight past me toward the doors. She was not wearing her happy face. Guess she'd heard back from the school about the disciplinary action.

Principal Lee had lectured both me and Kara while we waited for our parents. Fortunately, Kara the douche had chosen to attack me within view of a security camera. Had to love an idiot for making things easy. The fact that she'd obviously started the spectacle and reached for me first had been a big help, bless her. Due to the whole punching thing, no one was labeling me a victim, but still.

Outside, the summer sun was shining bright, the birds were singing. Despite my mom's downer of a mood,

I was feeling fine. The doctor had given me painkillers.

Mom still wasn't smiling. "I just got off the phone with your principal. You're suspended for a week. Given recent traumatic events, she decided to let you off easy."

"I'm not going back there."

"What?" Mom halted, glaring at me across the roof of her sedan.

"I never fit in and I never will," I said, meeting her eyes. "Especially after this. That place is survival of the richest—you have no idea what they're like. Kara will be out to make my life a misery and I'm not up for it."

"Honey—"

"I'm not going back," I said, voice clear. No doubt, no hesitation. My boundaries were all too clear to me these days. "I'll go to the local high school instead."

Mom frowned. "No. You won't."

I felt like shit fighting with her. Usually, we made big decisions together. Being a single parent, having to drop out of college to have me, Mom hadn't had it easy. She'd sacrificed. Grandma eventually came around and helped out, but it took time. Time during which Mom was utterly and completely alone. I didn't like to make things difficult for her. This time, however, I couldn't compromise. I couldn't back down. More than enough monsters were already in my head, feasting on my sanity, feeding my insecurities. Kara and co were officially too much.

"Edie, this is your education we're talking about," she said imploringly. "Your future."

"I know. And I can learn as well at the local school as

I can at that place." I leaned against the car, resting my hands on top. "Better probably. Grandma will get over it."

"I'll talk to the principal about keeping this girl away from you. I'll make sure from now on you're protected."

"That's a nice idea, but it's not going to work, Mom."

"I'll damn well make it work."

I gave her a most dubious look.

"Honey, she will not bother you again. I promise. But also, think about it this way. There's going to be people you don't get along with wherever you go. It's an unfortunate part of life, having to share the planet with a billion or so others," she said. "People just can be jerks. I know you've been through a lot, more than I can possibly understand. But running away every time there's conflict isn't the answer. It sets a very concerning precedent for you."

"I get what you're saying," I said. "I do. But there are limits, Mom, and daily persecution kind of goes beyond mine."

Her shoulders slumped. "Don't you think this is just going to add to how unsettled everything has been for you lately?"

"No."

Silence.

"Look, just...let's talk to the principal first. See if something can't be done." Mom's brows almost met in the middle. "You're in your senior year, Edie. Changing schools now would be a huge disruption."

"No, Mom," I said, tone sharper than I'd intended.

"Nearly getting killed was a huge disruption. Changing schools would be a relief."

For a long moment, she just looked at me. Then she slipped on her sunglasses, hiding all of the frustration and worry in her eyes. "Let's talk about it at home."

I shrugged, feeling bad that I would have to overrule her. As weird as it sounds, part of me was glad I felt bad about it.

To my ears, Georgia, Kara, and the principal sounded like they lived in an echo chamber. They could talk, but none of it really mattered. I knew what mattered now. What was life and death. Everything else was just bullshit everyday details.

But my mom still mattered. I clung to that.

chapter
eight

The local public high school had a lot more students than my former private one. Hopefully this would give me more opportunities to blend in and hide. Plus, three weeks had gone by since the Drop Stop, so it was old news. People had to have moved on by now. At least, no one seemed to be paying me any attention as I wandered down a hallway, map, class schedule, and other assorted paperwork in hand.

"Edie!" a voice yelled. "Edie?"

Great. I turned to find a girl running after me like her ass was on fire.

"You were supposed to wait at the office for me," she said, stopping to catch her breath. She was about my age, Asian, pretty. "We've got first class together. I'll show you where to find it. After that, you're on your own."

"Right." I just looked at her.

"Oh. Sorry. I'm Hang." She waved her hand in my face, giving me a smile. "Let's go."

I willed my feet to keep going when we passed a memorial to Isaac, the kid who'd died. So he'd gone to school here. Guess it made sense, if I'd stopped to think about it for a moment. There were plenty of pictures, poems, three-week-old wilting flowers, and a football jersey. It all told a story of tears and pain. Isaac had been missed and that was something. Wonder what my old school would have done if I'd died. I highly doubt the bulk of the student body would have cared. It's a strange thing, though, coming face to face with your own mortality.

If someone your own age could die, then what's saving you?

My school probably would have set up something tastefully fake. This didn't look fake. It reeked of loss and pain.

That fucking meth-head. Hate for him ate me alive. Isaac didn't deserve to die. They'd been crazy brave trying to save me, him and John.

Shit. Isaac would have had a funeral. The kid died helping to save my life and I didn't even go to his funeral. I'd been too wrapped up in my own self, trying not to think about the Drop Stop and what had happened. The kid behind the counter, too. He'd be buried or cremated by now. Meanwhile, I was alive and doing what? I'd gotten off easy. Just some scars and nightmares, both of which would fade.

"You okay?" asked Hang, snapping me out of it.

"Hmm?"

She looked from me to the memorial and back again. "He died at that robbery at the convenience store a while back. It was real sad."

"Yeah."

"I didn't know him personally, but he had a lot of friends around here."

I just nodded and kept walking.

"Honestly? They mentioned at the office that you were involved, but don't worry," she said, giving me a kind smile. "I won't say anything to anyone."

"Thanks."

Maybe, just maybe, I'd be able to integrate without too much hassle. I just wanted peace and quiet. A girl could dream.

All the way to English, Hang kept up a flow of light conversation. The kind of things they'd been working on in class, how many students were at the school, when the football and basketball seasons would be starting. At Green, sports hadn't been much of a big deal.

It was kind of nice to have someone at my side. Or at least, I felt less conspicuous. I tried to push off the guilt about Isaac. Like Mom would have let me out of the house to attend a funeral anyway. Going to the bathroom too often had sent her into apoplexy and yet another lecture about the need to rest. It didn't feel like enough of an excuse, however. Nowhere near big enough.

"Where were you before?" Hang smiled. She had a nice smile.

"Ah, Green."

"God, you must be glad to get out of those uniforms."

"Yes."

"Also." She presented the place to me like a game-show hostess. "We have a variety of genders here for your viewing pleasure."

"Green was definitely lacking in males," I agreed.

All of the usual labels were represented in my new school: cheerleaders, jocks, nerds, geeks, stoners, goths, emos, and all the rest.

Hang was wearing a cool vintage-looking floral dress, but I'd gone for dark colors. Less ninja, more panda with my sun-starved skin and tummy rolls. Still, I was comfortable and kind of confident that I looked good. Blue jeans with a rip in one knee, black T-shirt, black Doc Marten Mary Janes. Black was such a nothing of a color. A total absence of light. Maybe if I wore enough of it I'd be invisible to public attention completely and live my life in peace. Though I drew the line at dyeing my blond hair dark; instead I'd put it in braids. Made up my face with winged eyeliner and a subdued pale pink lipstick to distract from the scar.

Guess I still had some vanity.

Georgia had taught me how to do some of the trickier braids after watching YouTube videos. We'd learned how to perfect winged eyeliner the same way. My braids weren't as good as hers, but I didn't do too badly. Most of the ugly on my forehead was covered.

"My folks came over from Vietnam during the war and settled in this area," said Hang. "What about you, born and bred or an out-of-towner?"

"Um, yeah, I grew up around here."

58

"Cool," she said.

A sudden bang echoed through the hall. I jumped, spinning around, searching for the cause. My heart pounded, my throat shut tight. Some kid slamming his locker door shut. Nothing more. *Crap.*

"You okay?" asked Hang.

Awkward. I nodded. "Sorry. First-day nerves."

"Don't worry." She grinned, leading me into our classroom. I kept my head down and followed Hang to a seat near the back, dumping my bag on the vacant desk next to hers. "Any questions, I'll be right here. I can introduce you to some of my friends at lunch in the cafeteria, too."

"Thanks."

"No problem."

I sat and pulled out a notebook and pen, hiding a yawn behind my hand. Systems were not fully functioning; more coffee was required. Too big a chunk of last night had been spent stargazing instead of sleeping. Some nights, it seemed like Chris perpetually lay in wait, ready for me to close my eyes so he could pounce. I didn't want to think about him, but falling asleep let my guard down. Funny, I hadn't shot him, and he wasn't dead, but he haunted me anyway.

Curious looks were being thrown my way. I ignored them one and all. As per usual, my rear overfilled the seat and that crappy thought could get lost. Now it was the whole new-kid, first-day-of-school thing making me nervous.

Along with the latest panic attack and my general

surfeit of crazy these days, of course.

They were brought on by anything that I associated with that night, or he who shall not be named. I'd Doctor Googled the symptoms: anxiety, nausea, sweating, shortness of breath, heart going crazy, etcetera. I could control it all on my own. Who said I needed a therapist? Mom should be grateful about all the money I'd saved her. Honestly.

Grandma, on the other hand, had been beside herself at the news of me changing to a public school and saving her all that money. She'd insisted Mom deport me to Arizona so that she herself could deal with me immediately. Happily for me, Mom had said no. Threats had been made, removal from her will, us giving Grandma a stroke. Dramatics ran in the family.

An older woman walked into the room, taking everyone in with an iron glance. Silence fell hard.

"Good morning," she said, then turned toward the door. "Welcome back, Mr. Cole. Take a seat."

Agitated whispers circled the room at his entrance. Excellent. Someone to divert attention from the new girl. I couldn't have planned this better.

He strolled in, face down and backpack half hanging off his shoulder. Light brown hair had been tied back with a rubber band. He was tall, lean but not lanky. You could see it in the way his T-shirt stretched slightly over his shoulders, the muscles in his arms. He headed for the vacant seat at my back. Like me, his jeans had a hole in the knee, some fraying along the stitches. Unlike me, I'd bet his came from actual wear.

Holy shit. It was John. My fellow hostage and eventual savior from the Drop Stop. The familiar green Converse (happily minus the blood) were a big clue, along with the bandage peeking out from beneath his sleeve.

Mouth open, I gaped at him.

His bored gaze swept past me, then swiftly doubled back, eyes narrowing. He had blue eyes and the expression in them didn't seem particularly happy. I guess a Drop Stop reunion hadn't been on anyone's wish list. No other indication of recognition was given. He didn't say hi, I didn't wave, and the moment passed.

Without a word, he slid into the seat behind me and I wrestled my attention back to the front of the class. I was probably just being paranoid, but it felt like his gaze was glued to my back. Bet he hated me after all the shit Georgia had said on TV. A couple of people were watching us with interest, but I ignored it, staring at my desktop.

The teacher started talking, but I had no idea what she said. My mind was a mess, all of my attention on him. Of course he had to go to school somewhere. And presumably somewhere local. And with his friend Isaac. *Duh.* It just hadn't occurred to me it would be here. But then, I hadn't wanted to think about him at all, or anything else to do with that night.

John. Wow.

We'd probably continue to ignore each other, pretend we'd never met. It would be for the best. Maybe.

chapter
nine

Christ, the cafeteria was loud. I doubt Green's had been any quieter; my nerves were just closer to the surface these days. A book sat open on the table in front of me, along with a can of soda. I looked at no one. I needed no one. Alone was best.

"You made actual sustained eye contact with John Cole." Hang slid her tray onto the table, her smile wide. "You realize that's my lifelong dream."

I just shrugged, feeling all kinds of awkward. Again.

Behind her followed two others, a Latin girl with curls I'd kill for and a redhead gnawing on an apple.

"Oh," said Hang. "Edie, this is Carrie and Sophia."

"Hi." I smiled.

Both girls smiled back, taking seats at the table. Instead of eating alone, reading my book, I was suddenly surrounded. No cause for alarm. I could handle their curiosity; it was perfectly normal for people to wonder about a new kid in school.

"Back to John Cole, king of the hotties," said Hang,

poking a finger at her less-than-crisp-looking salad. She settled for picking out the tomato and cheese. "Honestly, that face of his is just made for sitting—"

"And staring at?" finished Carrie.

Hang didn't even blink. "Exactly. Yes, that's what I was going to say."

"Thought so."

"John who?" I slid a bookmark in to flag where I'd been up to, because only an ignorant, soulless monster doomed to burn in hell for all eternity would dog-ear a page.

"Don't even try," Hang groaned. "You nearly fell off your chair when he walked in. Which is a totally fine response to his manly beauty, no shame in it at all."

"My chair was wonky," I said, surprised to find myself smiling and genuinely enjoying myself. "I've broken chairs before. There's a lot of joy weighing me down."

Carrie laughed, taking another bite of apple. "Bullshit," she said. "Hang said he *looked* at you."

"You're probably mistaken," said Sophia. "Don't look at me like that. I'm not kicking puppies or being mean. None of us are cool or hot enough to get *his* attention."

"Or vapid enough," said Carrie.

"Or easy enough," threw in Sophia.

"Speak for yourself," said Hang. "I'd be easy for that."

"There's nothing wrong with liking sex," said Carrie. "Don't slut-shame."

Sophia bowed her head. "Amen. My bad."

"Holy shit. I've got it," said Carrie, interrupting their

banter and staring at me with an almost comical look of surprise. "You're that girl. The one from the robbery he was involved in."

"Oh," said Hang, finally seeing the tension on my face. "Shit, Edie...I got John-fixated and didn't think."

"It's okay. John wasn't involved in the robbery," I said, voice a touch sharp. "He was just there by coincidence, like me."

"Still, no wonder he looked at you."

I frowned and kept my face down, hoping no one nearby had heard.

"The girl..." Sophia's mouth fell open. "Oh my God."

"I thought you went to Green? You know, you're much prettier in real life," said Carrie. "That photo the news was showing didn't do you justice at all."

"Thanks," I said, avoiding explaining the change in schools.

"Sorry," mouthed Hang.

Carrie and Sophia stared at me in stunned silence. Which made it time for me to run and hide.

"You might as well relax and deal with it," said Sophia. "It hasn't been that long. We're not going to be the only ones to recognize you."

She probably had a point. Didn't mean I had to like it.

"Word will definitely get around," confirmed Hang, sipping on a soda. "John Cole is infamous around here."

"Infamous?" I asked.

"Oh, yeah." Hang pushed her tray aside, giving up on the salad. "He's the go-to local greenery guy. Best weed available, if you're into that. Even the jocks respect him. They need him for the weed, and apparently he's got connections to a great grower. Plus he's badass. His brother, too. Dangerous guys. They live together; the parents are out of the picture."

"You know a lot about him," I said, mildly perturbed. "And I thought marijuana had been legalized in California."

"I may have once had a small crush on him. Don't judge me. As for the marijuana," Hang shrugged, "everyone's underage, so it might as well still be illegal."

"I heard John's closed up shop," said Sophia. "Pretty much dropped out of school society. Just spends all his time out at the old skate park."

Carrie nodded, twirling a strand of her long hair around her finger. "Yeah, I heard he's stopped selling too. Ever since the robbery."

"All the police attention, probably," said Hang.

Of course, the fact that he'd even vaguely known Chris had made him dubious. But if he hadn't talked to Chris, kept him calm, I might not be alive today. At the very least, I owed the guy a huge thank you.

"I'd appreciate it if you kept me being part of the robbery on the down low, for now," I said, trying out a smile. It didn't quite hold, didn't fit right. "I just...I can do without the attention, you know?"

"Of course," said Hang, giving my hand a reassuring pat.

Carrie and Sophia both nodded, though their eyes

were skeptical, with a touch of excitement. Whatever. Be-sides wearing a paper bag over my head, there wasn't much I could do if someone recognized me. Hopefully other people in the local area were busy doing stupid newsworthy things and all memories of the Drop Stop would soon be forgotten.

"Thank you." I sighed, doing my best to relax, to trust.

He never made an appearance in the cafeteria. Not that I was waiting.

chapter ten

Either someone talked or someone recognized me. Whatever. It was beyond my control.

The first person who approached me after lunch was my new lab partner in Biology. Caleb drummed on the table with two pens, putting on quite the skilled performance. Beside him had been one of the only spare seats in the room.

"Hear you're tight with John," he said. "Could you do me a favor?"

I stopped fussing with my stuff. "No, I'm not, and no, I can't. Sorry."

"Don't be like that." He gave me a slimy smile. "What was your name again?"

Groan. "I'm telling you the truth. I don't really know him and I can't help you."

At that, he mumbled, "bitch," picked up his stuff, and moved to a different table. Funny, just like what had happened with Kara, the words didn't carry the usual sting. Having a gun held to your head helped sort out the big things in life from the little. So, some stranger's opinion of me given in the form an uninspired insult? Not a big deal.

Fact was, lacking mutant mind-control powers, I couldn't affect people's behavior or what they chose to talk about. If I was doomed to infamy for a while, so be it. New school, new mantra, new me—and I had no fucks to give.

A moment later, a tall black girl climbed into the seat at my side, giving me a friendly smile. She introduced herself as Marie, and at no time during the class did she mention John or hit me up for drugs. Much better.

The next John Cole-related encounter came at my locker at the end of the day.

"The natives are restless," said Hang, a wary look in her eye. "People have been talking about you."

"Yeah. I noticed," I said.

"With the whole John thing, you're too interesting to be ignored right now. Sorry."

I shrugged.

"I swear it wasn't me, Carrie, or Sophia. I threatened them both with physical violence if they said a word to anyone."

"Thanks." I smiled. "It's okay. Probably inevitable."

A boy on a skateboard pulled up alongside us with a hopeful smile.

"No," said Hang, going into beast mode. "She doesn't know him. Go away. That stuff kills brain cells, don't you know? Ask yourself, can you really afford to lose any? No, I don't think you can. Good-bye."

The smile fell from his face and he got gone.

"John was the guy with the connections around here." Hang sighed. "But they'll get the message eventually that you can't help them with getting weed out of him."

I nodded.

"You don't talk much, do you?" Hang hugged a Trig textbook against her body. "I guess I wouldn't either if I'd been through something like that. It'd seriously have to mess with your head. Not to say that you're unstable or anything. Just being exposed to that kind of violence right there in front of your face must really screw up the way you look at the world, right? I've never seen a dead body. I mean, my grandfather died at home, but my mom wouldn't let me go into the room and then the paramedics arrived and he was gone. So..."

I didn't want to think about her words, so I said nothing, concentrating on closing my locker. No blood, no bodies, no nothing. I was fine.

"Right, well. Good first day," Hang said, getting the message and backing up a bit.

"See you tomorrow." I attempted a smile, hefting my bag over my shoulder. "And thanks for showing me around and everything."

She gave me two thumbs up. "Later."

Like any sane school population, most of the students took the first opportunity to flee the premises. The parking lot was two-thirds empty by the time I wandered out. Someone had stuck a flyer under one of the wipers on my car. No, it was a piece of paper ripped out of a notebook.

My shoulders tensed, preparing for the usual round of "you're fat and ugly, we don't want you here, blah, blah, blah." Oddly enough, there was none of that. Instead, I had an invitation to a party that weekend. A girl by the name of Sabrina really, truly wanted me there and if I could bring John, all would be great.

Yeah, no.

I scrunched up the paper, throwing it onto the passenger seat. The mid-afternoon sun felt good on my face, a warm breeze blowing. Someone was staring at me from a couple of rows over. More eyes were directed my way from among a group hanging by the front stairs.

The ones on the steps, I could do without. But the boy standing beside the black chunk of old American metal held my attention. God, what a car. It looked like a baby-making machine, an environmental disaster, a threat on four wheels. Any money it was a Charger, a GTO, or one of those. No way could my sensible, economical white hatchback compete.

Sunglasses covered half his face, but I knew it was John. I'd known it before I turned around. Seemed there was something inevitable about his presence, as if we were bound somehow. I don't know. It might have just been more of the weirdness I'd caught from the Drop Stop. A braver girl would have gone over and explained about the Georgia-on-TV debacle. But my feet stayed put.

John's sun-glassed gaze passed over me without the merest hint of recognition, apparently more interested in the couple of other students loitering near us.

"JC!" A tall boy jogged out, bouncing a basketball. "Save me, JC. Deliver me from this evil."

They bundled into the black car of doom, engine rumbling to life, and off they went.

So much for inevitability.

I got in my car, went home, and told Mom how great my first day had been. How much more relaxed I felt there and how I'd already made a couple of new friends. She was hugely relieved, ecstatic even. Making Mom smile was its own reward. We made dinner together and watched some TV before she had to go to work. On the whole, not a bad first day.

Though it wasn't over yet.

chapter
eleven

I was lying on my bed listening to Lorde, doing my best to think of nothing and mostly succeeding. Right up until a face appeared in my open bedroom window. Screaming, I bolted upright, yanking out my earbuds. Yet again preparing for death, or whatever.

"Hey," said John.

"Holy shit," I said, hand pressed against my chest, trying to catch my breath. Just as well I hadn't thought to reach for the knife I now kept in my bedside dresser. "You nearly gave me a heart attack."

"Knocked at the door but you didn't answer." He made himself comfortable on the window ledge, coiling his legs against the frame in an easy mix of flexibility and balance. But a hint of a frown creased his forehead.

"I didn't hear."

A nod.

Slowly, my bodily functions returned to almost normal. There remained the issue of John Cole sitting on my windowsill, however.

I turned off the music and sat there in front of him in a black tank top with a shelf bra and loose cotton sleep shorts covered in little rainbows. Way too much skin on display.

What was it about this guy always catching me in my pajamas?

In my defense, the clock read almost midnight. I grabbed a pillow and placed it across my lap, reducing the amount of thigh exposed. Next, I smoothed a chunk of hair across my forehead, tucking it in place behind my ear. Hopefully covering the ugly scar.

He, of course, despite the unusually warm night, looked cool. Blue jeans, a gray shirt, long hair hanging loose. I'd never had the opportunity to really observe him up close before. The man/boy was intimidating. Hang had been right about his face. It was something special with the sharp angles of his jaw and cheekbones, the smooth high forehead, and those damn perfect lips. John Cole was stupidly beautiful, in that he was so beautiful it made me stupid. Not that I was staring or anything.

"Sorry about not going to Isaac's funeral," I blurted out. "And the stuff my ex-best friend said on TV about you, if you heard it. We both know things didn't happen like that. I never said—"

"Ex?" His voice cut across my babble of an apology.

"Yes."

Leaning his head back against the window frame, he nodded thoughtfully. "Sorry if I surprised you," he said. "Showing up like this. I wasn't going to come, but..." His voice broke off and his eyes flitted around my room. Thankfully, I'd insisted the hot-pink walls and matching lacy princess bedspread go a few years back. I'd painted my room a pale blue-gray and begged a fancy old-style white iron bed out of Grandma. Books were still everywhere; some things would never change. But Barbie's mansion was long gone and only my favorite soft toy remained on display, a battered old bear called Sugar. I refused to be embarrassed. In my younger days, Sugar had seen me through all sorts of trials and tribulations.

John's gaze returned to me and he took a deep breath, his frown turning into a determined scowl. "I wanted to thank you for telling the cops I wasn't involved, and that I tried to get us all out of there alive." He shifted his weight on the window ledge, balanced half-in and half-out of my room. "That's what I wanted to say when I called."

I cocked my head. His short words had launched a host of questions. I asked the last one first: "You called?"

"Yeah. A couple of days after. I talked to your mom."

Huh. "She never told me you called."

"Oh." He grabbed the back of his neck, rubbing at the muscles there. "Okay."

His face went neutral. Sometimes it was next to impossible to tell what was going on behind it. Why the hell hadn't Mom told me about him calling? Guess she'd been brainwashed by the cops and the drug-dealing accusations. Which still didn't make it okay.

Meanwhile, Mom would have a meltdown if she knew I had a boy in my room. Though technically, he wasn't *in* my room, just sitting on the windowsill. Highly doubt the technicality would get me out of being grounded, however.

"Sorry about that. That's kind of you to check up on me. It would have been good to talk." I tried to meet his eyes, but settled for staring vaguely at his shoulder. "I would have called you back—"

"Not a big deal, Edie." He shrugged off my concerns. "I just wanted to say thanks. It really made a difference." He nodded to himself, satisfied, as if in conveying his thanks he had done what he set out to do.

"How did it make a difference?"

Silence answered me. His eyes fixed onto mine, and for a moment his aura of badass cool deserted him, and he looked lost and alone. And young. Despite the sharp angles of his face and the scruff on his chin. "Isaac wasn't my friend," he said, taking a deep breath. "I was his dealer. I was selling that night at the Drop Stop. He was there because of me." He swallowed and looked away, scowling out into the night. I waited him out, and eventually he returned to my question. "The cops found two ounces in the back of the Charger. But they gave me a pass on it. They said there was a witness talking about me being a hero and saving her life. You must have been pretty persuasive. I've never had a cop cut me any slack before."

"Well, I'm glad it helped," I said, "but I was only telling the truth—you did save my life."

The trace of a sad smile flitted around the corners of his mouth.

I pulled myself forward on the bed and gathered the sheets up around my legs. "Why did you tell yourself not to come here?"

"Because I'm poison." His eyes fixed on mine. "I don't want to drag you down. That's why I didn't speak to you at school. If the teachers even see us talking they'll slot you in the 'don't bother' category without a second thought. There's no coming back from that. And the morons at school are no better. They'll just think they can use you to score some cheap weed."

"Yeah. That's happened already, actually."

John frowned. "Sorry."

"It's fine," I said. "Nothing I can't handle."

"Let me know if that changes." He frowned some more.

"It's fine," I repeated. "I couldn't care less about any of it."

"You should," he chided. "Especially the teachers. I tried showing up to a math study group during lunch a week ago, and the teacher wouldn't even let me into the room. Just thought I was there to deal or cause trouble."

"That's so unfair."

"No, it's not. I earned it." His voice dripped with bitterness, and his lip curled into a sneer. Whoa. Some serious self-loathing going on there. "But it would be unfair if any of it rubbed off on you. You don't deserve it."

His legs coiled up beneath him, and his body tilted away from me, as if he was about to slip off the edge and into the garden below.

"Do you have trouble sleeping?" I blurted. "Since it happened?"

He stopped mid-movement, as if surprised by my question. Then he settled himself firmly back on the windowsill, shifting around a little, getting comfortable. Facing half-away from me, his head tilted in a slow nod.

"Nightmares, too?" I asked.

"Every night," he said. A sudden smile flashed across his face, as if something in him had lightened at my words. He looked down and away, hiding his expression.

"I heard you hit someone at your old school," he said.

Guess news traveled fast. "Yeah. That happened."

Again the nod, this time followed by silence. He seemed happy enough, settled on the windowsill, one hand hanging down. His fingers rubbed absently at my scrunched-up bedsheet.

"How's your brother?" I asked, mentally high-fiving myself for coming up with something to say.

"Ah, yeah," he said, shoving a hand through his hair. "Haven't really seen him lately. Dillon's not much better than Chris. Moved on from selling weed to doing the hard stuff himself a year back. He'll probably be just like Chris in a couple of years."

"Sorry."

"Me too." He paused. "One thing I was wondering..."

"What?"

"When you took the gun..."

My throat tightened. "Yes?"

"You really think you could have pulled the trigger?"

"I did. It was out of bullets."

His brows arched. "You did?"

"Yes," I said, offering a tight smile.

"Huh." He didn't need to look quite that surprised.

"Don't be so impressed. If there had been ammo, I probably would have hit you by mistake."

He huffed out a laugh, and it was hard not to grin back at him.

John blinked once, twice.

"What?" I asked.

"Nothing. Just never seen you smile before." For a moment he looked thoughtful, as if his words were going somewhere. But they didn't.

"I'd better go." He dropped my sheet and moved to leave. "This is a nice area," he said, making his way out over the windowsill, "but you probably shouldn't leave your window wide open at night."

I shrugged. "I don't like having the AC on all the time, makes me stuffy."

He grunted disapprovingly, and jumped down from my window ledge. Fortunately, Mom hadn't gotten around to planting any flowers there yet. "'Night, Edie."

"See you at school," I said, moving to the window to see him off, and gathering the bedsheets around me, toga-style.

"Mm." Standing in the shadows of the garden, I could just see his jaw firm in the dim light. "I meant what I said. Best if I stay away from you."

"No. No, not really. When you think about it..."

We just looked at each other for a minute. Nothing was said.

"I just meant it felt good to talk," I fumbled. "I'm glad you came over. This whole thing has been kind of isolating, I guess."

He stared back up at me, his face inscrutable. "Yeah, I know what you mean. I lost a lot of friends when I stopped dealing."

"I don't know if they're really your friends if they're just using you for dope."

"Huh. Maybe not."

"Sorry," I said, hating the defeated slump of his shoulders. Me and my big mouth. "That was a little harsh."

"Probably true though."

I said nothing.

"'Night." Then he disappeared into the shadows. Soon enough, the growl of his car carried through the quiet. I hung out the window, listening until it faded into the distance. Stars twinkled up high, clouds drifting around.

What a strange night.

I closed the window and tried to get some sleep, but of course my mind wouldn't shut up. On and on, it kept going over his visit. Replaying the conversation, chopping and changing things. The version where he suddenly threw himself at my feet, declaring his eternal love and promising me all sorts of sexual gratification, was my favorite. I wondered if I'd ever get the chance to talk to him again.

chapter
twelve

"'S cuse me." Two girls stood near our table at lunch the next day, one watching me, her mouth in a fierce line. "You're Edie, right?"

"Yes."

"I, ah..." When she hesitated, the second girl started rubbing her back. They were both in cheerleader uniforms, pretty, and slim. A couple of days of turning down every request for marijuana assistance had cooled off the interest in me, happily. But here we go again.

"You were there when Isaac died," said the second girl. A statement, not a question.

I nodded, a little startled.

Tears slid down the first girl's face, her voice tightening. "Did he suffer? Or was it fast? Did h-he..."

"It's okay, Liv," her friend said softly, before turning to me with sad eyes. "They'd been together for nearly a year."

"I'm so sorry," I said.

Familiar feelings of hopelessness and loss stirred inside. Death and pain were all shadows and isolation. But seeing the desperation of the people left behind, of being part of the debris of someone's life, it tore me apart. Behind her tears hid the recriminations, the blame, and I had no words of healing, nothing real to offer.

Why was I still here when Isaac was gone?

Small chance something special would come of my life. Fate and luck were bullshit. Things just did happen sometimes, and searching for meaning in them didn't get you a damn thing.

"It was fast," I said, fingernails pressing into the flesh of my palms. "I don't think he even felt it. He was just gone."

Lips trembling, she nodded, though it looked more like a shiver.

"He saved my life, him and John. You should know that."

"He did?"

I nodded.

"We were going to take a gap year, go down to South America," she said through her tears. "There's this program for helping to build houses."

Useless, I just sat there.

"He'd be glad you got out all right," she said.

"Would he?"

"Yes."

Silence stretched. Finally, the friend led Isaac's girlfriend away.

I'd thought I was done with crying; however, the old

scratchy, swollen-eyed feeling came easily. "I have to go."

Hang sighed. "Edie…"

All but running, I headed straight for the nearest bathroom. Not stopping until I'd locked myself into one of the stalls. With the toilet lid down, I sat and just tried to breathe. In and out, lungs moving, there was nothing to it really. So why the hell was it so hard?

I stayed there for the rest of lunch. Sometimes, hiding was best. I should probably do it more often.

The problem started with *The Catcher in the Rye*.

Sure, it might be just a book. Pages, ink, and glue, nothing more. But it sat on my school desk, staring at me, taunting me, while the English teacher babbled on up in front of the class.

"…your essay will involve giving me an interpretation of the themes contained in Holden's journey through New York in the fifties, blah, blah, blah. It's due next Friday and will account for twenty percent of your grade, blah, blah, blah. Any questions?"

My hand shot up.

"Edith? Paying attention for once, are we? Good work."

So my focus was a little shot to shit these days. Everyone had their issues. "It's Edie. And can we please choose a different book?"

"No, Edie." Mrs. Ryder gave me a tired look over the

top of her glasses. "*The Catcher in the Rye is* the book." She turned to the rest of the class. "Does anybody else have any questions?"

I put my hand up again.

The teacher gave me a sour look.

"It's just that I already studied this book at my last school."

"Then you should have no trouble this time around," she said.

"But it's pointless," I continued. "He's a depressed kid wandering around New York, having random encounters with friends and strangers, none of whom particularly make him feel any better, then he gets sick and goes back to school, the end."

Absolute silence. Every eye in the class was on me. The ones behind me belonging to a certain boy held particular weight.

"It's a work of great American fiction." Mrs. Ryder's lips were pursed.

"But it's a book that comes with a body count." I couldn't shut up; I wouldn't. I had to make her understand. "People have died because of it. I'm surprised the NRA hasn't slapped a certification sticker on the front cover, for Christ's sake."

Behind me, John swore.

"Edith." Her gaze gentled and she rose to her feet. "Calm down. That's enough."

"But what if it happens again?" I asked, also standing, heart and lungs working hard. "What if Holden Caulfield's teenage masturbatory angst yet again sends someone into a rage and they go shoot a few people? What then? It's happened before, but this time it'll be on your head."

"Edie—"

"Holden Caulfield is a killer!"

The couch in the shrink's office was comfortable. Seriously comfortable. I could have curled up and gone to sleep if not for all the dumb questions.

"And how do you feel today, Edie?"

"Fine." I slumped back into the peach-colored sofa, a smile stuck on my face. Not sure if I could keep it up for the full fifty minutes; my cheeks were already starting to ache. "Thanks."

Everything in the office had been decorated in a soothing, nonthreatening off-white. A neat line of framed college degrees hung on one wall. Out the window, a lovely view of a park. Nice.

"Why don't we talk about the night of the robbery?" said Mr. Solomon, his eyes kind, curious.

I could do without either emotion coming from a stranger. "Because it was horrible, shitty, and messed up and now it's over?"

The counselor frowned.

"Look, let me explain my open aggression to you. You see, my mother made me come here," I said, wiping damp palms on the sides of my jeans. Like I needed more stress in my life. Honestly, I could have screamed. "I'm here to make her feel better. I don't want to talk about the robbery. Not to you, not really to anyone, not ever. You see, this can't help, us talking, because it'll just make me think about it more and I'm really doing my best to avoid that."

"All right. What do you want, Edie?"

"I want to leave."

Mr. Solomon looked at his watch. "With your mom waiting out in the reception area, I'm guessing you're probably not going to want to do that for another forty-five minutes."

Awesome.

"So why don't we talk about something else?"

I sighed, stared at the ceiling. "Do you read?"

"Mostly medical journals." He scrunched up his lips, obviously thinking deep thoughts. "I don't suppose you're into bowling?"

"Not in this lifetime. You watch movies?"

"Only every chance I get."

I leaned back, crossed my legs, and got comfortable. "Okay then. Let's talk."

At the end of the hour he referred me to a doctor for a prescription for some happy pills. Guess my predilection for zombie films gave him concern.

chapter thirteen

For the rest of the week, I had after-school detention due to tardiness (a.k.a. hiding out in the bathroom during a couple of minor freak-outs) and not paying attention in class once or twice. Or a few more times than that. I'd never had detention before; I was always the bookish and quiet type. A good girl. Punching people, arguing with teachers, and running late to class...good girls generally didn't do that sort of shit. Unfortunately, I found it hard to care. I mean, what did it matter? Life went on; no one had died as a result. The principal said it would go on my permanent record. Permanent? Please. Bullets were permanent. Everything else was temporary.

Mom would even get over it eventually.

The usual array of naughty types surrounded me. One girl with cool blue mermaid hair was scratching her name into her desk. Some were reading, doing their homework. Others stared at the ceiling or out the window. Up front, the teacher stayed busy on her cell phone, probably playing Candy Crush or sexting someone.

"Psst," came from behind me, followed by a sharp tug on the end of my braid.

"Hey," I growled, frowning back at the buffoon. "Don't touch."

"Sorry. I'm Anders." His grin was wide, his hair cut short. The package contained an excess of both cuteness and cooldom.

I said nothing.

"You're Edie," he said. "John told me about you."

"He did?" I frowned, realization slowly dawning. The basketball kid who'd caught a lift home with him the other day. Right. "Hi."

"Hi." Chin in hand, he looked me over. *God, here we go.* Shoulders tensed, I waited for the usual array of insults—fat, ugly, whatever. Maybe I had a chip on my shoulder. More than likely, I'd gotten used to expecting the worst from people. At any rate, instead, he said, "We should be friends. Spend time together. Stuff like that."

Huh. "Why?"

"Yeah, you, me, and John. I like it. Let's do that." His mouth just went on and on, rattling out the words. "Is it true you lost it in class the other day and started raving about a book killing people?"

I turned away. "Yes."

"Excellent." He chuckled. "What do you think about basketball?"

"I don't."

"That's a shame." He picked up the end of my braid again, swinging it back and forth between us until I smacked at his hand. What a weirdo.

"John talked about me?" I asked, trying not to sound excited because that would be dumb.

Anders shrugged. "Yeah, he said something like 'That girl was at the Drop Stop.'"

"That's not a lot."

"It's more than he's ever said about pretty much any other girl." He clasped his hands together and put them on the desk. "Generally, I do the talking for both of us. It's become a bit of a problem, actually."

"I see."

"No, you don't. Problem is, John's gotten a bit...how should I say this? Fucky. Yes, John's been in a bit of a fucky mood since the whole robbery death thing."

"Oh." I froze.

"But still, you're not seeing my real inner pain over this whole talking thing at all. You're not seeing how it affects me. I mean, I'm on the basketball team. This shouldn't even be an issue for me. But the thing is, Edie my friend, some of us have to actually talk girls into taking off their clothes," he said, one brow raised. "Fucky mood or not, he doesn't. JC just kind of looks at them and their panties and bras go up in flames. They spontaneously combust or something; I'm not sure what the exact scientific term for it is."

I winced. "I'm not sure I needed to know that. And actually, it sounds painful."

"Right?" He leaned in closer. "Between you and me, I think it's his Fabio hair."

"Fabio?" I asked.

"You don't know Fabio? Edie, friend, Fabio's an important and glorious part of American romance fiction history. My mom told me so."

"I'll look him up."

"You do that."

"What's going on with John?" I pushed, concerned.

"Good question." He chewed on the end of his pen, giving me a speculative look. "Going to the party this weekend?"

"What party? Sabrina's?" I seemed to recall that was the name of the girl who'd left the invite under my windshield wiper.

"Yep."

I frowned. "I hadn't been planning on it. I'm not really very social."

"No." Mouth hanging open in exaggerated surprise, Anders started slipping off his chair, catching himself only at the last second. "I cannot believe that. You seem so friendly and outgoing."

Smartass. "I do dazzle most people, it's true. Can we please talk about John?"

He just blinked. "Come to the party."

"Me? Why?"

"Is it not enough that I said to?"

And I contemplated that for all of a second. "No."

"Actually, I can respect that." He picked at his teeth with a fingernail. "What else are you going to do in this town on a Saturday night, hmm?"

Sit alone in my room, read a book, and eat a packet of Oreos. Pretty much exactly in that order. And it sounded like heaven. One of the true benefits of being an only child: no needing to share the snacks. But still, I was worried about John. And getting information out of this nut was difficult.

"Come to the party and bring your other friends," he said. "Ones that are girls, okay?"

I frowned. It's not like I usually got invited to a lot of things; maybe I should make an effort to be more social and fit in. I wondered if Hang and co would be up for it. On the other hand, a party. Ugh. Lots of people gathered in one place with social expectations, etcetera. "I don't know. Will John be there?"

"Anders," the teacher snapped. Guess she'd gotten tired of playing with her phone. "Be quiet."

Lips mashed together in frustration, he frowned.

We didn't talk again. At the end of the hour I strode out into the parking lot, a cool breeze blowing across my face. Everything shone gold in the afternoon light. I slipped on my black sunglasses, then began the twice-daily routine of searching for my car keys. One of these days I'd sort out the crap in my bag.

"Hey! Edie, wait." Anders loped across the pavement toward me on his long legs. No wonder the boy played sports. "Can you give me a lift?"

"To where?"

"Pipe over by Old Cemetery Road." He ran a hand over his shaved head. "JC didn't wait for me, the bastard, and my cell's dead. Can we go through In-and-Out Burger on the way?"

"That's not even remotely on the way. And why do you want to go to the old cemetery?"

"I don't, dummy," he said. "I want to go to the pipe near the old cemetery."

And that meant nothing to me.

"A skateboarding half-pipe. Oh, come on. John will be there..."

I gave him my very best nonchalant one-shoulder shrug. Even I could feel its inherent fakery.

"Please?"

"Fine." I unlocked the driver's-side door and slid inside, the air stale. When I let him in, Anders surveyed the wreckage of my vehicle's interior with curiosity. I wished he wouldn't. Empty water bottles rolled around on the floor, along with a scrunched-up Starbucks bag and a stick of deodorant. Hair ties in a variety of colors decorated the gear stick while a couple of items of clothing covered the backseat. Mental note: Clean car sometime.

He did the one-eyebrow-lift thing again. *Show-off.*

"I take it your car is spotless, wherever it is?"

"Actually, a sad thing happened to my car and my folks won't get me another. That's why JC gives me lifts."

"A sad thing?"

"I don't like to talk about it." He scratched at his chin.

"But I kind of drove it off road and down a hill, and I guess some sedans just aren't meant for that."

"I guess not."

"Hmm. Chicks." Anders sighed, back to cataloguing the mess. "So much stuff, so high maintenance. Is it any wonder I don't want to settle down?"

"I'm not high maintenance." Girls like Kara were high maintenance. My small amount of stuff couldn't even begin to compare to her gross displays of materialism. "You know nothing."

The idiot was laughing so hard he clutched at his stomach.

"You want to walk?" I snapped.

Immediately his face sobered. "No, ma'am."

"Tell me what's going on with John. What do you mean by 'a fucky mood,' exactly?"

"Hmm, I don't know." He bit at a nail. "Feels kind of disloyal to be talking about him behind his back now. Anyway, you'll see for yourself."

Frustration had me revving up the engine and pulling out of the school parking lot, tires squealing just a little. *Go, me.* Happily, Anders kept his mouth shut for a while. If he wasn't going to give me any useful information, then that was for the best. And here I was, reduced to giving veritable strangers rides just to see John again. Despite his superior status in the school echelons due to dealing, and his general attractiveness, the thought of us ignoring each other no longer appealed to me, if it ever really had. His fault. How could I not be curious after he appeared at my bedroom window in the middle of the night?

On the edge of town past the old cemetery was a park. Obviously neglected if the knee-high grass, scattered trash, and abundance of wildflowers were any indication. Graffiti in every color of the rainbow covered the wooden kids' play castle and swings.

"What is this place?" I asked, pulling the car in beside a couple of others.

"Some city benefactors' first attempt at a skate park. Problem is, it's so far out, you pretty much need a car to get here," he said. "Kind of defeats the purpose for most people."

"Yeah."

"Guess they didn't want us young hooligans hanging around, messing up the place where the good citizens could see."

"How'd that work out for them?"

He chuckled. "For them, not so good. They had to eventually build the one in town. For us, though, fucking fantastic. Come and see."

I locked the car, then followed him down a well-trodden dirt path. People were gathered by the skate ramps, some watching, waiting their turn. Others were throwing back energy drinks and sucking on cigarettes. Music blared, almost obscuring the sound of a set of wheels thundering across the pavement. I pushed my sunglasses on top of my head. Only one person flew up and down the sides of the pipe, his body and board moving and looking like a dream.

John Cole dressed in only faded black jeans and Converse dazzled my eyes. Add in the hardness of his chest, shoulders, and arms, glistening with sweat courtesy of the late-afternoon sun, and I was on the verge of writing him bad poetry.

Cool girls clapped and called out to him from nearby. One of them noticed me watching and sneered as if he was her property and she was marking her territory. Sadly for her, dirty looks didn't do much. Peeing might have worked out better. No one wants urine stains on their Docs.

"Hey," said John, pulling up at the top of the low ramp we were standing on. One foot stayed on the board, rolling it back and forth. "What're you doing here?"

"She gave me a lift. I invited her to come visit." Anders passed him a bottle of water with a grin. "I spat in that, by the way."

John drank without pause while I gave Anders a dubious look.

"Just joking," he cried, holding up his hands. "I met my new friend Edie here in detention."

"Detention, huh?"

"Yeah." I stuffed my hands in my skirt pockets.

"You shouldn't have brought her out here," he said to his buddy.

"Why not? You know her." Anders rocked back and forth on the balls of his feet. "She's a friend, right?"

John said nothing.

"But, yeah. Anyway," babbled Anders, "nice day we're

having."

John's jaw had locked with tension.

"Okay. Sensing a mood coming on. I'm going to leave you two to *talk*." Without another word, Anders wandered off to chat with the other people hanging out.

I took a deep breath. "We could definitely talk."

His brow descended.

"I mean, if you wanted to talk about anything, that would be fine. With me."

"No," said John without hesitation. "Everything's fine. What'd he say to you?"

"Nothing that made much sense." I tilted my head. "You sure you don't want to talk?"

"Yep."

Incredibly awkward silence.

"Sorry," he finally said. "It's good to see you."

My whole body eased, relieved. "You too."

John nodded, giving me a repressed half-smile. It consisted of wrinkled lips more than anything, and God help me, even that was attractive. In the light of day, his eyes were clear blue with brown flecks, his skin tanned, apart from the bandage on his arm. He was beautiful and I...I was nothing. An out-of-her-depth girl who wore too much black and feared the bulk of society. *Yay, me.*

"I'd better go," I said, taking a step back.

"I'll walk you to your car," said John, flipping his board up to his hand, and falling into step at my side.

"You don't have to do that."

He didn't respond.

I watched him out of the corner of my eye. My brain on high alert and my hormones and dreams on overload. Not once in my entire life had I ever been so curious about someone. What went on in his head, what was his life like? John Cole made for an enthralling mystery. I just hoped he'd been telling the truth and he was in fact okay. He did the stoic thing so well. It made it hard to judge.

Bees and other assorted bugs flitted around, the music fading as nature took over. It was nice out here, despite the cigarette stubs and occasional beer bottles hiding in the long grass. Summer had a smell, but so did he. I don't think I'd ever wanted to rub my face in someone's sweaty chest before.

Talk about unnerving. People shouldn't walk around half-naked unless they were at a pool or lake or something. Nipple viewing should really be reserved for special occasions. Christmas, birthdays, bar mitzvahs, stuff like that. Also, with every step he took, the waistband of his jeans slid a little across his lean hips. Not saying I was drooling exactly, but close.

Maybe I should attempt some self-love when I got home. The feeling building inside of me, this hyperawareness of him physically, mentally, and generally every way, had me growing increasingly agitated. Edgy. I don't know what.

"You okay?" he asked, frowning.

"Yes. Why?"

"Just had a weird look on your face."

Shit. "Ah, I was thinking about homework."

He tipped his chin. "How you doing with school?"

"Fine. Good. And you?"

A nod.

"Is your arm still hurting?" I nodded at the bandage.

"Came off my board the other week and opened it up again. It's fine though."

"Ouch." I flinched. "So, I take it Anders is one of the friends you kept when you stopped dealing?"

"Yeah."

"He's different," I said.

"That's one way to put it." John sort of smiled. "He doesn't care if I can score shit for him or not. A lot of the others, that's all they really wanted."

"Idiots." I scowled, angry on his behalf.

A shrug. "You settling in at school okay?"

"Sure. Everything's fine."

"Good," he said. "Thanks for giving him a lift out here. He would have blown up my phone otherwise."

"No worries."

Awkward silence.

"Anders was rattling on about some party on Friday night," I said, fiddling with the end of my braid. "Were you going?"

"Dunno. Haven't really thought about it yet."

I jingled my keys. "Some girl called Sabrina left a note on my car about it. Guess she's probably trying to sweet-talk you through me, like you warned about."

Brows knitted, he pushed back his hair. "Bree's not so bad. You should go if you want. Might be fun."

Bree, not Sabrina. Hmm. "This is me."

Without comment, he looked over my sedate white hatchback. Unlike his beast of a vehicle, it wouldn't be causing fear on the streets anytime soon. My car unlocked with a beep.

"See you at school," I said, getting behind the wheel.

"Yeah." He leaned in, resting an elbow on the open driver's-side door. "You gonna be okay with the gun lobby and everything?"

I winced, slipping sunglasses over my eyes—all the better to hide. "People have been calling me Holden."

"You were pretty spectacular."

"Ha, well," I drawled, going heavy on the sarcasm. "I live to impress. Who even wants to be boring and fit in when you can act like a complete head case in front of the entire class, right?"

"They'll forget about it." Pushing my door shut, he gave me a sly smile. "Eventually."

"Great."

"Seriously, don't worry," he said. "By this time tomorrow Anders will have done something so stupid no one will even look at you twice."

"Promise?"

He shrugged a shoulder. "I can pay him if I have to."

I laughed and he grinned, everything nice and friendly and infinitely better. This was what my days needed, more John Cole. (Insert happy sigh here.) Just as well my sunglasses hid the dreamy look in my eyes.

He gazed down at me, the tempting curl of his lips

easing slowly. "Don't worry about it, okay?"

"Okay."

Neither of us said a word. It seemed like forever before he looked away, rapping his knuckles once on the roof of my car.

"Later," he said.

"Wait," I blurted, grabbing his arm. Oh his sun-warmed skin, it felt so very good. I instantly ordered my hand to let go. "Give me your phone. Let me give you my number. Just in case sometime in the future you feel like doing the dreaded talking thing."

His face set in stubborn lines.

"I get it. Really. You don't want to talk about the Drop Stop, you just want to put it behind you," I said, stomach turning queasily at the mere mention of the place. "But you know what, I *get* it. We were both there. Sometime, speaking about it might help. Who knows?"

For a long time, he just looked at me.

"This isn't some pathetic attempt to get your number, by the way."

He snorted. "I know that."

"Well?"

Another long look. "I don't have my cell on me. Give me yours."

Moving much faster than I'd have ever thought possible, I grabbed it out of my schoolbag, unlocked it, and shoved it at him. He carefully wiped off his hand on his pants leg before putting in the info. Then he handed it back. "There you go."

"Thanks." I tried to keep my smile within acceptable non-triumphant limits. And failed.

"'Bye."

"R-right." I could have drifted in his dreamy gaze for days. Instead, I blinked, returning to reality. "'Bye."

He took a step back, watching me not so carefully reverse. For a very specific reason, it was hard to concentrate. My line of sight kept returning to him, and it took a concerted effort to keep my eyes on the road.

God, the way my heart kept bashing around inside my chest. It couldn't be good. Best if I went back to my room and tried to read a book, maybe listened to some music. Find my inner calm if it even existed these days.

Dust filled the air, stirred up by my tires. I watched him in the rearview mirror until he disappeared.

In all likelihood, he'd been looking at me counting his lucky stars yet again that the gun at the Drop Stop had been empty by the time I grabbed it. Or maybe he was just curious about me, the way I was about him. We had been through some crazy shit together. Still, stupid of me to become so angsty over someone so hot. Everything about the Drop Stop needed to get out of my head, and that included John. All we had in common was a night of blood and violence. End of story. Sanity decreed we should never want to cross paths again even despite the rules of high school hierarchy. The cool, the beautiful, and me didn't mix. Egos and bullshit always got in the way. I had to forget about him before I got my delicate little feelings hurt.

No way would I go to Sabrina's soiree. If Anders hadn't gone on at me about it, the stupid thing wouldn't have even crossed my mind. All of those people standing around getting loaded, judging each other's taste in everything, while gossiping about who might be hooking up with whom.

Nope, not for me.

chapter fourteen

"Thanks for inviting us along to the party."

"No problem." I forced a smile for Hang, sitting beside me on a low section of the garden wall. "Glad you could come."

Turned out Sabrina had a pool. The place was bikini city. Loud music filled the night air and people spilled out of the sprawling ranch-style house down the steps onto the wide back patio. Of course, there was also a keg and plenty of red Solo cups to go around. Stars twinkled overhead and the shadows of trees swayed in the wind.

"They're together?" I asked.

"Hmm?" Hang turned away from the pool, checking out the dance-floor area where Carrie and Sophia were kissing while moving to the music. "Yeah. You didn't know?"

"No."

Her gaze darkened. "I hope that's not a problem."

"No, of course not. That's great that they're happy," I said. "I just wish someone would get together with me."

"Right? Me too."

We both grinned. Before coming to the party, all four of us had gone to dinner at Old Town Pizza. There'd been no shortage of things to talk about. But Hang and I had the most in common. She too had a thing for Harry Potter and read fiction books outside of school time. Plus, she was calm, easygoing. And no matter who approached me about John, she hadn't mentioned him or the Drop Stop to me again. I appreciated that. Apart from avoiding that subject, whatever thought ran through her head came straight out of her mouth and I loved that. Why she put up with my moody ass I have no idea, but I hoped it got her some karma points.

Yet while Hang seemed like good people, I couldn't bring myself to trust anyone fully. Not after Georgia. My stories and secrets stayed safe inside my head.

We stuck to the edges of the party, watching. So far I'd seen no sign of John or Anders. Not that I was obsessively looking or anything. Mostly I just sat there sweating, worrying about everything and trying not to let it show. Appearances mattered. I'd almost died; therefore, attending a cool kid's party couldn't possibly be much worse. And sure, this was better than hanging at home on my own. Maybe. I don't know; I was trying to keep an open mind.

"Let's take a look around, see who else is here," suggested Hang. Without waiting for an answer, she grabbed my hand and tugged me to my feet. The crowd was thick. She said "hey" and "hi" to various people. I smiled and avoided eye contact. Nice to know the robbery hadn't changed everything—my social skills were still crap. Someone yelled out "there's Holden!" and others laughed, but I ignored it all.

"Want to get a drink?" I asked Hang, turning her back on the pool once more.

She nodded.

"Edie." An arm was suddenly slung around my neck, the scent of booze and tobacco thick in the air. "Good to see you."

"Anders! Hey." It took me a moment to catch my breath, to get my heart rate back under control. Not Chris, not a crazed lunatic. Sort of. "How are you? This is my friend, Hang."

"We've got History together, right?" he asked her.

"Yes," said Hang. "You asked me to do your home-work for you one time."

Anders's brow filled with lines. "Did you say yes?"

"No."

"Meanie."

Hang just laughed.

"Anders, you look hot," I said, trying again to remove his limbs from me.

"I know, right? Thanks, Edie."

"As in temperature-wise, you idiot. Why don't you take Hang for a swim?"

He turned back to my companion, doing some strange brow-waggling thing. "Shall we get wet?"

"What about you?" Hang asked me, ignoring his

comment.

"I'm fine," I said. "Go, swim. I know you want to."

She squinted, gaze moving between me, Anders, and the pool again.

"Seriously, I'm not much for swimming. Plus I didn't bring my suit." Not that I would have necessarily felt comfortable enough to do that even if I had known about the pool. "I'm going to get a drink."

"Edie, are you sure?" she asked.

"I'm sure."

"Ladies, please," cried Anders. "Make a decision."

"Okay." Hang shrugged. "Let's do it."

With that, Anders ran for the pool, dive-bombing in fully dressed. Water sprayed up into the sky, everyone cracking up with laughter. Hang followed behind at a more sedate pace, giving me a slightly worried look.

"You'll be fine," I said, giving her two thumbs up. God, I hoped Anders didn't accidentally drown her.

Cup of beer in hand, I sat off to one side of the pool, dangling my feet in the cool water. Nothing wrong with just watching. Especially since I didn't know the bulk of the people. Carrie and Sophia had disappeared inside a while back. Hang and Anders were chatting with some people down in the shallow end. Eventually, he'd thrown out his waterlogged socks and sneakers to dry. The rest of his clothing, however, remained. He was a strange one, but obviously popular. Others had a tendency to hover nearby, waiting for their turn to bask in his attention. To be the target of one of his bad jokes or to congratulate him on some basketball win or something. I liked how he kept Hang by his side, made her laugh. Given she'd volunteered to drive tonight, I could tell there'd be no leaving anytime soon.

Which was fine.

This wasn't so bad, being here. Sure, I might not be in the thick of things, but full marks to me for leaving the house and attempting a social life like a normal person. And I'd had a new book to read and everything. While no small animals had been harmed, sacrifices had definitely been made. As for staring at the night sky and not sleeping, why, I could indulge both of those hobbies right here. Awesome.

Mom had been ecstatic at the news of me going out with some new friends. It'd been the first time I'd seen her smile in days. I hated how a chunk of her happiness was dependent on me when I could barely keep my own head in check.

"The hell you doing hiding in the shrubbery?" John ducked and weaved to get through the garden planted at the water's edge.

"Oh, hi. Just getting back to nature. You know."

"Sure." He did not sound convinced.

"So you came." I smiled.

"You too." He sat down beside me, leaning back on his hands. Damn, he looked good, effortlessly so with his hair tied back, Converse, jeans, and a dark blue T-shirt. To think I'd labored over my makeup for almost an hour and changed outfits three times before settling on this dress.

It'd probably taken him all of two minutes to get ready.

"I'm not hiding," I said, taking a sip of beer. Ew. Still not my favorite thing, but it was what they had.

He just looked at me. Whatever; the boy could think what he liked.

For a while, we sat in silence, watching the party, listening to the music. It felt horribly right, having him at my side. I did my best to ignore those feelings.

"If you must know, I'm sitting down at this end because Anders was splashing around like crazy and I didn't want to get soaked." I smoothed the skirt of my dress down over my thighs. "He's like a duck having a fit or something. It's actually kind of scary."

John smiled.

"So that's why I'm here," I said with a smile. Because all of the bikinis and cool people hadn't set my insecurities to high alert at all. "What about you, shouldn't you be over there hanging out with Bree?"

He said nothing. Probably felt sorry for me or something. That made sense.

"You don't need to keep me company, you know," I said. "I'm fine on my own."

"Am I bothering you?" he asked, forehead lined.

"No. I just thought..."

He waited.

"Ignore me." I sighed. "I don't even know what I'm going on about and I'm going to stop talking now."

He blinked. "Okay."

Silence lasted all of about a minute. Probably less.

"It's just that you said you probably weren't going to talk to me in public," I pointed out. "And this is the second time since you said that where we've basically talked in public."

More frowning. "Yeah, well, there aren't any teachers here. Besides, we're not exactly in public. We're hiding among foliage in a dark corner at a party."

"True."

"So you admit about the hiding?" he asked.

"Shut up."

"Anyway," he said, holding back a smile. "I'm not dealing anymore. They'll get the message eventually. You didn't seem too worried about them bothering you, so..."

"I'm not. Really."

A nod. "That's your friend with Anders, right?"

"Yeah."

"You don't like swimming?" he asked.

I wrinkled my nose. "No. Well, not really in front of a crowd. I'm more of a non-public performance swimmer. I mean, yes, I do like the water. A lot actually, and I'm quite...just not in this sort of instance, basically."

"Um, Edie?" His brow wrinkled. "That was confusing."

"Okay." I sighed. "Can we just pretend that didn't happen and change the topic?"

"Sure."

A steady supply of John-centric information had been flowing my way all week, care of Hang. How he rarely slept with the same girl twice. There'd been great debate as to whether boredom or attempts of female possessiveness were to blame. How he'd inherited the marijuana trade when his brother left high school and moved on to other things. How he'd stopped skipping school and turned up on time every day since the Drop Stop. Due to a sudden belief in education or continued police monitoring, Hang and the girls weren't sure.

He made me curious; I just did my best to not let it show. Apparently my best sucked if Hang's preoccupation with the subject was any indicator.

"You mind?" The man/boy in question nodded toward my drink.

I handed over the cup of beer. "Help yourself. No cooties, I promise. Just plain old girl germs."

His smile slayed me. Then his face scrunched up something awful and he handed back the drink. "You've been here a while, haven't you?"

"Yeah. It's pretty warm." I laughed. "And beer's not really my thing, so...anyway. I don't know why I even keep trying it; I guess it's just what's available. Yeah. Sorry."

He cocked his head. "Do I make you nervous or something?"

Shit. "What? No! Of course not."

He just stared at me.

"You don't."

"It's just that you keep going to say stuff and then stopping and...yeah."

"Like what you just did?" I asked in a wry tone.

"Exactly like what I just did."

I laughed.

"You make me sort of nervous too." He didn't look at me; he didn't have to. "If that helps."

I stopped laughing and started having a tiny heart attack.

He cleared his throat. "You haven't called or texted me."

"Well, you didn't really want to give me your number."

"No, not at first." One shoulder hitched. "But then I did give it to you."

"True. Okay." Big sigh. "The truth is, I couldn't think of anything clever to say."

"So say something boring. I don't mind."

This boy wanted me to communicate with him. My heart basically sang with joy. "Okay."

"Anyone been giving you crap at school?"

"About Holden?" I did a one-shoulder shrug, trying to be cool. "Honestly, I don't care. It would have bothered me before, all of the carrying on. But now...it's nothing really."

"Mm." A reluctant smile crossed his face. "A lot of things don't seem so important anymore."

"I guess a near-death experience will do that to you."

In silence, he studied the party people once more. The guys gathered around the keg, the swarm of people on the dance floor, Anders and Hang having fun in the pool.

"Want to get out of here, go for a drive?" he asked.

"Sure!"

With athletic grace, he stood, dusting off his hands before offering me one. What a gentleman. No way would I be letting him get a feel for my weight this century, however. I pretended I hadn't seen his hand and climbed up onto my feet, all on my own.

Since we were sort of sneaking out, I sent Hang a text letting her know I'd find my own way home. We crept along the side of the house, avoiding most of the people. When the bitchy little voice inside my head said it was because he didn't want to be seen with me, I shut it down quick. Twice now he'd sought me out.

Up close, his old Charger was even louder, the engine grumbling and growling. It had cracked leather seats and smelled of grease and a fading pine car freshener. No air-conditioning, so I followed his lead and wound down the window. Unlike me, John actually kept his car clean. No wonder Anders had been frightened by the amount of stuff inside my vehicle. But really, my car was just an extension of my room, locker, and schoolbag. That and a set of wheels to get me places, of course.

Outside of Sabrina's party, the suburb was quiet this late on a Saturday night. Nothing stirred in the pools of light left by the streetlamps. A hot wind tossed around my long hair. To be safe, I leaned my elbow on the open window, covering my scar with my hand. I was really here, hanging out with John Cole. Hang would go nuts if she knew.

"Why didn't you give any interviews?" he asked, eyes on the road. "After it happened."

I didn't hurry to answer. The subject sat in my head behind warning signs and flashing lights. But if I was ever going to talk about it to anybody, it would be John.

He shot me a look out of the corner of his eye. "You didn't want the money?"

"I didn't want the attention and I didn't want to talk about it." Uncomfortable, I fidgeted with the seat belt, set a black bra strap back atop my shoulder. "All of the facts had already been reported. What was there to add, and why drag it out, anyway?"

He made a noise in his throat. God only knew what it meant.

"People died. The thought of turning that into entertainment for the masses did not appeal."

"Mm."

"What about you?" I asked.

"Didn't seem right."

"Did you get hassled on Instagram and all that?"

"Yeah," he said, pushing his hair back with a hand. "Just been ignoring them."

"I shut my accounts down. I kind of miss it, though. I mean, I only ever really put up pictures of books, but still."

He almost smiled.

"Hey. Did you have that guy from the local anti-gun lobby contact you?"

"No."

I huffed out a laugh. "They wanted me to be their new face, to give public talks and help them rally the youth to their cause."

"Seriously?"

"Oh yeah. I don't know, maybe I should have given it a try. I'm no fan of the NRA, obviously," I said. "But I do think meth had more to do with what happened than guns."

"Think he would have gotten as far with a knife?"

"Good question," I said. "I don't know. What do you think?"

"Lunatic like him all agitated like he was...maybe, maybe not."

"Hmm."

The road went on and on before us, the headlights cutting through the night.

"I can't even bring myself to talk about it to my mom," I said. "She keeps asking, thinking it might help, and...anyway. God knows what made them think I could give a speech about it in front of a crowd of strangers."

Nothing from him.

"I don't even want to think about it. But sometimes, it just gets stuck in your head, you know?"

"Yeah," he said quietly. "I know."

In an hour it would be the four-week anniversary. Almost a month since I'd watched two people get killed and had a gun in my mouth, John had risked death to save me, and I'd nearly shot Chris. Funny, it felt like it'd been both years and a moment since I'd left my youth and naivety behind police lines and crime scene tape.

"It's weird," I said, staring out at the houses flying

past. "Now I know how much there is to be afraid of and it terrifies me. But at the same time, I feel like if I could live through that, what happened to us, then I can survive anything. Like, what is there really to be afraid of? Weird, huh?"

"No. Not really."

"It could have easily been us in the ground tonight."

"Nearly was," he said.

"And I don't know about you," I said, twisting in the seat, all the better to see his face, "but I'm probably not going to be curing cancer anytime soon. Why do we get to live while they died? It's all just random."

"It's not all random," he said, his eyes fixed on the road. "It was my idea."

"What was your idea?"

"That moment, at the Drop Stop, when Chris dragged you to the door." His eyes flickered over me, his gaze hooded with something that looked a lot like guilt "I reached out and grabbed the neck of one of the unopened beers. To use as a weapon. Then I looked at Isaac to see if he'd back me up. That poor kid was white as a sheet, but he nodded. Just like that, in that split second, he made the decision to trust me. His *drug dealer*. Fucking insane, huh?"

"He was a hero," I said. "You both were."

"It's not random," he repeated. "He trusted the wrong guy, and now he's dead. Guess that's how it goes."

"What about the poor clerk? What did he do to deserve getting murdered?"

"What about Chris?" he countered. "Every step he took since he reached out to take his first hit of meth led him to that Drop Stop. Every choice he made just pushed him farther down that path."

I frowned in thought, my eyes scouring his face as he watched the road. "Is that why you gave up dealing?"

He shifted uncomfortably in his seat, gaze shifting from the road to me, filled with guilt. I clamped my mouth shut. He didn't need me psychoanalyzing him. Both of us had too much of that bullshit in our lives already. And yet...

"You're not what caused that situation, John. You shouldn't blame yourself."

He said nothing for a good long time.

Rock music filled the small space, spilling out into the streets as we drove. A female voice sang about the night belonging to lovers.

"What's this song?" I asked.

"Patti Smith. It's pretty old. Hell, the car's probably older than both of us put together." He glanced at the cassette slot on the stereo, sounding a bit relieved that I'd changed the subject. "But the, ah, the tape's stuck in there."

"It's nice."

His long fingers tapped against the wheel while the palm of his other hand rested on the stick shift.

"Why do you do that?" he asked, nodding toward the hand I had braced against my forehead. His gaze returned to the road. "Because of the scar, right?"

"Yeah."

He shook his head. "You don't need to hide."

I had nothing.

We drove in silence to the lake. All of the dark and silent little beaches and parks surrounding it were known to be prime make-out places. Of course, it's not why we were there. In fact, I had no idea why we were there.

"Let's go," he said, climbing out of the car and tearing off his T-shirt. What the hell was it with this guy and being half-naked?

Honestly, I just wasn't sure how much more my heart and hormones could take since the self-love hadn't worked. One moment I'd been happily picturing John's hands, John's mouth. Heat curling down low inside of me. The next, I'd been back at the Drop Stop surrounded by blood, adrenaline crashing through me in terror. Nothing worked anymore; both my body and my mind were against me. I'd wanted to scream, put my fist through a wall. I was disconnected from everything.

"Go where?" I asked, standing beside the car and watching him start in on his shoes.

"Swimming. Come on, there's no crowd here."

Oh shit. "But what are we going to wear?"

He just stopped and looked at me.

"Underwear. Right. Forget I asked," I mumbled.

Half of a moon hung high in the sky. Better than a full one for sure, but still. On my list of things to do, stripping down in front of John did not feature strongly. Or really at all.

"Something wrong?" he asked, stepping out of his jeans. "You're not scared, are you?"

"No." Yes.

"You've jumped off the rock before, right?"

"The rock?" I looked around, at last taking full note of where exactly along the lake we were. "You want to jump off a cliff into the water in the dark? Are you insane?"

He threw back his head and laughed loud and long. *Asshat.*

The sound did strange things to me. "You're serious."

"Absolutely—hurry up." His jeans went onto the driver's-side seat, then he shut the door and leaned back. "I won't look if it makes you feel better."

"Shit."

"It's okay to be afraid, Edie. You just can't let it stop you from doing anything."

I could do this.

No. No, actually I couldn't.

Oh, God.

Hands shaking, I lowered the zipper and pulled the dress over my head. Wrestled off my boots and socks and stashed it all in the car. Thank God I'd worn a decent black lace bra and plain cotton boy shorts. "Let's go."

Grass and dirt beneath my feet and the heavens overhead doing the sparkling, twinkling thing. People jumped off the rock all summer long. It was almost like some rite of passage, to be stupid enough to jump off the cliff in the first place, and then to be a good enough swimmer to get back around to the beach. I'd never felt the need to complete that particular passage.

"Do you normally bring girls here?" I asked, following behind him up the trail. All those bouncy white bits of me were out of his sight with him in front. My hands still roved, covering my chest, holding back my belly, fumbling over my thighs. Stupid insecurities. Though seriously, what the ever-loving hell was I doing? The temptation to turn and run ate at me. No way could I imagine any of the cheerleaders and assorted others Hang had pointed out as being among John's special private-time friends going hiking in the middle of the night.

"No." Amusement filled his voice. "Anders and I come here sometimes, but that's it."

"You guys been friends a long time?"

"Since the first day of first grade."

Georgia and I had been the same; funny how fast forever could end. Thoughts of her caused the usual pain, but I pushed it aside. Adventuring with John being way more interesting than inner turmoil.

"Careful here." He turned back, held out his hand. His fingers were stronger than mine, the skin rougher. Together, we climbed the rocky trail to the top of the hill and stood at the edge. Hands disengaged and all returned to relative normal.

"How you wanna do this?" he asked. "You want me to go first?"

"It's pretty dark down there. I can't see the water properly." I pushed some pebbles off the edge with my toes. They scattered and fell, eventually splashing.

"Don't worry. It's there," he said.

Interestingly enough, I'd been too busy hauling ass to the top of the hill and fretting about the fall to worry about my body. John's gaze did a quick up and down; no expression of horror or anything crossed his face. We were friends, apparently. It was fine. Still, the thought of him in the water looking up, watching while I plummeted, didn't appeal. Nor did him catching the view from above, either.

"Do you want me to push you?" he asked.

"Don't you fucking dare!"

More laughter from the ass. "Relax, Edie. I wouldn't do that."

Eyes all squinty, I gave him a disgruntled look.

"Sorry. You can trust me, I swear."

"Whatever," I mumbled.

"So," he said eventually. "What are we doing?"

"Can we go together?"

"Sure."

I held out my hand and he took it, grip strong and sure.

"Count of three, on three," he said. "Ready?"

"Yep."

"One. Two. Three." And we jumped.

I screamed and he laughed, the lake rushing up to greet us. Adrenaline surged through me, making me feel more alive than I had in a long time, but it was over so fast. Then we were in the water, submerged in the dark. Of course, I had to let go of his hand to swim to the surface. Still alive, thank you baby Jesus, blood pounded be-hind my ears. My underwear had even managed to remain intact.

John treaded water, wet hair hanging in his face. "You good?"

"Yeah. That was great!"

"What else haven't you done before?"

"I don't know." I swirled my arms around in the wa-ter, keeping myself afloat. Talk about an embarrassing topic of conversation. I wouldn't lie to him, but I wasn't willing to be specific, either. "The usual."

"Ever smoked a joint?"

"No, I haven't." And I felt a little foolish admitting it, too. "Good girls don't do that sort of thing. We stay home and contemplate God and shit."

"You're a good girl?"

"No," I said, pondering my answer. "Not anymore. I think I might've changed religion recently."

A fleeting smile crossed his face. The understanding in his eyes that I couldn't get anywhere else.

"Yeah, me too," he said.

"Race you back to the beach?"

"You're on."

"Ready. Set. Go!"

With seemingly effortless strokes he cut through the water, leaving me and my dog-paddling way behind. Not that I actually tried.

"You win," I called out and heard laughter.

Sports weren't my strong suit. Any kind of marathon

outside of shopping, TV, or reading and I'd be guaranteed to come in last. Never mind. Everyone had their strengths and weaknesses. Each and every one of us was a special little sunflower.

Coming in last also provided me with a most excellent view of John walking up the beach. Sodden dark gray boxer briefs were plastered to his butt, and what a butt it was. Whoa. A photographic memory would be so great. Not that I was objectifying my new friend or anything, because that would be wrong. And foolish.

Like an oversized dog, he shook the water from his hair. I wrapped mine around a hand and wrung it dry, following him slowly, trying to catch my breath. My makeup had probably dripped halfway down my face, but whatever. Most of my nervous energy had been burnt up in the fall. From inside the car, he grabbed a lighter and a little baggie.

"Sit on the hood," he said, climbing on up and leaning back against the windshield.

"That won't hurt your car?"

"No. But it'll keep our asses warm and help us dry."

"Good call." I carefully climbed onboard, hoping the metal wouldn't start groaning or something beneath my weight. Probably, I should have just put the dress back on. That would have been the smart thing to do. But screw it.

Flames leapt and John lit the blunt, then held it my way. "Go hard, Edie."

"Shut it." My smile wavered from nerves.

Carefully, he handed it over, smiling back at me.

Without too much hesitation, I put it to my lips and drew back slowly, taking it deep into my lungs, before letting it out. A puff of smoke floated out of my mouth and my eyes stung a little. Then I tried unsuccessfully to cough up a lung.

"You all right?" he asked.

Nodding, I coughed some more into my hand and passed the joint back. "Absolutely. I'm a rebel."

"You're badass. I'm actually a little afraid of you."

"Thanks."

"You've got to puff a bit gently," he said. "Weed burns hotter than tobacco."

We passed it back and forth, relaxing against the car, staring up at the stars. My body unraveled, all of my earthly worries and weight falling away. So my thighs were thick and my belly bulged. *So what.* I was alive and allowed to take up space.

"Fuck being unhappy," I said.

"Fuck being unhappy?" John repeated, giving me a curious look.

"Yes. Absolutely."

The side of his mouth curved upward, his gaze lingering on me. From my face to my chest and back again. In all likelihood, the boy was inwardly laughing at how red my eyes were or something. I crossed my arms over my breasts, feeling self-conscious.

A breeze blew in off the lake, cooler than before. He'd been spot-on about the benefits of sitting on top of a warm engine, and who knew muscles cars could be so comfortable?

"You don't look like a drug dealer," I said quietly.

"Probably a good thing. For the business, I mean. It's a hassle if the cops know straight away you're dealing."

"True." I crossed my feet at the ankles. "Think you'll start up again?"

"No, I'm done with that." He pushed his hair back from his face, saying nothing for a minute. "Dillon started the business; I kind of inherited part of it when he left high school. But the heavier stuff he moved on to selling, it wasn't good."

Mouth shut, I listened.

"You were right about the Drop Stop changing things. Part of me felt like looking at Chris was maybe like looking at what Dillon will be like before long. And then looking at Dillon made me wonder what I might be like before long." Again, he breathed the joint in deep, letting the smoke out slowly. "So yeah. I told Dillon I was finished and moved in with my uncle."

"You don't live with your parents?" One of the girls had mentioned as much. Still, weird.

"Dad got a job up north," was all he said.

I nodded. It seemed like some response was required.

"Anyway, dealing pot's got no future. Need to figure something else out."

"Yeah, you're probably right," I said, studying the shadows on his face. The girls had wondered over his sudden interest in attending school and getting an education. Guess this answered why.

We didn't speak for a while, each busy in our own head. Funny, the lurking signs of adulthood showed in him more clearly. His height and build, the depth of his voice, and the knowledge in his eyes. He turned back to staring at the night sky. Despite the draw of him, I did likewise. It wouldn't do to get any stupid ideas, no matter how high I flew.

Midnight came and went, my curfew broken for the first time ever. With Mom at work, it wasn't like it much mattered. Still, the good girl would have been scared stiff of somehow getting busted. Her fears were small, stupid things. Nothing that actually mattered.

"It's such a beautiful night. Nature and stuff is great. This is my favorite thing, watching the moon and stars." I took my turn with the joint, not coughing quite so much this time. Talking to John came easier every moment. I don't know if it was our recent history, the jump, or the dope. But it felt good, letting the words flow with him listening. I happy sighed. "Along with books, they're my favorite. And cake and coffee and music and...movies and shopping. You're allowed as many favorites as you need."

"Right."

"Your turn."

"Hmm." He took his go doing the illegal drug thing. "Skateboarding."

"Yep." I waited. "And?"

He frowned as he thought. Apparently he had fewer words to let flow. "Shooting hoops with Anders."

Thus he had his body and I had my body, and never

the two shall meet. Sad but true. "Things besides sports?"

"Movies are okay. Action, horror, stuff like that."

"Yes, agreed. What else?"

Quiet descended while he thought. Bugs, night birds, and the breeze shaking the trees took over. Finally, he gave a long sigh. "Honestly, I spent most of my time selling weed."

And hooking up with cheerleaders, I silently added, because jealous bitch, etcetera. "You need a new nonillegal hobby."

"Yeah." His eyes narrowed on the heavens. "Bet that clerk from the tech college had plans. There were hundreds of people at his funeral. I saw his girlfriend; she was devastated."

"You went to the funeral?"

He nodded. "Seemed like the right thing to do."

"I was taking it easy with cracked ribs and stuff." I frowned, unsure I'd have had the courage to go even if I'd been able.

Overhead, the moon did nothing. It was dependable in that way, circling the sky all nonjudgmental like, just doing its thing. Me and the moon were great friends, especially now. It kept me company during the long, awful nights. The moon kept my secrets, telling no one how many times I woke up in a panic, covered in a cold sweat.

"What are your nightmares like?" I asked.

He turned to me, eyes dark. He didn't speak.

"I don't want to sleep anymore."

A nod.

"Think of all the time we lose sleeping anyway," I said. "It's a waste. I mean, I love my bed, but I could do without the dreams."

Nothing from him.

"Thanks for tonight," I said, keeping my voice low. "This is nice."

He smiled. "Yeah, it is."

"We should be friends."

Brows arched, he gave me an amused look. He had nice lips. "We are, you goose."

And John Cole teasing me, that felt damn good too. Another feeling, however, suddenly came front and center. "God, I'm hungry."

We went to In-and-Out Burger before he dropped me home. Even without the high, talking to him now after everything felt easy, soothing. He understood because he'd lived through it too. Was still living through it. I even got to sleep without too much tossing and turning. Best night of my life.

chapter fifteen

Sunday night...

Me: You awake?

My cell buzzed a minute later. "Hello?"

"Hey," he said in a low voice. "How you doing?"

"Good. How about you? What are you up to?"

"Just give me a second." In the background, a girl asked John who he was talking to. Guess that answered that question. He mumbled something and I heard rustling, followed by the closing of a door. Eventually, he sighed. "Sorry 'bout that."

"No problem." I'd interrupted his Netflix and sex session. Awesome. *Go, me.*

"What'd you do today?"

"Ah, I hung out with my mom. Tried to do some studying, the usual. What about you?"

"Did some work on my car. Read *Catcher in the Rye.*"

I snorted. "What'd you think of it?"

"Thought you were a bit harsh about it, to be honest."

"Maybe," I said. "Though the heart of my loud, embarrassing, and irrational rant was more fear over what idiots have done in the book's name."

"Can't really blame the book for that."

"I suppose not." I hummed. "Apparently, it's a *trigger* book for me. Because I have triggers now..."

"Probably to be expected."

Silence.

"Bad dreams again?" he asked.

"Yeah."

"The one where you're flying, but can't get high enough to get out of trouble? Or the one where you die instead of Isaac?"

Crap. "I told you too much last Friday."

A soft chuckle. "You're safe with me. I get it, okay?"

"Yeah," I said, more to be polite than anything. Exposing what a hot mess I was to this cool, beautiful boy. How much more insane could I get?

A pause. "I keep waking up, hearing the gunshot, thinking the bullet's got me in the chest this time instead of just winging me."

"God. That's horrible."

Silence.

"I keep smelling blood, even when there is none," I said.

His laughter sounded entirely without joy. "I was never great with blood. Now...it fucks me up a little."

"How long do you think it takes to get past this sort of thing?"

"I don't know if you do." He sounded down and a little lost. A lot like how I felt. There came a click, followed by him breathing in and out real deep. Smoking. "Can't imagine forgetting it."

"Guess it just becomes a part of you. You get used to it."

I lay on my back on the bed, staring out at the night sky. Deep thoughts. Deep, pointless middle-of-the-night thoughts of life and death and pain and dismemberment. "I forgot to say, thanks for turning up to school Monday morning. You really did me a solid."

"How's that?"

"You took the attention off me being the new girl."

"Ha. You're welcome," he said.

"I owe you one. If you run into trouble with any English assignments, I'll help, okay?"

For a moment there was no reply, and I wasn't sure if he was still there.

"John?"

"Okay, deal." His voice sounded cautious. "Math, I'm fine. But if they start in on poetry or shit like that..."

"Understood." I laughed. "You get numbers? I've never known what to do with them. Numbers and I are not friends."

"We'll trade." Another heavy exhale. "I'm serious, Edie."

"Okay." I smiled and then stopped. "Oh. Under the

weird requests category, I was wondering, would you visit the guys' graves with me sometime? You don't have to. It was just a thought."

"Yeah, that's...we can do that. Tomorrow night work for you?"

"That would be great."

"I got to get home," he said. "You okay to try and sleep now?"

"Yes. Thanks for talking to me."

"Anytime."

Beneath my ribs, my heart stuttered. "Night, John."

"'Night, Edie."

chapter
sixteen

I brought two bunches of flowers with me. John brought a six-pack of beer. Both seemed apt in their own way.

We wandered through the cemetery, moonlight shining off of burial stones and winged statues of angels. Never would I have had the guts to do this in the dark by myself. The whole place made me nervous. He'd had work after school, so we couldn't go until later in the evening. This worked for me, because I didn't have to mention anything to Mom about the Drop Stop or why I felt the need to go visiting dead people. Both would have worried her and I was sick of being the cause of Mom's high stress levels.

Luckily, John knew the way, leading me through the graveyard without any hesitation. He smelled different tonight. Spicy, like he'd put on aftershave. And God forgive me for noticing such details in a place like this. I was headed straight for hell's barbecue, and that was the truth.

"Where do you work?" I asked, watching the ground so I didn't trip over anything.

"Landscaping business my uncle owns," he said. "Just started a few weeks back. I've gone from selling grass to cutting it. Ironic, huh?"

"Ha." I grinned, even though he had his back to me. "I have to get a job. That's next on the list."

"You don't get an allowance or something?"

"Not anymore with my behavioral problems."

"Another first?"

"Yes, it will be. My very first job. Does that make me sound like a spoiled, bitchy private school girl?"

"Nuh. You're not mean enough."

"I could be," I said, looking down my nose at him with my very best judgy glare. "Though really, who has the energy?"

He stopped. "Here we are."

A mixture of fresh and fading flowers covered the ground in front of a dark gravestone. I tried to remember the boy behind the counter, the clerk. The details of his face and the startled look he'd given me when I put my basket full of junk food on the counter. Details of that night were either scarily pristine, ingrained on my memory, or hazy and on the verge of being lost. Any moment now they might fade off into the recesses of my mind, gone for good.

"I can't remember his face," I said, adding my flowers to the rest. "Why can't I remember his face?"

John placed a beer by the headstone, then passed me

an open bottle before taking one for himself. "He'd worked there a while, didn't mind me dealing there. Used to buy from me sometimes. Always seemed nice enough."

I gulped down the cold liquid, ignoring the taste of the yeast and hops. Beer would never be my thing. Especially now that it was linked to that night, sitting on the floor bleeding, listening to John trying to keep Chris from losing it completely and killing us all. But I wouldn't let bad memories stop me, not even in this case.

"He was a student working night shift at a crappy job and he died for no good reason." I blinked, fighting back the threat of tears. Useless things, they never helped.

"Yeah."

"Fucking Chris." Hate burned bright in my heart. I'd never wanted anyone to die a fiery death to the extent that I wished it for him. It weighed on my mind heavy and dark, and churned deep in my belly. Forgiveness didn't even exist.

John took a long pull of his beer. "Come on, Isaac's just over here."

I stumbled along behind him, the beer hanging forgotten from my hand. Flowers and burnt-out candles covered Isaac's grave. Here too, John left one of the beers. I lay down my remaining flowers, staring sightlessly at the petals and thorns, the white sympathy cards so bright in the dark. Death was a stone, dragging me deep. Life had been so much simpler and easier before all of this. I'd been immortal, but tomorrow didn't exist. It was all now, here, today. Until Chris and his gun destroyed everything.

"He died because of me," I said, swaying on my feet. Some facts weighed heavy. "If you guys hadn't tried to help me, he might—"

"Stop it. Don't take that on yourself." Shadows covered his face. But he reached out, the rough palm of his hand cupping my cheek. The movement, the connection, totally unexpected. "We made our own choices, Edie. Chris would have turned on us next. He wouldn't have even hesitated."

With him touching me, I could barely breathe, let alone speak.

"Do you understand?"

I managed a slight nod and his hand fell back to his side. The loss stung.

My head filled with chaos, a multitude of questions, ifs, and buts. Answers about life and death didn't come so easy. I tried not to think about what remained of the body buried below. About what his family must be going through. Fate was a bitch and luck was no better. Yet we were always searching for meaning, for some hidden truth. What bullshit.

"It's not your fault," repeated John. "If it's anyone's, it's mine. I pushed him into charging at Chris—it was my idea."

The raw pain in his words hurt my heart. I breathed out heavily. "No. You're right; Chris would have turned on you two next."

He said nothing.

"And I'd have been dead too. He wasn't going to stop,

and no way were the cops giving him what he wanted. The whole situation was fucked. We just got caught up in it." I shook my head, drank more of the crappy beer. Not that it helped.

"It's not on either of us." Sadly, he didn't sound any more convinced. He took another mouthful of beer, stared up at the stars. "It was all Chris, the fucking meth-head."

Before I could think to censor myself, I blurted the words out. "Sometimes I wish there'd been ammunition in that gun. I know the two of us were basically out of trouble by that stage. The police were there. But..."

John's laughter was hollow, unhappy. "Yeah. Sometimes I wish you'd shot him too."

It both was and wasn't funny. Maybe I should be ashamed. Or maybe my sense of humor had taken a turn toward the dark and morbid, and that was okay. I don't know.

"Of course, that would make me a murderer," I mused.

"No, we were still fighting then. Would have been self-defense. Think you'd feel better or worse if you had?" he asked, watching me carefully.

I frowned hard, thinking. "I don't know. I'd have killed someone, but...maybe it would feel more like justice had been served, you know? I highly doubt I'd be standing at his graveside drinking a beer."

He nodded.

"I needed to do this, to come here," I said. "Thank you

for doing it with me."

"Sure."

"You think things will ever feel the same, like they used to?"

"No." He dropped his empty bottle on the ground and started in on another. "Honestly, I think if it did, we'd be even more messed up than we are already."

I watched the moon, the rich golden glow spreading across the dark. "You know, you just might have a point there."

chapter seventeen

Officially, the punishment for punching Kara and disturbing class had been the cessation of my allowance. Term of sentence undecided. There'd been a big discussion about how I'd recently been through an extremely traumatic event, but how Mom still felt certain rules needed to be followed. Like not assaulting people, even raging bitches who possibly deserved it. I gave a good blank face and kept my thoughts to myself.

Mom allowed for transport costs to and from school, lunch, and not much else. But it had become a problem since I'd started indulging in the odd late-night drive when I couldn't sleep. John was right: it did sort of help. At first, the lack of money had been no big deal. I'd had a bit of cash squirreled away from Christmas and I'd been off my reading game anyway. But that was then and this was now. New books had been released. New books that I needed. Mostly number three in a YA fantasy series that I'd been dying to read, but had been waiting until all of the books were out.

If anything could fix my gnat-like attention span, this book could. And yes, I could have gone to the library and reserved what I wanted to read. Patience and I, however, didn't get along. Not these days, anyway. If you wanted to do something, then you had to get it done fast. Before some psycho with a gun finishes things. Or a car crash. Or whatever.

Given how unhappy Mom had been over my detention, though, money wouldn't likely be flowing my way anytime soon. And Gran didn't approve of students diverting their energies with part-time jobs. We should all be studying all of the time. But Gran was in Arizona and apart from a weekly grilling over the phone, her power was limited since she no longer paid for my education. Here, for me, things were changing, and it felt good.

"Carrie, does your mom need anyone at the salon?" asked Hang, Monday at lunch.

"No." Carrie shook her head, holding up a slice of pizza to her mouth. "She's got me and an apprentice right now, sorry."

"I need a job," I said.

Hang groaned. "I need one more."

"I have no allowance."

"I dropped my cell in the toilet last night."

"You win." I winced.

"No wonder you didn't return my call," said Carrie. "Dad dropped his in once, ruined a brand-new smartphone."

"Shitty." Sophia grinned and bumped Carrie's elbow

with her own. "Get it, get it?"

Face pained, Carrie groaned loudly. "Um, yeah. It wasn't that subtle."

"No, it really wasn't," confirmed Hang. "I'd only give that like a two out of ten, max."

"It was a number two!" Sophia thrust her hands in the air.

"No." Gently, Hang banged her forehead against the table. "My bad. I walked right into that."

"Shame on you for encouraging her," said Carrie, laughing and chewing at the same time. "And as for you, you're terrible, Soph."

"Aw, I'm sorry." Sophia laid her head on Carrie's shoulder and looked up at her. "Do you still love me?"

Sophia's gaze softened. "I suppose so. Yes."

God, they were so sweet together it made my heart hurt. Not that there was anything wrong with being alone. Alone was fine and dandy. It lacked the thrill of being with John, though. Together, hanging out with the right person, had benefits too.

"Where are you going to start looking for jobs?" asked Sophia. She had a part-time gig at a clothes store. Futile for me to ask about openings there, however, since they didn't even stock my size.

Hang shrugged. "Check out the local paper."

"And we should do up some résumés, start handing them out to businesses," I said. "Did you try putting your phone in a bag of rice to suck out the moisture?"

Hang nodded. "It's dead, and my parents won't get

me another until Christmas. I can't wait that long."

"It's definitely job-hunting season."

"Agreed."

We bumped fists across the table. Yay, sisterhood. The bell rang and we all gathered our stuff.

"Later," said Sophia, after a quick kiss from Carrie.

Hang and I made our way together through the crowded halls. At least I didn't flinch anymore when we passed Isaac's memorial. I still averted my eyes, however, not that it mattered. All of those dead flowers and photos seem to be imprinted on my memory.

But it wasn't the deceased making me nervous today.

Those were not butterflies in my stomach. Today's mystery meat had probably just given me gas. Deep breaths; seeing John in English was no reason to get all giddy. I clutched a textbook to my chest, calmly talking myself down from overexcited heights.

Someone knocked into me and my book went flying. My head shot up, an apology ready on my lips for not watching where I'd been walking. Except, the sneering girl from the skate park with the long, dark hair stood in my way. Not an accident. And I was not doing this; I was not standing silent and scared, playing the part of her victim. Girls like this have so much, yet they always want more. It wouldn't end here.

"He's mine," she hissed, pretty face distorted with hate.

I cocked my head. "He who?"

"Don't give me that shit. You know who I'm talking

about." Behind her, her girl posse smirked, looking me over with great distaste. "Like I'd just give him up to some fat bitch like you."

"Okay, have fun with that," I said, shrugging her off. Presumably this was my new school's version of Kara. Funny how every school seemed to have one.

Except then she turned to Hang to spew some more of her venom. "And if you think Anders is serious about you, you're dreaming, you slope-eyed twit."

"Whoa now," I said, voice firming. I inserted my hefty self between her and Hang. "None of that racist bullshit, thank you."

"Shut up, you stupid fu—"

"I mean, why can't we all just get along? Wouldn't life be better without this judgmental, small-minded crap?" I asked. My voice was cool, nonchalant even. It was as if Chris's gun had been able to reach deep inside my mind and trip some crucial circuit-breaker. And just like that came the nightmares, and the insomnia, and the impatience. But that same switch had changed whatever hold people like Kara had ever had over me. I still didn't like being the center of attention, but I couldn't remember what if felt like to actually be scared of them. It was just gone. "Right, Hang?"

"Oh, absolutely," she confirmed.

Bitchy girl just sneered at us.

"And it's so boring," I drawled, rolling my fingers into fists. "You're a slut because you like to wear your skirt high and have sex. While your other friend there must be a frigid bitch because she likes to wear her clothes baggy and I hear she turned some dude down. And on and on it goes, all of it superficial and meaning absolutely nothing. They're just pointless, insulting labels that don't even come close to who any of us really are as people!"

"Actually," said Hang, "that's a valid point."

"What the hell are you on about?" asked the bitch queen.

"Everyone should just do their own thing without assholes like you giving them a hard time," I said. "Would that honestly be so bad?"

"What did you just call m—"

"You're not even original about it," I said. "God, the fat thing. Do you have any idea how often I've had that flung at me? I mean, what if I only take the word as being a descriptor? Then you're screwed. But I bet if you tried, you could make up much better insults. Give it a try; I'll wait because your opinion really, really matters to me. Whoever you are."

Her mouth opened, anger turned into confusion before morphing into rage.

And there was my moment. Fists made correctly this time, I drew back, ready to swing. A strong hand gripped my arm, halting the whole process.

"No," he said, forcing my fist back to my side.

"Uh-oh," said Hang.

"John." The girl nervously flicked her hair. "Hi."

"What's this about?"

I cleared my throat. "I believe your girlfriend was just

staking her claim or something."

"Christ. We screwed a couple of times, Erika. That's it." The look he gave her was grim. "Don't hassle Edie again."

"But—"

"I might not be around next time to stop her from knocking you on your ass."

Eyes wide, the girl pulled herself up as tall as can be. Not particularly impressive. I could take her, easy.

John picked up my book, handing it to me with a nod.

"Thanks," I said.

With a final displeased glance at the girl, he ushered me into class. His fingers brushed against my lower back, something I liked a little too much.

"That was exciting," said Hang, following behind. "I've never nearly been in a fight before."

I gave her two thumbs up. She'd stayed by my side, right up until John's intervention. That deserved respect.

"Fighting at school again? Seriously, Edie?" said John.

"She started it." I slipped into my seat, shoulders rounded. Feeling like the naughty child did not go with my outfit.

"Yeah, and you were about to end it." He took the desk behind me, face still distinctly unhappy. "The amount of shit that hitting Erika would have landed you in is not worth it. You know that."

"I should have just let her insult my friend?"

"You'd made your point. You didn't need to throw

any punches."

"Right." I turned back to face the front. He didn't understand and I wasn't in the mood to explain. Someone like him had probably never been bullied in his life.

"What happened to not caring what people say, hmm?" he continued. "I'm trying to get things together here and I've already got a record. I won't get dragged into your bullshit again, understood?"

Outraged, I turned back. "My memory must be faulty. John, can you run the bit by me where I asked for your help?"

The blue of his eyes turned ice cold. He likely thought "bitch."

I definitely thought "asshole."

Lucky for all, the teacher walked in then, calling for order. The weight of John's pissed-off gaze drilled into my back throughout class, however. What with him not being my keeper, this did not impress me at all. Neither did the niggling idiotic, completely wrong feeling of guilt.

chapter eighteen

We got lucky with the job hunt. A new smoothie place was about to open at Rock Creek Plaza. Hang and I got there just as the manager began sticking the Help Wanted sign in the front window. Talk about timing. The store consisted mostly of shiny stainless-steel juicers and blenders and the like. Giant pictures of fruit and lots of eye-bleedingly bright orange trim.

Bouncing on the balls of her feet, Ingrid, the manager, told us to come back the next afternoon for training. It turned out she did a lot of bouncing. I don't know if she was snorting sugar or just high on life. Either way, Ingrid had energy to spare. I liked her, even if just watching her did wear me out.

"This is the Summer Sunrise," said Ingrid with great enthusiasm, waving her gloved hands around as she spoke. "A handful of raw squash and pumpkin pieces, some orange segments, a squeeze of lemon, a couple of leaves of lettuce, a cup of ice, and a sprinkling of chia seeds."

Hang studied the lumpy concoction with an impressively straight face. "Awesome."

"Isn't it?" With practiced ease, Ingrid put the ingredients into the commercial blender and the blades whirred to life. "It only needs thirty seconds. Any questions?"

"No, I don't think so," I said, pasting a professional smile on my face. "Looks tasty."

"It really is. We're going to have so much fun working together, girls. I can't wait." Ingrid poured the murky orange mixture into a cup and handed it my way. "You can have this one, Edie."

"Oh. Thanks." I took one tiny hesitant sip, trying not to taste anything, doing my best not to gag. When I started coughing, however, Hang smacked me on the back, forcing the Summer Sunrise to slide down my throat.

"What do you think?" asked Ingrid.

My eyes watered. "Wow. Yummy."

"Right? We'll make the Green Berry Blitz next for you, Hang," said Ingrid. "It's got kale, cabbage, celery, and strawberries in it. I can't begin to tell you how good it is for your digestive tract."

Fear filled Hang's eyes. "I can't wait."

"You're so lucky, Hang," I said.

"Drink up, Edie," she bit back.

"Ingrid?" A woman stood in the doorway, viewing us with open disgust. She was all sharp edges, dressed in a designer tracksuit.

"Susan! What great timing." Ingrid put a little something extra into her bounce. "These are the part-time girls

I hired, Hang and Edie."

Susan said nothing, nor did her look of abhorrence lessen.

"Girls, this is the owner, Susan," Ingrid continued, unaware. "She invented all of these fantastic recipes by herself—isn't that amazing?"

Our best smiles in place, we both dutifully nodded.

"Outside. Now." Susan turned on her heel, marching back out.

"Sure thing!" With a wave of her fingers, Ingrid followed. "Won't be a moment, girls."

We watched them go in silence.

I poked a straw into the cold orange mush, stirring it round and round. "For someone with a healthy digestive tract, Susan doesn't seem very happy."

"I was just thinking that."

And for all of her niceness, Ingrid didn't seem to exactly be the brightest. She'd left the door wide open. Fragments of their conversation, or more accurately, of Susan tearing into the woman, floated through the store. "...we're selling people the idea of good health. Does that girl look healthy? Does her body say Susan's Smoothies to you? Or does it say 'I just ate a box of donuts and I'm going back for more'? Well? I can't believe...The little Asian one can stay. We don't want to look racist. But you need to get back in there immediately and fire that..."

Ouch. What a bitch.

I stood tall, aiming for blasé. "I never could have sold this sludge, anyway."

Without a word, Hang snatched the Summer Sunrise out of my hands and slammed it down on the counter, icy goop slopping everywhere. Then she grabbed my hand and led the exodus.

"Are you sure?" I asked, knowing she needed the money.

"I'm not even going to dignify that with a response," she snapped.

Whoa. "Okay."

"Hang. Edie." Ingrid had stopped bouncing. "Wait."

I lifted a hand in farewell, but Hang didn't even slow down. The girl was on a mission to get us gone from this place of raw vegetables and misery.

"You're great, Ingrid. Seriously. But you, you're a cunt!" I waved cheerily at Susan. "Bye."

Hang barked out a laugh.

"Guess it's still job-hunting season."

"Yep."

chapter
nineteen

The week didn't improve.

John and I still weren't speaking, ignoring each other throughout Thursday's English class. It sucked. I missed him. But he was wrong to say I should just put up with being insulted. For years, I'd let Kara push me around and she hadn't lost interest or moved on to tormenting some other poor sap. She also hadn't experienced any inner awakening leading to her deciding not to be a complete and utter bitch. Things had only escalated. I wanted to explain all of this to him, except pride got in the way.

How dare he blame me?

My foot pressed harder on the gas pedal, the hatchback flying down the empty back roads. Window open, wind tangling my hair, and The Kooks screaming about having a bad habit. This was good. John had been right about the therapeutic value of driving late at night. If I went fast enough, I could outrace all of the bad memories and terrifying dreams. Leave them far behind in the darkness.

A noise like a gunshot shattered the night as a tire blew. Swerving wildly, the car screeched and shuddered. I braked hard, my head whipping forward, body slamming into the seat belt.

Holy shit.

Carefully, carefully, I steered the hatchback over to the side of the road and turned off the engine. All I could hear was the hammering of my heart. My hands shook, still holding on tight to the wheel. Not dead, just really shaken. Okay.

One at a time, I pried my fingers loose of their death grip. It wasn't easy. Driver's-side door open, I stepped out, knees knocking only a little. Everything was fine. No need for anyone to lose their shit.

The smell of burnt rubber filled the air. Only ragged strips of tire remained on the rear wheel. It could have been worse. Still, I swore up a storm, then popped the hatch, pulling out the jack and spare wheel. Mom and I had practiced for just such an occasion. The first three nuts came off fine, but the fourth one...I pulled and I strained and I called it every vile name ever invented, along with a few new ones even Shakespeare might have appreciated.

Nothing worked.

Over and over, the boom of the tire blowing echoed through my head. Not a gunshot. I needed to pull myself together. Except strange noises came from out in the dark, beyond the limits of where the lights could reach.

The scuffle of a foot sliding over gravel, the mumbling of voices. Tonight, nature most definitely wasn't my friend.

"Stop it," I whispered. "It's just your imagination. There's no one out there."

Chris stepping out of the blackness, walking toward me with a gun in hand. That smile. That creepy, crazy, murderous smile.

"You're just freaking yourself out, you idiot," I muttered.

Mom would still be at work. Never mind what she'd say if she knew I'd been out cruising at one in the morning. Hang would come to my rescue. If I couldn't get the damn tire off, though, then neither of them stood a chance of doing it, either. I held the cell phone to my ear.

"Edie?" he asked, voice husky from sleep.

I took a deep breath. "John."

"What's wrong?"

"The, uh, one of my tires blew. I tried to change it myself, but—"

"Where are you?" There were rustling noises in the background, the jangling of keys.

"Bell Road. A couple of miles along."

"Get in the car and lock the doors," he ordered. "I'll be there soon."

"Okay. Thanks."

I let down the jack and did as told, sitting in the dark, cell held tight in my shaking, sweaty hands. Deep, calm breaths and nice thoughts. I closed my eyes, concentrating on good things. Kittens and cake and books and shit.

Happy things. At least I'd gotten semi-dressed in black yoga pants and a tank top, a pair of flip-flops on my feet.

Years passed. Or at least twenty-three minutes. Someone tapped on the window and I shrieked. John. I flipped the lock and slowly climbed out of the car.

"You all right?" he asked, face set.

I nodded. "Thanks for coming."

"What were you doing out here?"

"You were right," I said. "About driving at night. It helps."

He nodded.

"Here, hold the light." He pressed it into my hands and dropped down onto one knee beside the busted wheel. Evilest tire in all of creation. Of course, for him the nut came off on his first try with ease. Bastard of a thing.

"I must have loosened it for you," I said, the tips of my ears burning with embarrassment.

He just grunted.

"I do know how to change a tire. It was just, you know, the nut."

A nod.

John had the car roadworthy again in about two minutes. God, for him it'd all been so simple. The boy probably thought I'd lured him out here under false pretenses. Because I wanted his attention or something stupid.

"You okay to drive?" he asked.

I hid my shaking hands behind my back. "Absolutely."

"I'll follow you back to your place," he said. "Make sure you get there okay."

"Thank you."

Back at home, I don't know what I expected. A wave of the hand, a chin tip maybe. But he parked his car and got out, moseying on over to where I stood.

"Your mom home?" he asked.

"No. She doesn't finish until four."

I'd left on the light in the front hall and the bedside lamp in my bedroom. Walking into a totally dark house had a tendency to freak me out these days. Meanwhile, my stupid hands were still trembling. The noise the tire made when it blew had been shocking, true. But that had been nearly an hour ago. I shook them hard, trying to dislodge the fear, to get the tremor to ease.

When I looked up, John stood silently watching. "I can stay for a while if you want."

"No," I said, guilt making me refuse. "Really, you should go home, get some sleep. I'm going to as well."

He just looked at me.

"Thank you for rescuing me. I would have been in real trouble if you hadn't come."

A brief smile flitted across his lips. "No problem."

I smiled back at him, took a deep breath, and raised my hand in farewell. "Good night."

"'Night."

"Or morning."

"Right."

The curve of his lips could have kept me occupied for

hours. Wings stirred in my belly, both scary and thrilling at the same time. Friends again or not, liking John in a more-than-that way was dumb. Insane even. Still, just to be sure where we stood, I wanted to ask if the fight had been archived, forgotten. Except just bringing it up again seemed risky during this time of peace. Maybe I should, though. Clear the air and all that.

"Edie," he said, shaking his head. "I'm waiting for you to go inside."

"Oh. Right."

"You sure you don't want me to stay?"

More than I could say, and for reasons less than pure. "Oh, no. I, um..."

"I don't mind."

"No, no. I'm fine. Really. Thanks." I rushed to the front door, unlocking it with all due haste. "'Bye."

"I'll see you tomorrow at school." He took a step backward, watching me all the while. Then he turned, heading straight for his car.

"Today at school," I called out.

He laughed. "Whatever."

Such was the magic of John Cole, I even managed to get to sleep. Bet I still had the stupid smile on my face, too.

chapter twenty

John: Hey

Me: Hi. How's 1:38 am treating you?

John: Shit. You?

Me: Same

John: No driving at night alone again right?

Me: I'm guessing you want to hear no...

John: correct

John: Been worrying about it

Me: Alright. I'll text you first if I do.

John: Ok thanks

Me: And you'll let me know too

John: You want to know when I go out?

Me: That's what you're asking from me

Me: Hello?

John: Ok deal fine

John: I can look after myself though

Me: I put a baseball bat in my car.

John: You're weaponized now?

Me: Or ready for impromptu baseball games

John: Right

Me: So...what else shall we talk about? What do you usually discuss when you text girls at one in the morning?

John: I don't

Me: Sure you do. Come on. Tell me.

John: You don't want to hear that

Me: I absolutely do.

John: lets talk about movies or something

Me: Waiting.

John: Shit Edie

John: I ask them if I can come over

Me: That's all?

John: Yeah

Me: You don't text them anything else?

John: No

Me: None of the "what are you wearing" thing first?

John: No

Me: Let me get this straight, you give them no lead-in whatsoever?

John: Already told you no. Can we talk about something else now?

Me: Man, you're so lazy.

John: It works

Me: I'm actually disappointed in you right now.

John: FFS

John: we both get what we want. Why complicate things?

Me: I'm beginning to think life is about the complications.

John: Enough shit in life is complicated thanks. Sex can stay easy

Me: Not even a prom date on the horizon?

John: not going

Me: Got other plans?

John: hang at the lake maybe. What do you think

Me: You're inviting me?

John: yeah

Me: Cool. Sounds good.

John: We could jump off the rock again

Me: Okay. But just to warn you, I'm wearing a prom dress even though I'm not going to the dance and this isn't a date. It'll be something truly sparkly and stupid.

John: Remind me to bring floaties so you don't sink.

Me: Thanks, I appreciate that.

John: No problem

Me: You seriously wouldn't be embarrassed to be seen with me?

John: No. If that's what you want, go crazy

Me: You're sure? Because I'm talking big hair, a corsage and fluffy skirts, serious amounts of sequins and tulle.

John: whatever makes you happy. I'll even buy the corsage for you.

Me: ☺

John: I'll bring the flowers and drinks and you wear the dress.

Me: Done.

John: Tell me something good

Me: We're in our last year of high school.

John: So?

Me: So time to get the hell out of here.

John: And go where?

Me: Everywhere.

John: What about college?

Me: College is out of this town. It's a start.

John: yeah

Me: You thinking of going?

John: maybe. Been looking at a certification for landscape technology and construction management. But my brothers not doing well so leaving him could be hard

Me: I'm sorry.

John: going to try sleep. Need to keep my strength up for fishing you out of the lake soon

Me: Ha

John: How about you?

Me: I might try to sleep too. Night John

John: Night E sweet dreams

chapter
twenty-one

The next night, a hand waved in front of my face and I sat upright, screaming. The motion ripped my earbuds out, but Marina and the Diamonds played on without me.

"Hey," said John, as calm as ever.

"Holy shit," I whispered, hands clutching at my chest. "I really wish you'd stop doing that."

"It's only the second time."

"Let's not have a third."

He lazed on my windowsill, backpack in hand for some reason. "You didn't answer your door. What am I supposed to do?"

"Okay. All right." I grabbed a pillow, covering up my baby-blue sleeping shorts. Little could be done about the slightly tight tank. At least it had a shelf bra and nothing was hanging naturally. "So what's going on?"

"We're studying."

"We're what?" I scrunched up my face, hitting stop on the music. "It's nine o'clock on a Saturday night."

He just shrugged. "Working all weekend. Now is the time I've got."

No wonder he had such a great tan, mowing lawns and landscaping all weekend. And muscles. Let's not forget the muscles. I respected him heartily for them.

"You didn't do that well on the book essay," he continued. "Better than me, but still."

"Hey. C-plus is a passing grade."

"But you usually do better, don't you?" He didn't wait for an answer. What with my guilt-ridden face, he didn't need to. I didn't exactly feel guilty for my own sake. I couldn't care less if I got an F. But I knew Mom would be disappointed. "Every time I look at you in class, Edie, you're staring out the window. Not paying attention."

My heart sped up once more. "You look at me?"

"You're seated right in front of me," he said with a smile. "I can hardly miss you."

Stupid heart. "Right."

"It's not like I've got anyone else I can study with," he said, face turned away. "Anders is barely getting by for his basketball scholarship. Anyway, he's at some party."

"I would have thought you'd be there too."

"Nuh. Not in the mood." He pushed back his hair. "Plus I don't want to fail English, and you said you'd help me."

Without further ceremony, his backpack was dropped onto my bed, making the mattress bounce. He'd either packed every textbook known to mankind or a bowling ball. Odds were sadly on the latter. Not that I was even any good at bowling.

"Of course I'll help you," I said. "And you're right, I've had issues focusing on books and classes since *it* happened. It's stupid; my brain just doesn't want to seem to do its thing."

"You still seeing that shrink?"

I nodded.

"You told him about this?"

"Not exactly."

His gaze narrowed. "Why not?"

"I don't know." I turned away, embarrassed. "People died that night and I'm popping pills over issues like night terrors and panic attacks. Poor me."

"On the other hand, not much point being alive if you're not willing to get your shit together." His voice was no-nonsense and his face the same. "Is there?"

"Ouch."

"Am I wrong?"

I hung my head. "No."

"Tell him everything. Let him help you."

Scowling at the floor, I searched for a change of subject. Anything would do. "And what about you, John? Who do you have to talk to?"

He leveled his gaze at me pointedly.

"I'm not particularly qualified," I objected. "You don't talk to me that much, either."

"So I'll talk to you more."

Huh.

"That a problem?" he asked, tipping his chin.

"No. Of course not." My heart just about beat out of my chest. "I like talking to you; you know that."

"No, I don't," he said, gaze turned aside. "Half the time I'm not sure if I'm bugging you or what."

"You worry you're bugging me? Seriously?"

Not bothering to reply, he climbed in after his bag. He had on his usual attire of a T-shirt and jeans. Immediately, he started pulling off his Chucks.

"Lucky you took those off," I said, watching him toss them onto the floor with an approving nod. "Mom would be super pissed about shoes on the bed. A hot guy hanging out in my room with me though? Not a problem. Hell, she'd probably give me a high-five."

"You think I'm hot?"

"What? No. I was just making conversation." My face heated. Mental note: Duct tape mouth at first opportunity. "Geez, the ego on you."

Huffing out a laugh, he shook his head. "So you are or you aren't supposed to have boys in your room? I can't keep up."

"Boys are definitely not allowed," I confirmed. "Actually, I'm also not supposed to have anyone over while she's at work. Not without permission."

"I'm here to study."

"That would still be a hard no."

Lines filled his forehead. "You want me to go?"

"No, of course not." I smiled. "I like you bugging me. I like it a lot."

He laughed softly.

"Got it?"

"Got it. Bit of a rule-breaker these days, aren't you?" Pulling back his hair, he secured it with a rubber band he'd had around his wrist.

"That's not good for your hair. Use this." I grabbed him a hair tie off my bedside table and he took it with another one of those looks. Lips drawn wide in a vague smile, yet his brows drawn down. Interestingly enough, he used the look a lot around me. As if he didn't quite know why he was going along with what I'd said or something. Like I amused and confused him both at once. The feeling was pretty much mutual.

"Would your parents mind?" I asked, curious. They weren't something he tended to talk about.

"Doubt it. I only talk to them on the phone now and then since they moved a year ago. Dad got offered a job in Anchorage. Dillon was of age and the money was good, so they moved," he said, like it was no big deal. "I had the business to look after and I didn't want to change schools, so I stayed."

"I know you'd said they moved up north, but Alaska?"

"Hmm."

"Never occurred to you to change your mind after the Drop Stop?" Escaping to an icy land of few people sounded pretty appealing to me.

He pursed his lips. "I never thought I'd miss not having my parents with me. When they said they were thinking of moving away, all Dillon and I cared about was freedom." He shook his head. "But no, I didn't want to leave here. My uncle, he's pretty good, and he'd been on me to work for him for a while. Moving in with him for my senior year's a lot easier than starting over up north. And it still gives me some space from my brother."

"Wow."

"Even when Mom and Dad were down here, things weren't much different. Mom didn't like the people Dillon had hanging around, but she sucked at saying no to him. Plus she had church groups and stuff going on. Kept her busy," he said. "Dad was working just about around the clock and was dead tired whenever he was at home, so we tended to keep any friction away from him."

"Did they know about the dealing?"

One side of his lips drew out a ways. "Mom definitely had to. I think she was just really good at not seeing anything that didn't suit her, you know?"

I frowned.

"I'm not sure about Dad. Can't remember me or Dillon ever having to ask for permission," he said. "As soon as Dillon hit high school he was always going out somewhere. Most of the time he didn't mind me tagging along. He had this piece-of-shit truck that was always breaking down and I was better with engines than he was."

"I can't believe your parents moved away, just leaving you with your brother," I said with more bite than intended.

"Think they'd pretty much given up by then."

Just the thought made me furious. And yet..."Now here you are, wanting to study on a Saturday night. They were wrong."

His gaze lingered on me, assessing. "Sure you don't want me to go? I don't want to cause trouble with your mom."

"No, stay," I said, answering the earlier question. "You know, I have a theory that most of the rules we're given are nonsense anyway. I'd rather make up my own mind about things. Take for instance you being here. There's nothing for my mother to worry about. Nothing's going on. Nothing's going to happen."

"Only I just happened to sneak in your window to hang out with you on your bed." He scratched at the beginnings of stubble on his chin.

"Now you're thinking like my mother. Don't do that."

"How old are you?" he demanded.

"Seventeen."

"See, you're not even legal yet. Practically a baby."

"Please." I scoffed. "You've only got a couple of months on me."

"Beside the point. Edith Millen, you are under the age of consent and living in your mom's house," he said, pushing on. "You're smart and you're nice and you've got no fucking business being alone with someone like me and you know it. I'm an ex-drug dealer, for Christ's sake. Apart from math and technology, I'm failing everything. Oh, and PE—I'm passing that too. Seriously, though, you couldn't have picked a worse friend if you tried. Your mother would freak."

"Don't put yourself down like that."

Nothing from him.

"And don't call me Edith." I stood tall, angry all over again. "So what if you've got a history? That's what it is, history. You're trying at school and you've got a proper job. You're also the sort of person who risks his life for a complete stranger. How many people do you think would do that?"

His mouth stayed shut.

"I'm honored to be your friend. You idiot."

"I was just pointing out that your mom cares about you," he said with a hint of a smile. "Considering how pissed you were at my folks for giving up on me, her rules aren't so bad."

"Even if we are breaking them."

"To study," he clarified. "But thanks. Grab your books."

"I'll get my math textbook too; I think I'm failing," I said. "You said you could help with that, right?"

"Absolutely, I'm great with numbers. Ran a successful business for years, didn't I?"

"You mean selling dope?"

"Yep."

Wide-eyed, I looked him over. John as an entrepreneur. An illegal one, but still. "Guess I never thought of it that way."

Leaning back against the wall, he got comfortable, legs stretched out, crossed at the ankles. John Cole on my bed acting right at home. Happiness. Still, I tried not to let my body or brain get overexcited. We were just friends, after all. And the more I kept reminding myself, the sooner it would hopefully sink in. Crushing on friends wasn't smart. God knows, his friendship was a big part of what kept me sane-ish these days.

"Building the customer base, getting and keeping their loyalty, dealing with all of the different suppliers, keeping track of everything," he said. "I'm not just a stoner, Edie. Hell, I didn't even smoke that much. Well…"

"Well?"

"Most of the time. Anyway, I was in it for the money, and that meant taking it seriously."

"And your brother's still dealing?"

"Oh, yeah. He's his own best damn customer." Pain filled his eyes, there and then gone in an instant. Shoved aside.

"I'm sorry. I'm glad you got out, though."

"Me too." He patted the mattress. "Stop delaying. Come on, you explain this Poe guy to me and I'll help you with your math issues."

"Deal."

"And hey, Edie?"

I got busy rifling through the contents of my schoolbag. "Hmm?"

"You're cute when you're pissed off."

My head snapped around like the chick from *The Exorcist*, but he was reading his textbook, not even looking at me. Weird. "Thanks. But I prefer the word *fierce*."

chapter twenty-two

Me: I'm bored. Text with me.

John: About what?

Me: Anything. What's your favorite color?

John: I don't know. Green. I'm guessing yours is black

Me: Truth. Tho it's not really a color, it's a shade or a tone or some shit. Favorite food?

John: Pizza. You?

Me: Tacos.

John: Good call. Music?

Me: Lots. Too many to have a favorite.

John: Me too. Movie?

Me: Deadpool. A perfect balance of funny, hotness, and wrong.

John: It was good. TV show?

Me: Used to be Stranger Things but now I'm not so sure. You?

John: Samurai Jack. Why are you not sure?

Me: I don't know. Maybe I need more happy and light in my life.

John: Fair enough

Me: I loved Orphan Black too.

John: Excellent show

Me: You didn't say your favorite movie...

John: I dunno. Star Wars

Me: A worthy classic. Tell me something I don't know about you.

John: Like what?

Me: Anything you like.

John: Hell

John: Sometimes I eat pop tarts for breakfast

Me: What?! No...truly you've exposed your innermost self to me. I never would have picked you as a pop tart guy. My entire mental image of you is messed up now. It's like the whole world has been turned upside down.

John: Great. Your turn

Me: I like texting you.

Me: And occasionally I eat pop tarts too.

John: ☺

Because happiness is overrated, things fell apart again between John and me the next week.

It came in the form of John standing by his locker covered in Erika's hands. The girl couldn't seem to decide what part of him to publicly grope first. His chest, his lean hips, the hard lines of his arms. So classy, the way she tried to dry-hump his leg. I sincerely hoped he remembered to wash himself in disinfectant when she finished.

Why that bitch? Any other female and I'd have dealt. But no, poor delicate feelings and wounded heart, broken loyalty, etcetera. Without a doubt, it was my fault for getting all dreamy and delusional about the boy. Even though he's just my platonic friend, to let that ho fondle him in the hallway after everything she'd said...how could he?

Before either of them saw me, I about-turned and made for the nearest exit. The brave thing to do was to immediately run away. God knows what would happen if I stayed. A limb might fall off or something. I'd made it through a solid three-quarters of Friday without hiding from reality by locking myself in a bathroom stall for a half-hour or more; to expect anything else of me this week would be insane.

"Hey," said Hang. "You're going the wrong way."

"No. Nope." I shook my head. "Unless, of course, you *want* to watch that Erika chick attempting to mount John next to his locker."

"What?" Hang wrinkled her nose. "Ew."

"I know," I said. "And while I realize the school's sex education policy could be seen as inadequate, actual real-life demonstrations are not what I'm after."

"Fair enough."

"So I'm ditching school for the first time. It's my next new experience, I just decided." The smile I gave her was in all likelihood slightly unhinged. "Take notes for me, pretty please?"

She shook her head. "Screw that, I'm going with you. Let's get out of here."

First we stopped at Auburn Coffee Company, because caffeine. Next, decisions were made. An empty Friday night loomed ahead. This would not do.

I won't lie: some fear and guilt lived inside of me over skipping school. But I valiantly ignored those trash-talking fools. So what if I got detention again or they told Mom? Actually, I'd prefer if Mom never found out; her stress levels over me were high enough. It was, however, one measly class in my entire school career as opposed to the end of the world.

"I was abducted by aliens," said Hang, sitting cross-legged on her bed. The aforementioned plans included a sleepover at her place. Since her parents had a very well-stocked bar and they'd gone out for dinner with friends, we'd finished our coffees and started on some beer. "They stole me straight out of a school hallway. There was nothing I could do but allow them to carry out their sick and perverted tests on me."

"God, you poor thing." I sipped at my drink.

"Did I mention that all of the aliens looked like male models?"

"All those probes. You're so brave."

"I try." She sniffed. "What about you? Why did you miss your last class?"

"Oh, I slipped and sprained my left breast," I reported with a straight face. "Had to go home and rest it immediately."

"Absolutely. That sounds excruciating."

"Very." I gave my boob a pat. "The doctor said I mightn't be able to wear underwire for weeks. We're talking possible sagging here. The pain is real."

Hang cracked up. "These are problems us flat-chested girls will never have. You and your rack stay away from me. I'm sticking with my sports bras and comfort, thank you very much!"

Some reality television show played in silence on the small flat-screen hanging from her wall. Pictures she'd drawn or painted covered another wall, the subjects ranging from self-portraits to friends, houses on her street, and small everyday things from around the house.

"You really are crazy talented," I said for not the first time.

"Shut up."

"You are."

"No." She downed a mouthful of beer. "Dad is crazy talented. I'm average."

I just shook my head.

"Me and my brother are lucky," she said. "Between Mom being an accountant and Dad an art teacher, we've got both the left and the right side of the brain covered."

"I'm not sure I've got any of the brain covered," I joked. "Mom is smart. She had to drop out of college to have me, though. The sperm donor wanted nothing to do with us. His loss."

"Bastard."

I shrugged.

Sure, it sometimes stung, but that didn't change the truth of it. I was loved. I would not allow the douche canoe who'd broken Mom's heart and let us down so badly to mess with my head. No emotional reunion would be coming up, no understanding and ultimate forgiveness. For me, he didn't exist. One parent who loves you can be more than enough. The end.

"So," she said, lying on her side, holding the beer back up to her lips. "When do we start texting insults to John?"

"Um, never?"

Her mouth opened wide in surprise. "No, come on. He let that bitch touch him after she said all of that shit about you. Where is the loyalty?"

"I don't own him. If he wants to have bad taste in women, that's his problem." It made me die a little on the inside, but no biggie.

"No way, you can't let this go. Friendship! Comradery!"

Maybe I should have told her the tale of him coming to my rescue when my back tire had blown out. But even though I really liked Hang, trust still didn't come easy. My privacy had been invaded enough in the last few weeks for me to now value it deeply.

She held out her hand, fingers beckoning. "Just give me your phone. I'll send him one small, concise message, that's all. Something along the lines of 'I hope you had a nice day and that your penis falls off.'"

"No. We are not drunk-texting John."

Two hours later...

"Is *cock splash* one word or two, do you think?" asked Hang, chewing on her bottom lip while she studied the screen of my cell.

"You're calling him a cock splash?"

"Inventive, isn't it?"

"Yeah." I stretched out on the bed at her side. The ceiling seemed to be doing some trippy spinning thing. "I wish I'd thought of that one."

"It's like I told you, vodka helps with creativity. It unleashes the artist within."

"Obviously."

"My brother is not going to be happy that I stole that bottle out of his room. Though I really don't drink that often. Still, we should hide the evidence and not tell him. And we should definitely not let my parents find out." Her cell chimed again and she grabbed it off the bedside table. You had to admire the girl's ability to multitask. Who knew how many different people she'd been carrying on text conversations with tonight? "Oh, that's nice. Carrie and Sophia's dinner with Sophia's parents is going well."

"That's good." I sighed. "Everyone should be happy and in love and shit."

"Hmm. Either that, or drinking and sending boys imaginative and angry texts."

"Yeah."

A pounding noise came from the front door. We both sat up, startled, then we began laughing for some reason. I don't know, it made sense at the time.

"My brother must have forgotten his key." Hang climbed off the bed and I followed because curiosity, but also bathroom break time. Fortunately, we hadn't changed out of whatever clothes we'd worn to school. No one would be meeting me in my pajamas, for a change.

The house was a long, low-set brick ranch, the walls covered in big, bright, beautiful canvases. All of the paintings done by Hang's dad. If he'd been my parent and I'd been into art, I'd be intimidated too. He was good.

More pounding on the front door.

"Patience," called out Hang, flipping the lock and swinging the door open.

"Ladies." Anders filled the doorway, his smile wide. "You were wrong, JC. They're not messily drunk at all."

Something inside of me—my stomach, my pride, I don't know—sank lower than the floor. I grabbed Hang's arm, whispering, "You told them we were here?"

"Anders tricked me."

I frowned. "How?"

"He asked me where I lived."

"H-how is that a trick question?" I asked, bewildered. Hang flailed.

The boy in question, however, chuckled his ass off. *Jerk.*

John pushed him aside, striding into the hallway. He was not happy. "Any particular reason you sent me the address for every STD clinic in the state?"

I opened my mouth, closed it, and then opened it again. "Well, you know, that's actually really useful information for anyone to have."

He remained unconvinced. "And you want my tiny, useless dick to shrivel and fall off why?"

"Man," Anders laughed. "That one cracked me up.

Though they were all pretty good."

Hang grinned. "We did half each."

"Nice work." He held up his freakishly large hand and they high-fived. Awesome.

Meanwhile, a vaguely homicidal expression filled John's eyes. "Edie?"

"Like you don't know," said Hang, all goodwill and joy now gone from her face. "Turncoat."

John just looked at her, brows drawn tight.

"Erika," she spat at him.

"Erika?" John turned to me. "What about her?"

I looked elsewhere. The floor, the walls—these were all super-interesting things greatly deserving of my immediate attention.

"Beside your locker this afternoon," said Hang. "After all that shit she said to Edie. How could you?"

Anders whistled, leaning against the wall, getting comfortable.

"She was so upset, she ditched school for the first time ever," Hang continued, standing tall. "Her education is ruined. Because of you."

Smite me now please, baby Jesus.

John bent over, getting into my line of sight. "Edie, she came up to me and I told her to get lost. Is that what you need to know?"

"I...You did?" I asked. "But you let her grope you first?"

"Christ. I told her to get lost, okay? She just took a while to get the message." He straightened, pulling the usual rubber band out of his pocket and tying back his hair. "Plenty of girls out there. Why would I mess around with one who insults my friends?"

I didn't get to grope him, so why should she? Still, in the end he'd done the right thing. I sighed in relief, ignoring the quick jab of jealousy. "Oh."

"Well, this is awkward," whispered Hang.

John stood in front of me, waiting.

"Sorry," I said, grimacing. "But you have to admit, it looked really bad."

"We dating? We together or something and I didn't notice?"

"What? No."

"Well then?"

I frowned.

Arms crossed, he said nothing.

"Okay, so the insult texting...we got a bit carried away. I, um, I promise in the future I'll only use your number for good instead of evil."

"I'd appreciate it." His eyes, they still weren't happy. Couldn't really blame him, either.

"Okay kids." Anders clapped his hands together, rubbing them. "We're here now. What entertainment can you offer?"

"Want to watch a movie?" asked Hang, closing the front door.

"Solid idea."

Together, they wandered off toward the family room, discussing which film to pick. John and I, however, stayed put.

Fingers twined together, I offered him a small repentant smile. "Sorry for being a rampaging bitch."

"Next time you got a problem with me, Edie, come to me directly," he said. "You're right, I probably should have cut Erika off sooner. But how was I supposed to get her hands off me, hmm? Pushing a girl back in front of school cameras doesn't look good."

He might have had a point.

"I'm used to people thinking I'm shit, but I expected better from you," he said, eyes wounded.

"I don't think that."

"So why didn't you trust me?"

My alcohol-soaked brain had nothing.

He looked away, shoulders still stiff. "Only reason I talked to her in the first place is 'cause she had a message from my brother. She still buys from him."

"Oh."

For a long time he said nothing. "Tell Anders I'll see him later."

When he left, he didn't slam the door or anything. The quiet dismissal was almost worse.

chapter twenty-three

"**W**hat about this one?" Mom asked, holding up another top. "It's cute."

I squinted at the item over the edge of my sunglasses. "Notice the part where it's not black?"

"Everything you wear has to be black?"

"Yes. Pretty much."

"Okey-dokey." With a heavy sigh, she returned the top to its rack.

We were in the approximately two square feet of space the department store had designated as being "Plus Size." Whatever. Usually, the internet had some goodies for me to wear. Like hiding those sizes away in cyberspace made the bigger, more fashionable brands remain cool and distanced somehow. *Jerks.*

"Can we go look at makeup now?" I asked. Sephora being the main reason I'd suggested driving down to Roseville to hit the Galleria. At least there, I didn't have to worry about squeezing into things.

"Sure," said Mom. "You do know you're not fooling

anyone with those sunglasses, right?"

"I'm cool and mysterious."

"No, honey. You're hung over," she corrected. "I'd tell you off, only I did the same thing a time or two at your age and I prefer not to be a hypocrite whenever possible."

"And I love you for it."

"Hmm. Doesn't change the fact that I worry about you," she said. "I hope you were reasonably sensible and in a safe environment. You were at Hang's the whole night, yes?"

"I was." I pushed my glasses up on top of my head, rubbed at my weary eyes. "Bad things happen, I know. Promise we weren't doing anything dangerous."

Her frown continued. "And you know you can call me anytime, no questions asked, if you need a lift home."

"Yes."

"Okay. Thank you."

A strand of gray hair had escaped mom's neat blond bob. It glinted bright beneath the harsh store lights. Grandma had gone gray in her thirties too, as she loved to point out to me with creepy glee. Yet Mom had always seemed indestructible, tough and ready to take on the world for me. I resented that gray hair mightily.

"You're growing up way too fast lately. I can't keep up." She cupped my cheek with a cool hand. "Did you have a good time with your new friend?"

"Yeah, I did." I smiled, covering her hand with my own. "Hang's nice. I think she might even be trustworthy —shock, horror."

"You're really not going to forgive Georgia, are you?"

I turned away, our hands falling from my face. "No. I just...I can't."

"Edie." Mom frowned. "You two have been friends since you were tiny."

"Sure." Nausea twisted my stomach. Hangover or Georgia, I couldn't tell. "And then she completely sold me out, insulting the person who saved my life in the process."

"People make mistakes."

I shook my head. "I know. Believe me I know. Her talking to one journalist about me, I could forgive. Going on every show and speaking to anyone who'd give her the time of day? Not so much."

"Oh, kid." Public space or not, Mom wrapped me up in her arms. "Things have been hard for you lately."

I attempted a smile. It didn't quite work.

"I'd like to meet your new friends sometime."

"Sure. Sometime." No way did I want to know what her reaction to John would be like. If there ever came a time in the future when he felt like talking to me again. Mom had watched him get taken away in cuffs from the Drop Stop, just like I had. She'd also heard about his former life as the friendly neighborhood drug dealer.

Nope. Even if I managed to pull a miracle and win him back, Mom and John didn't need to meet.

"I did kind of mess up something last night," I said, sort of needing to talk about it. God knows it owned my poor alcohol-damaged mind. My fingers knotted all on their own. Talk about a guilty conscience.

"What do you mean?" asked Mom.

"I jumped to the wrong conclusion about one of my new friends and might have slightly been a complete ass to them."

Mom's nose wrinkled and she took a step back. "Damn. Did you apologize?"

I nodded.

"It didn't fix things, huh? Well, if they're important to you, you keep apologizing," she said, patting my cheek with her cool hand. "And find new and varied ways to apologize. Bake them brownies, write them a song, build them a cabin in the woods, go wild with it."

"Maybe."

"You know I'm here for you, don't you?" she asked, eyes bright.

"I know." I grasped her hand.

"Whatever you need to talk about, I want to hear it. The robbery, your new school, how things are going with your therapist, relationships, friends, boys, girls, anything..."

"It's okay, Mom. Really. I'm fine." If you overlooked the insomnia, occasional panic attacks, and general crazy going on in my head. "Things are calming down."

She sniffled.

"Oh my God, we're in public. Do not cry," I ordered. "This is not a moment."

"Of course it is. We're hugging it out in the middle of a department store." Mom squeezed me tight. "It's a beautiful mother-and-daughter moment. Let's ask that passing stranger to take our picture."

I rolled my eyes. Then a mark on her neck caught my attention and I squinted. "Mom? Is that a hickey?"

"What?" Her hand flew to the tiny bruise below her ear. "No, of course not!"

"It is." My mouth, it gaped. "You're seeing someone."

Guilt was pinched lips and wide, panicky eyes. "Of course I'm not. Don't be silly. When on earth would I even get the time?"

"Mom—"

"Between you and work, my hands are full." She smacked a kiss on my cheek and smiled. "I pinched a bit of skin taking off a necklace last night, that's all. The lock caught."

"You know I wouldn't mind," I said, watching her carefully. Not quite believing. "You're allowed a life. Just disregard my disgust at the thought of you getting it on with anyone."

"I appreciate that, honey." She gave me a dry look. "But Edie, I'm not seeing anybody."

Slowly, I let out a breath. "Okay."

"Coffee and cake-pop?"

"Would be potentially lifesaving right now."

She grinned. "A girl after my own heart. C'mon."

And all was well again. Mostly.

chapter
twenty-four

On Monday, I put a bag of homemade cookies on John's desk in English. He raised a brow, then stowed them in his backpack. We didn't talk.

On Tuesday, I handed him a cupcake as we passed in the hall. The word *sorry* hadn't quite fit on top, but I thought the *S* done in green icing said a lot. We still didn't talk.

On Wednesday, out of both baked goods and money, I slipped a haiku titled "I'm the Worst" into his locker. Writing a song was out. At first I'd attempted a sonnet, until the realization that I sucked at poetry struck home, and anyway haikus were shorter. I didn't actually see him that day.

On Thursday, in English once again, I placed a small, neatly wrapped brown paper package on his desk. Tired shadows lay beneath his eyes. He cocked his head, curious or confused, I couldn't say.

"Lettuce, ham, Swiss cheese, and pickles," I supplied.

"You made me a sandwich?"

"Yes."

"Huh."

"You don't have to eat it if you don't want to."

"No," he said, placing a proprietorial hand on the sandwich. "I want to."

"Okay." With that settled, I turned in my seat, facing the front of the class.

"Edie?"

I looked over my shoulder. "Yes?"

"You're forgiven," he said. "You can stop with the presents."

I exhaled slowly. "That's good. I'm running low on ideas. Tomorrow it was probably going to be me offering to carry your books."

"You were gonna carry my books?" Amusement filled his eyes.

"Sure. Why not?" I asked. "If it went on into the weekend, I figured I'd wash your car or something."

He paused. Then shook his head, long hair falling forward to hide a grin. "I should have held out."

"John, I don't think you're a bad person—and I do trust you."

He just stared at me. "Thanks."

Suddenly, breathing came easier. Like my now healed ribs had shrunk, but now returned to their normal size. If John had decided I'd been too much drama, I'd have survived. I know this. Forgiveness felt much better, though. The clip-clopping of heels announced the arrival of our teacher. I faced forward with a smile.

chapter twenty-five

That night...

Me: You awake?

John: Yes

Me: What are you doing?

John: TV. You ok?

Me: All g. Want to study?

John: there in 15

Guess he was antsy because as soon as he arrived, he suggested a drive instead. We went to a roadhouse out on the highway leading into the state forest. It was a long, cabin-type building with a big Bud sign lit up on top. Bet they hung dead animal heads on the walls. Even in the middle of the night, a few trucks and bikes were out front.

"I don't have a fake ID," I said, asphalt crunching beneath my feet.

"You won't need it. Owner's an old friend of my dad's."

"Wow. First time under-age drinking in a bar."

He held up a hand and we high-fived. A warmth filled my chest that had nothing to do with alcohol or drugs. It felt good to have my friend back.

Inside, there were booths and a long wooden bar, tables in between. Country music poured out of an old-style jukebox. Dead animal heads—I knew it. A small dance floor and a couple of pool tables sat to the side.

"Do you play?" I asked, heading in that direction.

"Sure."

"John." A waitress in her mid-twenties sidled up to him with a very welcoming grin. Very pretty with a tight denim skirt. Next came a full body-contact hug. They either already knew each other in the biblical sense or she wanted them to. Lay your bets.

"Ruby. Hey." He gave her a squeeze before stepping back. "This is my friend Edie."

"Hi." Her smile wavered slightly as her eyes flicked over me. They'd definitely done it. "Welcome."

"Can we get a cider and a beer?" he asked.

"Coming right up!" Ruby sashayed off, throwing a little extra something into the sway of her hips. Of course, John watched.

I set up the balls and selected a stick, rubbing a little

chalk on the tip. As for me, not jealous because that would be pointless. Completely and utterly futile. The stupid part of me that insisting on mooning over him could just shut up.

John cleared his throat. "Hope that's okay?"

"What?"

"Cider? I noticed you're not really that into beer, so..."

"Oh, right. Cool. Thanks." Shoulders relaxed, breathing easy. "Do you want to break?"

"No, you go."

Leaning over the table, I lined up my shot. The white ball smashed into the side of the neat triangle of colored balls, sending them scattering in every direction. One kerplunked into a corner hole. Very gratifying.

"Nice," said John.

I loved this, the brush of the felt against my fingers and the feel of the stick in my hand. Especially the satisfying crack the balls made upon impact followed by the sound as they rolled through the tunnels beneath the table down to the end. I was in the zone now. For the next shot, I sent another ball down. And then another.

"You've played before," he said.

I squatted a little, lining up the next shot in my head. "Mom had this boyfriend for a while. He was great. He had a table, taught me how to play."

John made a noise in his throat.

"I think he wanted to take things further with Mom, but she wasn't ready. Pity." The shot went wild and I winced. "Damn. Your turn."

Ruby came back with the drinks, setting them on the tall table beside John. She winked. He smiled. I gulped half of my drink.

"Here's to friendship," I said, and set the glass back down.

John took down a stick and bent over the table, taking his shot. I tried not to look at the way his jeans melded to his butt, and failed. As per usual, what I screwed up he achieved with reckless ease. One ball went down, followed fast by another.

"Have you seen your brother lately?"

"Yeah." A storm cloud moved across his face. "He came over the other night, wanted to talk to me about getting back into selling. I told him no. Again. My uncle won't have him in the house; he knows what shit Dillon's into. There was some yelling. It wasn't good." He missed the shot, came over to the table, and started in on his drink. "Anyway, how's the therapist going?"

"Well, we've moved beyond only talking about movies." Guess we'd hit the no-holds-barred part of the night. I took my shot and the ball sunk. "I told him about you."

John's face went blank. "Yeah?"

"His professional opinion was that our being friends after going through such a traumatic experience together could be both beneficial and harmful."

He said nothing, bringing the bottle of beer to his lips.

"Therapists talk in circles sometimes."

A grunt. "But you're talking to him about your focus

and insomnia and stuff now?"

"Yeah." I nodded. It hadn't been easy, but I'd done it. And been given another prescription and some coping techniques in the process. We'd see if they worked.

"Good," he said.

Another ball sunk. "Should I not have mentioned you?"

"Whatever helps, I guess."

"Are you sure?" I asked. "I can stop talking about you with Mr. Solomon if you'd rather I not. He was just asking about my friends."

"It's okay, Edie."

"I don't talk about you with anyone else," I said. "Just in case you were wondering. I know what it's like to have people talking behind your back. Gossiping and shit."

"Not even with Hang?"

"No. Well..." I scrunched up my nose. "Generally, no. Nothing personal. Apart from the unfortunate incident with the texting."

An ironic smile from him. "Right."

"Sorry." I got into position, bent over the table, the stick in my hand. "Again."

"You're forgiven. Again." He swallowed some beer. "It was the sandwich that did it. Never had someone bring me lunch before."

Smiling, I took aim and shot. The ball fell into a corner pocket. I moved across the table from him, lining up the next one. Almost time for me to oh so graciously win.

John watched me in silence. I'd have loved to know

what was going through his head. Except then his gaze dropped to the gaping vee of my shirt's neckline and there it stayed, stuck on my breasts.

No way.

And it wasn't like I hadn't worn a bra. They weren't freestyling or anything. Also wasn't like he hadn't seen me in wet underwear at the lake. If memory served me right, he'd noticed them then too. Briefly. Still, the way he now stared enthralled you'd have thought the boy had never ever seen a pair. Like a girl was some strange foreign object.

Slowly, I straightened.

Trance broken, he looked at me, eyes wide. He'd been busted and we both knew it.

"You're about to get buried," I said.

He blinked repetitively. "Edie, I—"

"Six feet down, John." I nodded to the balls on the table.

Frown in place, he turned his attention there too. "Oh."

"Mom says I shouldn't joke about death, but I don't know...gallows humor feels about right after what we went through."

He said nothing.

"Don't you think?" I asked, stalling, giving him time to pull himself together. Praying things wouldn't get weird. Weirder. I'd only just got him back as a friend; I couldn't lose him again. It'd been a random ocular accident, no more. After all, we both knew I wasn't his type.

Still, maybe I should make more of an effort to get laid. Apparently, sex made for a wonderful stress-buster. And right now, my best male friend was making me feel a little wound up.

Yes, genius. I'd found my next first to strike off the list.

"Yeah, I do," he said eventually and nodded toward the table. "Best of three?"

I smiled. "You're on."

After I'd beaten him another time or two, he drove me home. Nothing happened between us. I mean, of course it didn't.

chapter twenty-six

"I'm just saying, I think that educationally the movie had a lot to offer," said Hang, chewing on a straw.

Friday night and we were at a party in the field past the Old Cemetery Road skate park. Far enough out of town to avoid any interest from concerned parents, citizens, or the police. Yet close enough for plenty of people from our school and a few others to show up.

Car lights lit up the space. One had its hatch up, speakers blasting music out of the back. Another had the prerequisite beer keg and red Solo cups working overtime.

"Beast Man," said Hang in a low, deeply disturbing voice.

I wept for me. Or pretended to. "It was so wrong. I still want to gouge my eyes out."

"Please. You loved it."

"No, I didn't."

"Yeah, you did. Another first gone—you've now watched a porno." Hang grinned. "I can't believe my brother had that on his computer. That's blackmail material for life."

"I'm never watching anything like that ever again," I said, taking a sip from my cup of beer. Like it or not, it was the only thing on offer at this party. "I feel dirty, like my soul is stained."

"Oh, it is. You'll be burning in hell with the rest of us now."

Sadly, I nodded. "And I keep seeing that poor, innocent cave girl sacrificing herself to Beast Man's unnatural lusts. She was so brave."

"She saved the clan."

Hand to my heart. "A role model for all young women."

"Yes," sighed Hang. "I want to be just like her when I grow up."

We both lost it, exploding with laughter.

"Good evening, ladies," said Anders, appearing out of nowhere as per usual. How someone so big snuck around so easily, I didn't know.

"Hey, Anders." I smiled, wiping away tears from laughing so hard.

"What are you two on?" he asked, eyes curious.

"Life. We're high on life."

He did not look convinced. "JC's skateboarding. I got restless, figured I'd come talk to you guys."

"Lucky us," said Hang. "You know there's plenty of other girls here you could bother."

Anders gave her a look. No idea what it meant.

Hang's elbow knocked against mine and she nodded to someone nearby. Red hair, medium height, cute. The boy from Trig had arrived. Apparently, the very same person who had asked my new bestie about me and expressed a keen interest in meeting same. I drank some more beer, trying to be cool as opposed to the usual sweaty, nervous wreck. It didn't work.

"He's here," said Hang.

"I see." *Deep breath in, slowly let it out.* "I don't know."

"Nice, nonthreatening, knows what he's doing if his last girlfriend is to be believed."

"What are we talking about?" hissed Anders, bringing his head down to our level. "Who are we looking at?"

"Nothing. Go away," said Hang.

"But I want to be one of the girls!"

"No." She put a hand over his face and pushed.

He made a weird kind of "ugh" sound and retreated into the night.

"You were the one who wanted to get your v-card punched," she said calmly. "But it's totally up to you, Edie. You're in control."

More beer. "Remind me. What was my reasoning again?"

Holding up her hand, she ticked off her fingers one by one. "It can be messy, painful, potentially embarrassing. And you just want to get it over and done with so when you meet someone you want to be in a relationship with, which could be years from now, you'll be equals."

"Right, that makes sense." I nodded. "The logic is sound."

"Plus, if he really does know what he's doing, there should be an orgasm in it for you. Win! But, it's also another first you wanted to experience in case you somehow die tomorrow in a bizarre accident," she said. "Caught in a stampede of runaway llamas. Mauled by a pack of rabid shih tzu. That sort of thing."

"You mock me, but it could happen." I snapped my fingers. "Just like that you're gone, dead. The end."

"All right, my morbid friend. Whatever you say." She took my beer, finishing it off. "Bump into him as you go get a new drink. Talk to him—I hear guys like that."

My feet stayed put.

"Or not. You're sleeping over at my place, so you've got the whole night," she said. "You can always decide later. No pressure."

"No pressure." Apart from the hand holding down my heart, fingers slowly squeezing. I would not have a panic attack. I would not freak out.

"You could wait a little longer, magically meet someone wonderful and want him to be your first." Hang shrugged. "You just never know. You've only been at the school a couple of weeks."

"True."

"Or maybe that guy over there's the one and you'll fall in love, get married after college, and have babies." A dreamy smile appeared on Hang's face. "Then you'll be able to tell everyone you married your high school sweetheart."

"Mm."

"And you'll only ever have sex with one person."

I frowned.

"Yeah," she said. "I'm not so sure that's a great option after all. Forever is a long time."

"I am only seventeen, so me neither. Though we could be wrong."

"We could be," she agreed. "Let's just concentrate on getting you de-virginized and save the happy-ever-after for another time."

"I think that would be best."

Hang had dated a senior last year. They'd broken up when he went away to college. Her card had long since been punched in the name of love.

"Your long blond hair is shiny, your winged eyeliner is perfect, your boots are cool, and I really do like that dress you're wearing," she said, giving me the once-over.

"Thanks." I straightened the black cotton skirt. "Got to love a good maxi."

"True."

"It's just a meaningless bit of skin with a lame name," I said, shoulders back, boobs out, standing tall. "I don't need it."

"No you do not." Hang shoved the empty beer cup into my hand, face serious. "Go hard. Slay. Or do whatever you're comfortable with, you know. It's your body and your choice and I respect that."

"I'm glad we're friends." With an arm around her

shoulders, I gave her a half-hug. Her lips parted in surprise. Guess me showing affection didn't happen often. Mom wasn't particularly touchy-feely either, generally.

"Me too," she said, eyes misty.

No more hesitating. Empty Solo cup in hand, I headed into the crowd. My every thought revolved around what the hell to say to him. It shouldn't come as a surprise that I almost ran the boy down.

"Oh," I said, stopping suddenly, standing much closer to him than intended. "Sorry. I should have been watching where I was going."

The friends at his side kept on talking. But he turned to me, looking at the cup. "You're a woman on a mission."

"Yes. Yes, I am." I forced a grin. "I'm Edie."

"Duncan." His gaze was warm, friendly. "We've got Trig together, right?"

"That's right."

We were about the same height, but his arms were thick with muscles. Clearly, he worked out. A dusting of freckles fell across his nose. Up close, he was cuter than ever. "How are you liking the school?"

"Much better than my last."

"Good. Here, let me help you with that drink."

"Thanks." I handed him my cup and he forged a path through all the people. Frequently, he'd look back at me to smile. Tonight was the night. Something about it just seemed right, despite the nerves running riot through me.

Quite a few people watched us; I have no idea why. One of the dudes gathered around the keg slapped Duncan on the back while another said "hi." Beer flowed, and he filled my cup to the brim before passing it back and getting his own. The cold beer cooled my hand for only a minute before John took the cup, spilling the contents out on the grass.

What the hell?

"Never let other people get your drinks," he said, lecturing me like a child. One who'd been particularly naughty.

"I was standing here the entire time," I said.

"He had his back to you when he poured." Blue eyes turned to ice. "Could have slipped anything in there."

"I wouldn't do that," said Duncan, tone aggrieved.

John barely spared him a glance. "Edie, do you even know the guy? How could you be so stupid?"

"Stop it," I said, dropping my voice and moving in closer. "You're right, I should have gotten the drink myself. But you need to calm the hell down."

"Forgive me if I find the idea of you getting drugged and raped a little disturbing."

"John!"

"Cole, you asshole." Duncan pumped the muscles in his arms, hands in tight fists. "You're the dealer, not me. I didn't do anything to her drink. I wouldn't do that. Edie —"

"You don't talk to her," John growled. "Don't even look at her."

"Whoa," I said.

People had started gathering around us, pressing in,

getting excited. Testosterone filled the air like a stinking miasma. Jaw rigid and the veins in his neck standing out, John took a step forward. Obviously ready to fight.

I put my hand on his chest, holding him back by sheer force of will and one hell of a pissed-off expression. "That's enough. Let's go."

His furious gaze flicked between my face and Duncan's.

Duncan said nothing. Interestingly enough, for all his earlier flexing, wariness now filled his eyes.

"John." I slipped my free hand into his, forcing his fingers to open and accept mine. "Come on."

Ever so slightly, his stance relaxed, the set of his broad shoulders easing. Good enough. I half led him, half dragged him through the crowd. Away from the people, lights, and music. Away until it was just me and him alone in the parking lot, standing beside his car.

It was over. Okay.

"Oh, boy," I whispered, the pounding of my heart gradually slowing down. I dropped his hand and took a couple of steps, breathing hard. Wonder if this had been what he went through, breaking up the scene between me and Erika. The thought of him getting hurt, of him getting into trouble with the police or something, made me want to vomit.

"Holy shit, John," I said. "What the fuck was that?"

"You were going to give it up to Duncan Dickerson?" he sneered. "Are you serious?"

I halted, staring at him. This was not good. "How do

you know about that?"

"Anders overheard you and Hang talking."

"Bastard."

"Well?" he demanded, acting all authoritarian. *Idiot.*

"To be fair, I didn't know his last name was Dickerson," I said. "That's unfortunate. Though, I wasn't actually planning on marrying him, so..."

"Not funny."

I shrugged.

"You barely know the guy."

"Um, yeah. None of your concern. We're not talking about this." How mortifying! My face burned bright. People should just gather around and cook s'mores. "I appreciate that we're friends. You mean a lot to me. But this is going to have to fall under definitely none of your damn business, so go away please."

"We're talking about it." He advanced a step.

"No we are not." And I retreated.

"You were going to let a complete stranger touch you." Advance.

Retreat. "People do it all the time. *You* do it all the time."

"But you don't," he said, taking the final step, backing me up against the side of his car and getting all in my face. "Edie, this is your first time we're talking about. Isn't it?"

"Yes, and it's going to be messy and painful and probably horribly embarrassing and I just want it over and done with." I tried to meet his eyes but failed, settling for a spot on his right shoulder. "You're not a girl; you wouldn't understand. Also, last time I checked, you're not the gatekeeper of my hymen, John Cole. So back the fuck off."

He said nothing.

Deep, calming breaths. "Look, someday I'll meet someone I really like and we'll have a deep and meaningful relationship and go at it like bunnies. But I don't want to be the dumb virgin in that scenario."

He slowly shook his head.

"Also, I do not want to die a virgin."

"What? What the hell are you talking about?"

"Hey, you and I both know death can occur at any time."

"This is crazy."

"I'm seeing a therapist!" I told his shoulder. "I don't know if you noticed, but I'm a little bit messed up these days. It's hard for me to trust people. That's not going to change anytime soon."

He screwed up his face at me. "Wha—"

"I'm just trying to be practical."

"Well, you're being ridiculous. None of this makes sense."

"It does to me."

Again, he said nothing.

In fact, he said nothing for so long that I finally looked him in the eye. The anger had left him, replaced by an emotion I didn't recognize. Worst of all, he still smelled like summer. A little sweat and the open night air, everything I loved. Liked. I meant liked.

"What?" I said, finally.

He let loose a breath. "I'll do it."

My mouth opened. I blinked. Somehow, it seemed my brain had stalled. He couldn't possibly have just said what I thought he'd just said because that would be crazy.

CRAZY.

"What?" I asked. "What did you say?"

"I said, I'll do it." He hesitated, face grim. "If you want."

"Wow."

Both of us stood in utter silence for a minute, everything bizarre as all hell. Then he swallowed hard. "So you want me to do it or not, Edie? Yes or no?"

"Y-yes. Okay."

A grunt.

"Thank you." I stood immobile, a lot perplexed. "I thought you didn't like virgins? You know, the possible sight of blood and stuff."

"I don't, normally. But I like you. Come on."

"Is this going to affect our friendship?" I asked, uncertain and maybe just a little scared.

"No." He got into the car, reached across, and flicked the lock on the passenger-side door.

I climbed in, put on my seat belt. "We have to make sure it doesn't."

"It won't," he said, sounding so sure of himself that a lesser woman would have been insulted. No hesitation, no second-guessing. His face was set. "One time only. Then that's it."

"Okay."

"We'll go to my place. My uncle's out."

Anxiety had me in a stranglehold. I did my best not to fuss, but to sit still, face calm, looking straight at the road ahead. John and I having sex. Getting naked. Doing it. My mind couldn't begin to fathom the enormity of the situation. Luckily, I remembered to text Hang and tell her John and I were going for a drive. The way I kept disappearing on her at parties, it quite possibly made me the worst friend ever.

Time began to behave strangely. The drive took forever and yet we got there too soon. We pulled up outside a two-story house surrounded by tall trees. The porch light had been left on in welcome.

No words were spoken as I followed him inside the dark house. Suddenly light dazzled my eyes, showing a room littered with books on horticulture, football paraphernalia, photos of hills and lakes and stuff, and the largest flat-screen television in creation. Nothing here really said John. His boots thumped up the stairs and I trailed slowly behind. I found him standing in the middle of a bedroom, looking around. A lamp on the bedside table glowed softly.

"It's a mess," he said, before springing into action. Shoes and clothes were thrown into the closet, his schoolbag and books shoved aside. "I only changed the sheets yesterday, promise."

I lingered in the doorway, uncertain how to proceed.

"Okay."

He hadn't unpacked everything; a stack of boxes sat to one side. Yet photos of him and a similar-looking, slightly older boy hung on the white wall. Had to be his brother. Next was a full family shot including his mom and dad, then came a picture of a much younger John and a woman posing beside the Charger. Navy-blue curtains, a Ramones poster, and his big bed.

Okey-dokey.

"Sorry about this," he said, still cleaning with a vengeance. "I don't usually bring girls here."

"It's fine."

He paused. "Come in. Sit down."

I did as told, taking the final fateful step into (gasp, shock, horror) a boy's bedroom. Once I started moving forward, things seemed easier. As instructed, I sat on the edge of his bed, the mattress sinking a bit beneath me. Firm but bouncy.

"John, really it's fine. Stop fussing."

A furrow sat between his brows.

"It's just me," I said, attempting a smile. "Relax."

He huffed out a laugh. Guess we were both nervous. Then he said, "Condoms," and raced out of the room. Rifling noises came from the bathroom across the hall and he returned triumphant, a string of silver packages hanging from his hand.

"You sure about this?" he asked.

I nodded. "But what about you? Are you sure about this?"

He closed the bedroom door, the lock clicking.

My heart punched hard. "Are *you* sure about this?"

John just looked at me. "Shoes are awkward. Let's get rid of them now."

"Right." Instructions were good. I could follow instructions. My fingers fumbled over the laces, hands shaking as I pulled off my boots. Neatly, I tucked my socks inside, then pushed them under the bed, out of the way. "Done."

With his back to me, he stood, flicking through a book. An expensive-looking new laptop sat on his desk. Wonder if it was part of his getting-serious-about-school thing.

He sat beside me, placing the open book in my lap. "Here," he said.

"What's this?"

"In case you had any questions," he said. "Are you okay at telling the boy and girl things apart or do you need some help?"

If I had, the biology text he'd provided me with had several large and neatly labeled diagrams explaining the relevant anatomy and the process of fornication in depth. Not only informative, it was a heavy book and would make a fine weapon. I slapped it shut, using it to try and hit him over the head. Sadly, the boy was too fast. He dodged my blows and tore the book out of my hands, sending it flying. I settled for slapping him around, instead.

"I'm sorry." He laughed.

"You're not forgiven," I hissed.

He grabbed my hands, wrestling me back onto the bed. The fool. In this position, I could use my legs as well.

"Shit," he said, struggling to keep my knee out of his groin. "Edie, you want that working, remember?"

"I changed my mind."

Despite my wrath, he won. His hands caught my wrists, holding them above my head. His body he wedged safely between my thighs. The worst I could do was beat my heels against the back of his legs in protest. And I did.

"I'm sorry," he said again. "Really."

"You're still laughing."

Somehow, he managed to calm himself down. "You didn't really change your mind, did you?"

I sniffed as disdainfully as possible.

Realistically, however, I doubted I could hold out for more than a minute or two, maximum. Some of his weight he took on his elbows. Still, the feel of his body pressing me into the bed made all sorts of things stir inside.

Patiently, he waited.

"Hmm. I guess not," I said.

"Need a definite from you."

I swallowed. "No, I haven't changed my mind. Yes, I still want to have sex with you."

A slow smile crossed his face, turning me inside out. Lying on top of me, being right there, he looked more gorgeous than ever. It wasn't fair. Whatever happened after tonight, however this changed things, I'd never regret stepping into this boy's bedroom. I couldn't.

"It would seem we've already assumed the position," I said, the corner of my mouth twitching in an attempt at a smile. "Was that your nefarious purpose with the textbook all along?"

"Maybe." He licked his lips. "Mostly I just wanted to annoy you. Distract you from being nervous so you'd stop making me nervous. I had no idea you'd try to damage me."

"I'm badass."

"You are."

"You're not really nervous, are you?" I asked.

He didn't answer.

Instead, his mouth came down on mine, gentle, hesitant almost. As if he still had doubts about my commitment to this whole losing-of-virginity thing. That wouldn't do. In a surge of action, I rolled us, putting me on top and him on his back against the mattress. Surprise turned into a smile, his hands sliding down my sides over the cotton of my dress. Knelt over him, I kissed him how I'd wanted to, how I'd imagined in my very best daydreams. Sweet, deep, and hungry. No holding back.

The noise he made in the back of his throat sounded like something between a gasp and a moan. Either way, it was full of approval. A kiss had never been so good, so all-consuming. We were all lips and tongues and teeth. His hands moving tirelessly, stroking my feverish skin, holding me to him. To be this close, touching him how I wanted, feeling his solid body beneath me. My fingers searched out his chest, sliding under his T-shirt, needing no barriers.

I wanted it all. Every part of him.

Stubble scratched my cheek, my lips moving down to his neck. The scent of him there was stronger, warmer. I kissed and licked and did what I liked. Bit him just because I could. John swore in a voice about a billion times deeper than normal, running his hands up the back of my thighs. My face pressed against his neck, I could have hidden there forever. Strong fingers grabbed at my ass, pressing my body against him.

"Edie," he whispered.

"Mm?"

"Whatever you want."

"I want your shirt off," I said, panting just a little, hands tugging at the offending item.

He sat up, forcing me to do likewise, and then he tore the shirt off over his head. The expression in his eyes, the absolute focus. God, everything about him. All of that golden skin, mine to explore. I pressed the palm of my hand over his heart, feeling it beating fast. Inside of him seemed every bit as stirred up as inside of me.

"Lay down beside me?" he asked.

I nodded, and his hand guided my leg over him, my body back down onto the mattress. Raised up on one elbow, he stared down at me. Fingers traced patterns up my arm, around my shoulder, and over my collarbone. We kissed like we'd never be parted. Life and death, time itself, none of it mattered. Tonight would be endless and nothing beyond the bed existed.

His hand cupped one of my breasts, taking the weight of it, his eyes huge. It was impressive, the string of truly filthy words spilling from his lips. Basically, I guess he liked my tits. And I liked him liking that part of me. God, I liked it so much.

Lightly, the back of his hand trailed down my chest, over my breast, then farther still. Not stopping until he reached the hem of my dress, sitting high on my thighs. My thunderous, bulky thighs. My bulging belly. Embarrassment over body parts still sadly endured. How horribly crappy. I broke the kiss, breathing heavy, my hands tangled in his hair.

"You okay?" His whole body stilled. "Want me to stop?"

"No."

"What's wrong?" The hand that had been sitting high on my hip, under my dress but above my underwear, moved to cup my cheek. "Hey."

A mass of doubt and negativity raged in my head, chasing away the happy. *No, absolutely not. Not here, not now, not ever.*

"Don't stop." I grabbed his hand, putting it back on my hip. "My brain is just being stupid. Ignore it."

Brows knitted, he remained on pause. "Stupid about what? Talk to me."

Oh God, the embarrassment. I covered my face with my hands, unable to look him in the eye. I was the worst. Trust me to kill the mood. "You're just doing this out of pity."

"No. I'm not."

Maybe I should just crawl under the bed or disappear into the closet. Wait for him to go to sleep, then hightail it home. If I asked nicely, kept bringing him sandwiches for a while, we might even be able to pretend this never happened.

"Edie?"

I didn't respond.

Oddly enough, there came the sound of a zipper being undone. Next, John grasped one of my hands, pressing it first to his mouth, then to his cheek. "Look at me."

I sighed, but did so.

"You're hot and soft. And you felt fucking amazing beneath me."

"You're kind."

"Not even a little." He pressed my hand to his heart, still beating double time. "Feel that?"

I nodded.

Then he led my hand down into his jeans, pressing my palm against the hardness beneath his underwear. "Now you feel that? That's what we call a penis. You saw one earlier in the book, remember?"

Stunned, I said nothing. Of course I knew he had one and it would be involved in tonight's activities. Though I don't think I'd fully comprehended touching, feeling him. Even over the cover of his underwear. Attribute it to a lack of opportunities to fondle boys. I'd never gotten much beyond kissing and occasionally having a boob groped. Now here I had a penis almost in my hand.

"To be fair, I hear they get hard on some pretty flimsy pretexts," I said.

"I'm eighteen, Edie, not twelve." Once, twice, he kissed my lips. "I'm not closing my eyes and imagining someone else. That's not what's happening. I'm here with you. I want you, understood?"

My throat tightened, my eyes sore.

"Because you putting yourself down isn't okay," he said, gaze open, sincere, and a bit angry.

"Fine." I sniffed, getting control of myself. So high maintenance, it was a wonder he didn't kick me out of bed. Slowly, carefully, I gave in to curiosity, wrapping my fingers around him. "It's not tiny."

A hint of a smile curled his lips. "It's not useless, either."

A grunt and his hips pressed into my hold. His mouth covered mine once more and then my hand got firmly but gently relocated back to his chest.

"Later," he mumbled.

Talented fingers followed the waistband of my boy shorts, teasing sensitive skin. Back and forth, he gently trailed his knuckles over the front of my underwear, from my navel to between my legs. Low in my belly tightened, the blood rushing through my veins.

When he finally slipped his hand into my underwear, I wanted him to feel me there, needed him to. Even the most delicate of touches made me shake. My bare legs shifted restlessly against the mattress, every muscle in me drawing tighter and tighter. John knew things, magical things. And while yes, I could have done this myself, having him with me made it so much better.

No time to be self-conscious or nervous. The sensation coursed through me, thrilling and complete. Sparkles and stardust and the best rush of endorphins. My whole body seized, fingers sinking into his back, mouth gasping for air. It took a while for me to come back down.

A finger sat hooked in the front of my waistband, questioning.

"We could stop here," he panted.

"Don't you dare."

"Thank God."

In a moment, my underwear went flying into a corner of the room. Together we got my dress up and off, over my head. His hot mouth covered my chest in kisses, fingers fighting with the back of my bra. Meanwhile, I attempted pushing down his jeans. We were an overeager catastrophe, a mess of mouths and limbs. God, it felt good.

I passed him one of the condoms off the nightstand. Determined though quietly freaking out. He got rid of his underwear and put on the protection. Face sober as he climbed on top of me, covering my body with the hot length of his.

"You're definitely sure?" he asked.

"John! Please, would you just fu—"

His mouth fell on mine, hand sliding over my side before reaching between us. Slowly, he pressed forward. Strange, to be so impossibly physically close to someone.

Over and over, he broke the kiss to check on me, always returning to my lips. I closed my eyes and hung on tight, trying to be relaxed.

It hurt. Natural though it might be, my muscles tensed just the same, resisting the intrusion. From nerves or the slight edge of pain, I don't know. Then he was inside, burying himself deep, his body rocking against mine. One strong hand held my thigh, keeping my leg up and around him. Warm breath heated the side of my face, my neck. I stroked his back, slick with sweat, trying to memorize everything about him being so close. I held onto him and waited.

After a while, his movements grew jagged, faster. Body tense, he groaned, holding me hard against him. Puffing out breaths, he slumped on top of me, only taking some of his weight on his arms.

I'd done it. I'd had sex. How amazingly bizarre.

"You okay?" he asked in a quiet voice.

"Yes."

Carefully, he withdrew, falling onto the mattress beside me. Then he looked down at himself. "Shit."

"What?"

He grimaced. "Blood."

Crap. Things between my thighs were a bit of a mess. "Oh, um, excuse me."

I got off the bed and rounded up my bra, dress, and underwear. After cracking the bedroom door and listening for any signs of life from the rest of the house, I broke land speed records racing into the bathroom across the hall.

The girl in the mirror didn't look any different. Mussed hair, pink cheeks, and swollen lips. Nothing permanent, however, seemed to have changed on the outside. Inside, things felt a little tender. I cleaned myself up and dressed. Then searched for a face towel to wet and take to John.

"I'd momentarily forgotten you don't like the sight of blood," I said, slipping back into the room.

A grunt.

"You okay?"

"Back in a minute." After snagging his jeans off the floor, he took his turn in the bathroom. Apparently he wouldn't be answering my question.

At a loss for what to do with myself, I took a seat at his desk and started putting on my boots. Sitting on the bed didn't seem right. We'd done what we'd set out to do, and John didn't strike me as the type to cuddle. Time to go back to being just friends.

Right, I could do this.

The toilet flushed and he reappeared, tying back his hair with a rubber band. He didn't look at me. Guess we'd entered the part of the evening where we avoided eye contact. Awkward. This wouldn't do.

"John, look at me."

He did as told. "Yeah. Everything okay?"

I nodded, smiled.

His smile slowly returned. "You sure?"

"Yes."

"Okay. Good." He sighed, relaxing a little. "You want me to give you a lift back to your place?"

"To Hang's would be great. Thanks."

A nod.

I grabbed my cell and shot off a text.

Me: Back in 15

Hang: ???!!!

Me: You still at party?

Hang: No, come to my house.

"We're fine, right?" I asked, not at all slightly nervous. "Still friends?"

He looked up in surprise. "Of course."

"Good. That's good."

Shirt and shoes back on, he stood, hands on his hips. "Nothing's changed."

"Right," I said. "Thanks for that. For what we did."

"Sure." Another smile. "Ready to go?"

"Absolutely."

chapter
twenty-seven

That weekend, I did the laundry as a non-virgin. I also cleaned the kitchen, attempted to study, and then tried to start reading a new YA sci-fi series. Studying didn't work as well without John, but texting him to come over so soon after last night's events felt a bit weird. Eventually I gave up and took a nap.

Still, all of these miraculous feats were performed minus a hymen.

Remarkably, nothing much seemed to have changed. I still succeeded in doing the laundry, and failed on both the studying and reading fronts. Just like my previously hymened self. When we went out for lunch together at a local taqueria on Sunday, Mom didn't even notice how her daughter had apparently become a woman. Of course, Hang guessed what had gone on. She'd taken one look at my messy hair and makeup and squealed with glee. Though, she'd been in on the planning stages.

I didn't wake up the next morning feeling particularly wiser or more mature. Things down there were a bit sore,

KYLIE SCOTT

but that was about all.

Honestly, so long as there was consent and protection, the biggest danger in doing it for the first time seemed to be the memory you'd make and carry with you for the rest of your days. To be able to live with your decision and the whole reality versus expectations, etcetera. But once you'd started, did that automatically mean you should continue and just automatically do it with the next person you liked? Though that didn't really make sense. Guess it depended on how you felt about the next person. And also, the risk of things getting emotional. If the person you'd had sex with ignored you after, or talked crap about you, that would suck. (Learning how to deal with assholes did, however, seem to be an unfortunate part of life.) I don't know. Everyone's different. And how I'd feel when I saw John again, I had no idea.

Found out first thing Monday morning in English class, though.

Ripped jeans, a faded T-shirt, and the mother of all yawns. He gave me a chin tip. I gave him a smile. Awesome. Not awkward at all. We'd survive this whole having-had-sex thing no problem.

"Hey, how you doing?" I asked, turning in my chair.

"Good. You?"

"Good."

He pulled out his book and a pen, getting sorted. "Want to study tonight?"

"I'll text you later." I turned back to face the front of the class.

This was great. How stupid of me to have worried about how having sex would change things! Why, the scent of his sweat, feel of his skin, taste of his mouth, warmth of his breath, noises he made, weight of his body, strength of his hands, and his eyes, oh God, his beautiful eyes, never even entered my head.

We were still just friends. Excellent. Everything was perfectly fine.

chapter
twenty-eight

While all remained apparently cool between John and me, the school grapevine was abuzz. Gossip had apparently been flying all weekend. We'd left the party together. Ooh!

There'd been some scuffle between John and Duncan over me. OMG!!

But at the end of the day, the possibility that *the* John Cole could be interested in someone like me was just so fantastically HAHAHA!!!

No one could bring themselves to believe such a ridiculous thing.

Duncan had attempted to corner me outside of Spanish class. I'd made vague gestures at my watch, apologized profusely, and done one of my finer disappearing acts. Now that I'd had sex with John, now that I knew exactly what was involved and how it felt...the thought of doing anything remotely similar with Duncan (or anyone else for that matter) freaked me out just a little. Sex was so intimate, so private. I'd hung a closed sign over my girl parts for the time being. Much easier. Not even the thought of dating appealed.

"How about pole dancing?" asked Hang in the cafeteria over lunch. "Any experience in the live adult entertainment industry and/or exotic dancing areas?"

"No. Sorry."

"Damn. Sadly, that rules out a big chunk of the employment market." She flicked through the local newspaper employment pages on her cell. "Cat grooming services?"

"Maybe."

Hang tapped a finger against her lips. "I'm sort of highly allergic. But they have good allergy medicines these days, right?"

I just looked at her.

"No. Okay." She took a sip of her soda. "I'll keep searching."

"Good idea."

"What's a good idea?" asked Anders, squeezing his sweaty self onto the seat between Hang and me.

"You going and having a shower," said Hang. "Yuck. You stink."

"I smell manly."

"No. You smell like unwashed feet."

Anders threw his hands up into the air. "Why are you so mean to me? What did I ever do to you?"

"Go. Shower. I'm done with this conversation." After pushing her glasses higher on the bridge of her nose, Hang returned to studying the want ads. "Edie, do you have any secret business credentials you haven't seen fit to share with me?"

"Um, no." I bit into my apple, crunching away. "In fact, I'm reasonably certain I'm going to fail math."

"We can work on that some more tonight," said a familiar voice. He sat down opposite me, blue eyes inscrutable.

I just froze. I don't know why. Or worse yet, I did.

Truth was, I'd gotten off easy having him seated behind me in English. Faking it hadn't been so hard. With him right there, however, staring at me, all of the complicated and difficult stormed through my head. A hurricane's worth of *oh shit, what the hell have I done with my best friend.*

Time. That's what I needed.

The time and space to put him firmly back in the just-friends box. No need to panic; everything would be fine. I had a plan. After all, it's not like I had so many friends that I could afford to lose one to lust. Especially not one as important to me as John. Yet all I could think when I saw him was how I'd had my tongue in his mouth. He'd had his penis in my vagina. And despite the actual sex part kind of sucking, maybe with my hymen out of the way, next time would be better. Hell, maybe next time would be awesome. With someone who wasn't John Cole, of course.

Yes, he and I would go back to being just friends. Just. Friends.

"Well?" he asked.

"Ah, maybe?"

"Let's talk later."

I kept my face pleasantly blank as Hang's gaze switched from John to me and back again with interest. Luckily for me, John didn't notice. Also, Hang did subtle well, God bless the girl.

"We shooting hoops?" asked Anders. "Or you going to the library again like a loser?"

"Hoops."

"All righty then." After wiping the sweat from his brow, Anders trailed a damp finger across Hang's cheek. "Later, babe."

"Oh God, gross!" she cried, ducking out of reach. "Get away from me."

"I know you want me," he said, getting to his feet.

Nose crinkled, Hang stared at him in disgust. "However did you guess? Hooking up with a feral raving lunatic is absolutely my dream."

A crease appeared between John's brows. "Leave her alone, man. See you later, Edie."

And the recipient for the Best Fake Smile award for the year was (insert drum roll here)...me. "Bye."

"God, now I'm going to have to decontaminate myself with bleach or something." Hang scrubbed at her cheek with a Kleenex.

"What was that?" asked Sophia, moseying on up to our table. Carrie stood beside her, holding her hand. "Are there things going on with you and basketball boy?"

"Good question," I said, despite my own need for privacy. "Seems like he's into you."

"No, no. Absolutely not," said Hang. "I'm not the slightest bit interested in that too-tall idiot. And it's a testament to our friendship that I'm still talking to either of you."

When Sophia turned to me for answers, I gave a small shake of the head. Most definitely not going there anytime soon.

"You sure there's nothing going on?" she persisted, taking a seat. "Are you really really sure?"

"I saw them talking outside of History earlier," said Carrie. "Looked cozy."

With great zest, Hang slapped her hand down on the table. "That's it. You're both dead to me and I'm not even going to mourn you."

"Ooh," Sophia chortled. "The bitch pack won't like that. First Edie and John, now Hang and Anders. You should have seen their faces when the guys were just here. Ouch."

The table full of girls in question sat on the opposite side of the cafeteria, laughing just a little too loud, flipping enough hair around to cause permanent neck damage. I didn't care who the cool girls watched or what they thought, yet conditioning from my early years whispered that it mattered.

As if.

Hang cocked her head, eyes unimpressed. "Seriously, guys?"

"I'm not with John," I said, finishing off my apple.

"We're just friends."

"You two doth protest too much." Carrie and Sophia shared a look.

"Don't you two have something better to do than listen to dumbass gossip?" asked Hang. "Like, live your lives or go make out or something?"

"Actually." Sophia leaned into the table, her chin in her hand. "I come bearing good news."

The frown stayed on Hang's face. "What?"

"My old manager is running a home decorating place at the mall and just so happens to be in need of a couple of people for Saturdays." Sophia grinned. "I just might have told her about two mature, honest, and hardworking friends of mine who are looking for jobs."

Hang clapped her hands. "You're alive to me again! Oh my God, that's great, Soph."

"Really?" I asked, excitement building inside me.

Sophia nodded. "She wants you both to stop by one day this week after school."

"That's great." I smiled. "Thank you."

Hang and I beamed at each other. This was it: money, fame, and fortune would be ours. I could feel it.

chapter twenty-nine

John: U awake?

John: Edie?

chapter
thirty

"If you had to make a list of everything you'd need to survive the apocalypse, how high would napkin rings rate for you?" asked Hang.

I put on my thinking face. "Hmm. Food, water, napkin rings."

"You'd put them ahead of the napkin itself?"

"What use is a napkin without its decorative ring?" I asked.

"True."

Carefully, I attached the price sticker she'd handed me onto another shining example of the aforementioned item. "What about you?"

"Yeah," said Hang. "Pretty much the same."

We were gainfully employed. Or at least employed. Box and Jar had a wide and wonderful selection of everything you could possibly require to fulfill your domestic needs. It boggled the mind, half of the stuff. I mean, who the hell felt the need to invent three different varieties of dill pickle extractors? Pickles were great on a sandwich or burger. Absolutely awesome. But did getting the damn things out of the jar really warrant such a complex array of tools?

Apparently so.

"I hear there was another party at Sabrina's last night." Hang watched me out of the corner of her eye. "Apparently it was lit, going off, super-duper, and all of these things."

"Anders called you?"

"Texted," she corrected. "Wanted to know why we weren't there."

"What did you tell him?"

"That we had work today and needed to get some sleep."

I nodded. "Which is the truth."

"Yes, it is."

"You know, Anders really does seem to like you. Are you sure you're not into him just a little bit?"

"Let's talk about John."

I shut up.

"Girls!" Miriam swept past us on one of her regular checks. "How are you doing?"

Head to toe, the woman exuded class in her neat white linen shift dress and navy apron with the company name embroidered across her chest.

Meanwhile, I was all bulges in the tight straight dress, the largest size Miriam had been able to locate. Boobs, belly, butt, and thighs. And white was such a meh of a color on me. The navyk apron seemed only barely up to the job of holding me together. Any sudden wrong movement on my part and a seam might split. I lived in perpetual fear of it all falling apart. Here's hoping the dimples in my knees would distract people from my slightly overwhelming show of curves.

"You're already finished pricing those?" asked Miriam with a brilliant smile. "That's great. You know, that job would have taken the last lot all day and they still would have messed it up."

We both smiled back at her.

Earlier, she'd confided that the previous employees who held our positions had been busted smoking a joint in the storeroom. This worked out great for me and Hang. With them being so amazingly crappy, Miriam's expectations were low. So long as we turned up every Saturday, were coherent and got stuff done, she'd be happy.

Best job ever.

"I'm so glad Sophia told me about you two." Hands on hips, she surveyed our work. "And they're all sorted correctly. How do you feel about cushions?"

Hang turned to me.

"Ecstatic," I said.

"Great." With all the grace of a game-show hostess, Miriam directed our attention toward a full wall of shelving in disarray. "Some customers went through them yesterday. Left everything a complete mess. Do a cushion display that wows me, girls."

"You got it," said Hang.

I surveyed the wreckage of ruffles and fringing, buttons and bows. A few had been stuffed back into shelves, but most were still on the floor. "I'm thinking a rainbow, gay pride sort of statement."

Hang nodded. "I like it."

We got to work.

"Things got awkward with John post-sex, huh?" she asked, picking out all of the navy and dark blue cushions.

My lips slammed shut. Again.

"It's okay, Edie." She gave me a wry smile. "I know you don't like talking about him. Or anything at all."

"I'm a shitty friend."

"Nuh. You've just been through a lot. I get it." A cushion was held high. "Would you call this cobalt, royal blue, or sapphire?"

"Cobalt, I guess? It's not you, Hang," I said, trying to figure out how to explain and getting frustrated with myself in the process. Me and my many issues. "My last friend really screwed me over."

"That sucks."

"Yeah," I agreed sadly. "Having her put it all out there, making my private stuff public, it wasn't a good feeling. People were already talking about me, saying all this weird shit about the robbery. One conspiracy theory idiot was convinced I was in on it with Chris. That I was his real girlfriend or something. It was all such bullshit. When they didn't have any real information to report on, they just made things up."

Hang's lips were pinched, her gaze a mix of anger and sorrow.

"That kind of attention, it's not a good thing. There's nothing fun about it," I said, fingers curling into fists. "It's like there's this spotlight on you and there's no escaping it. You're not a person to them; they don't care about what you think or how you feel. The only thing that matters to them is getting what they want out of you."

Nope. I didn't sound bitter and twisted at all. Not even a little.

I shrugged. "Anyway, it's pretty much over now. Moving on."

"And John went through that too."

"Yeah."

"No wonder you two bonded. I mean that in a non-sexual way."

I nodded. Fluffing up a denim-colored cushion, I placed it into the correct cubbyhole-style shelf for our rainbow scheme.

"Sleeping with him was probably a mistake," I admitted, reaching for the next blue pillow. "I *need* him as a friend. He's the only one who gets what it was like that night. And afterward."

"Sex can make things tricky."

"I'm seeing this now."

"Okay," she said. "Obviously, we need to invent a time machine. Go back to that night, and have you sleep with Duncan instead."

And lose all of those lovely memories of John's skin against mine. What a horrible thought. Also, Duncan did nothing for me. Not in comparison to John.

"Or not?" she asked tentatively.

"Honestly, I've always had a bit of a crush on John. But now my pelvic region wants to do bad things with him all the time. I'm doomed." My shoulders drooped. Then I pulled them straight back up. "No. Things will return to normal. It'll just take some time. If I can avoid him for a while, all will be well."

"That's why you ran off to have your lunch outside recently," she groaned. "I was worried we'd insulted you somehow or something."

"No. I was hiding like a coward," I admitted. "I do that sometimes."

Slowly, she nodded. "Okay. Well, you're a strange one, Miss Millen. And I mean that with great affection."

"Why, thank you." I beamed. "I think you're quite odd yourself."

"But back to the problem at hand. Sure, you could keep avoiding him." Her gaze, it didn't fill me with confidence. "It might work."

"Absolutely it will work. He's always got so much going on, I bet he won't even notice if I drop out of sight for a while. I mean, I have to think positively. After all, we only bumped hips once." I held up a finger. "Just the once. You could almost say it was an accident."

"Yeeeaah. No," she said. "I'm not buying that. You've just lost all credibility there."

"Fine. But plenty of people have sex and it's nothing more than recreational. It means nothing to them, zip, nada, zero," I said. "It's just horizontal cardio with no clothes on. An orgasm or two and they're good to go, hitting the road."

"Some people, yeah."

I puffed out a breath. "Well, that could be me."

Hang said nothing. A whole lot of it.

"It could be."

"Maybe." She grimaced. "But, if it was you, in this case, wouldn't we *not* be having this conversation?"

I snapped my mouth shut. Turned away from my new female best friend and thought deep thoughts. Or at least tried to. Obviously, the validation I required would have to be found elsewhere. And while it was comforting that apparently Hang wouldn't be lying to me anytime soon, still...

"Get away from me with your logic," I pouted.

She held up a cushion. "Sky, arctic, or cornflower?"

"Pale-ish light blue?" My brows rose in question. "I don't know. Let's just do this damn thing."

"Right on." Carefully, she arranged it on a shelf. "So I shouldn't tell you about the field party Anders said is happening tonight?"

"No. Best not to."

She looked up at me from beneath her lashes. "Do you mind if I go? I mean, it's just...you know how Anders gets. The idiot will be texting me every other minute if I don't make an appearance. For some reason he's decided I'm fun to have around."

"Absolutely, you should go. I'm sorry to be such a loser and bailing on you. It's just going to take me a while before I can go near John without imagining him with no pants on. I need to stay away from him," I said with great conviction. "At least for a little while."

With a big sigh, she nodded. "Honestly, Edie, that might be for the best."

chapter
thirty-one

With another attempt at the book in the new fantasy series, a pint of chocolate-chip cookie dough ice cream, and the starry sky overhead, I had my own Saturday-night party for one. It was perfect. Mom had said she was going out with some friends from work, but I don't know. Something was going on with her. Something that, I'm pretty sure, caused hickeys. At any rate, I had the house to myself. Ah, silence, peace, and serenity. I'd forgotten how good being in your own sacred space could be.

I wasn't missing John at all. And I was absolutely not imagining that the hero in the book resembled him, because that would be wrong and directly contrary to what I was trying to achieve. Though it did sort of help with my focus issues.

"Hey."

I screeched, heart hammering inside my chest. A familiar size-and-shaped shadow stood outside my open window.

"John," I said, breathing just a wee bit quickly. Honestly, you'd think I'd be getting used to his sudden appearances by now. "Holy shit."

"Saw your bedroom light on, figured I'd just come around."

"Of course you did." I set aside my book, shuffling over to the far side of my bed as he climbed up to sit on my window ledge. "Thought you'd be at the field party."

"Could say the same of you."

Guilt hit me hard. "First day of work, I was kind of tired. You know. Had a bit of a headache from all of the stupid scented candles."

Head cocked, he nodded. Blue jeans and white shirt, his hair tied back into a ponytail. The cut of his cheekbones cast stark shadows on his face.

"Yeah, it was big, real busy," I said, blathering on. "You know, napkin rings and cushions and stuff. Lots of necessary household items."

"Right."

I smiled.

He didn't. "Want to tell me why you've been avoiding me, Edie?"

"I haven—"

"Don't!"

I stopped. The tone of his voice didn't encourage debate. And yet. "John, I get that you're upset. But if you raise your voice at me again I'll push you out the fucking window. Understood?"

For a second his eyelids squeezed shut, searching for

control or something. "Sorry. But I'd really appreciate it if you didn't lie to me, Edie."

"Okay." I took a deep breath. "All right."

"What's going on?"

I bit my lip and studied my hands, fingers twisted together in my lap. "Things have just gotten a bit weird for me. I just, I've been trying to deal with them, is all. Get them sorted out inside my head."

"What things?"

"You things."

His face was like stone. "This is about us fucking, isn't it?"

I flinched. "Yes."

"Dammit, Edie. It's just sex. It didn't mean anything."

Deep down inside, a small and hopefully insignificant part of me died. Some dumb hope that should never have existed in the first place. "I know. I'm screwing things up. I'm sorry."

"We talked about exactly this before we did it. Why would you even get confused?"

"I don't know," I cried. "I'm sorry, my feelings sometimes do their own thing. They don't always wait for permission. They're funny like that."

He huffed and puffed and swore some more. "This is why you ignored my text the other night. I am always there for you when you need me."

"You're right; that was extraordinarily crappy of me. I'm sorry." My stomach turned, a sour taste on my tongue. "Though it's not like you have problems finding company if you really want it."

His eyes glinted cold. "I didn't need someone to fuck, I needed a friend. You."

Then he turned to go, jumping down from my windowsill in one smooth move.

"Wait. Wait!" I cried, throwing myself across the bed and hanging out the window. "John, don't go."

The shadow of him hesitated.

"I shouldn't have said that." The window ledge dug into my belly. "It was bitchy and unnecessary."

"Yeah, it was."

"You're right—I'm an asshole," I said, loud enough to include my neighbors in the conversation. FFS. "But to be fair, I've never done the sex thing before and you're really important to me. So maybe can you just cut me a little slack here, please?"

He didn't turn back to face the dim light from my bedroom, his expression a mystery. "You're the one that wanted to lose it, Edie. It was all your bright idea. I just wanted you to be safe, to get treated right."

"I know."

"Nothing was supposed to change. That was the agreement, remember?"

"Yes," I said. "But feelings don't just turn on and off, John."

A grunt. The boy did that way too much.

"Look, you're right. I should have talked to you about it instead of going into hiding."

"Yeah, you should have. You're important to me too."

"Thank you."

"But this is still on you." Nice to know he had no interest in making this easy. He crossed his arms over his chest. "One way or another, you need to deal with this."

"How?"

"I don't know," he said. "Just...do whatever it is you need to do to forget about us having sex so we can go back to normal."

I frowned, tongue playing behind my cheek. "Hold up. Are you suggesting hypnosis or that I sleep with someone else to get over you? I'm confused."

The most pained sigh of all time. Truly, I felt bad for the boy. "I gotta go. I promised Anders and Hang I'd give them a lift home."

I said nothing.

"We okay?"

"Yes. We're fine." My fibbing skills were off the charts. The CIA or Hollywood or someone would probably be calling for me any day now. "No problem. I promise no more avoiding."

"Good. Maybe we could hang out tomorrow?"

"Sure." I half lifted a hand in farewell. "'Night."

chapter thirty-two

John: What do you feel like doing?

Me: Sick, sorry. A bit of a mess. Talk to you later.

My cell started buzzing. "Hello?"

"Thought we sorted this out," he said. "You avoiding me."

"I'm not avoiding you."

"Yes. You are," he said, voice sharp with tension.

"No, I'm not." My jaw tightened. "I promised I wouldn't do that. I'm honestly just not feeling well, John. It happens sometimes."

"Oh yeah?" he scoffed. "You were fine last night."

"You're right. I *was* fine last night." The girl in the bathroom mirror scowled back at me, every bit as furious as I felt. "But then blood started gushing from my uterus this morning and now my insides feel like they've been twisted into knots. It's really not pretty."

A long silence.

"Yeah. The cramps hurt like a bitch, John. So as you might have guessed by now, I'm not in a very good mood," I said through gritted teeth. "Also, my breasts ache and I kind of want to kill something."

"Um, okay."

"Great, glad we could talk this through. 'Bye," I finished, stabbing at the end call button.

Give me strength. I could have hit something, preferably him. Instead, I'd take two Advil, go back to bed, and feel sorry for myself. In that exact order. It would have been nice to hang out with John and further clear any lingering weirdness. But curling up in fetal position took precedence right now.

A couple of hours later, Mom came wandering in with a curious look on her face and a big white paper shopping bag in hand. "I'm concerned. Any chance you have a creepy yet practical, wealthy secret admirer or stalker you want to tell me about?"

"What?" I sat up, setting aside my book.

"I just found this sitting on the doorstep," she said, handing the bag over. "Tampons, Midol, and a box of chocolate cupcakes. Unoriginal but quite apt."

I burst out laughing.

She cocked her head. "Please explain."

"I scared a boy with my menstrual rage," I said, going through the contents of the bag. "Though to be fair, he kind of deserved it."

"Huh." Her brows remained knitted, her gaze perplexed. "Is he going to be leaving things on the doorstep often? Should I set up a motion sensor camera so I can get a look at him?"

"He's *just* a friend, Mom."

"Yeah, right." She gave me a look. *The* look. "Those cupcakes are from the fancy-pants bakery. Not cheap, kid."

"Yum." I opened up the box, salivating. "And they're all for me."

"I taught you to share—I know I did." She smiled. "So, what's his name?"

"Just a friend."

"Unusual name."

"Isn't it?" I passed her a cupcake. "Here."

"Oh, I shouldn't," she said, reaching out a hand. "Just a taste, maybe. You're not going to tell me about him, huh?"

"There's nothing to say. We're just fr—"

"Friends. Yes, I get it." She took a bite, an expression of bliss crossing her face. "Well, I love him, whoever he is. He already has my approval. These are divine."

Biting into my cupcake, I smiled. Then, once Mom had gone, I picked up my cell and hit his number.

"Hi," I said.

"Hey. You got the stuff?"

"Yes, I did. Thank you."

"No problem." A huff of breath. "Sorry 'bout earlier."

"You had a right to be dubious." I sighed. "We're always saying sorry to each other. What's with that?"

A laugh. "I don't know."

"My therapist would probably say we're interesting personality types working through our issues within the bounds of our relationships."

"Christ," he mumbled.

"Hmm." I took another bite, chewing with delight. "These cupcakes are amazing."

"Good. I gave Ruby a call and she clued me into what you'd want."

"The waitress from the roadhouse?"

"Yeah."

"She knows her stuff," I said, licking some chocolate frosting off my fingers. "And don't worry, I'll get over my weirdness. Chocolate has all sorts of magical healing properties."

"Okay. Good."

Neither of us said anything for a minute. Yep, it was a very comfortable long, drawn-out silence. Not awkward at all.

"Anyway, I'd better go," I said eventually. "Mom wanted to—"

"Right. Yeah. See you at school, Edie." And he was gone.

chapter thirty-three

Unknown: SOS!!

Me: Who is this?

Unknown: Me, dummy.

Me: ?

Unknown: Anders!!!!!!!!!!!!!

Me: What do you want and how did you get my number?

Anders: JC gave it to me. His car's died. Come get us we need a lift to school.

Me: Be there soon.

Anders: For him you do stuff. WHAT ABOUT ME?

By daylight, the two-story home looked even more in need of work, despite the perfection of the garden. Flaking paint and climbing vines hid the potential glory of the place. Guess his uncle was too busy running a business to do much work on the house. It wasn't a bad neighborhood or anything. Most of the other homes were well maintained, immaculate even. Only John's place seemed at odds, in need of a little love.

He was bent over the engine. But by the time I got out of my car, he'd progressed to throwing a wrench at the ground before really releasing his frustrations by kicking one of the beast's tires. "Fucking asshole."

Whoa.

"Johnny." A man strode out of the house, wrapped up in an opulent green silk robe. His long hair was thrown over one shoulder, face neatly shaved. "Hey, come on. Calm down."

Hands on hips, John glared at the beast. "He's taken the distributor cap."

The man, in his late thirties maybe, put a hand on John's shoulder, giving it a squeeze. Whatever the man said next, I stood too far away to hear. He gestured to an aging silver sedan parked alongside the beast and John shook his head, lips pinched white with fury.

Meanwhile, Anders sat on the lawn, just hanging. "Hey, check it out. Edie's here, what a happy coincidence!"

John turned to me with a frown.

"'Morning," I said, pushing my sunglasses up on top of my head.

The heavy frown was redirected to Anders, who just shrugged it off. "What? She goes to our school and we need a ride. Problem solved—you're welcome."

Nothing from John. Guess he hadn't given my number to Anders and asked him to text.

"Hello," said the man, coming toward me with a hand outstretched for shaking. "I'm Levi. John's uncle."

"Edie," I said. "Nice to meet you."

Levi beamed with pleasure, happy crinkles appearing around his familiar blue eyes. "Grab your bag, John. You don't want to keep the lady waiting."

Still looking all sorts of unhappy, John slammed the beast's driver's-side door shut before stomping off into the house.

Uncle Levi offered me a wary smile. "He hasn't had a good morning."

"No. Doesn't look like it."

Once John reappeared, bag on his back, we got moving. He sat slumped in the front passenger seat, staring out the window, his jaw set, while Anders whined about having to take the backseat all the way to a local drive-through coffee place. No matter how mad John was, I needed my fix.

"Want anything?" I asked my passengers.

Anders shook his head.

"Coffee." John fished a ten-dollar bill out of his pocket. "And I'll buy yours."

"That's not necessary."

The tone of his voice hadn't lightened any. "Call it gas

money."

"All right."

A few minutes later, John had his Americano and I had my double-shot latte. Hopefully caffeine would cheer him up. God knows I found mornings more bearable with some coffee in hand. The rest of the ride to school passed in silence; even Anders kept his mouth shut for once.

"Thanks," John mumbled upon arrival, spilling out of the car and quickly walking away.

Slowly blowing out a breath, Anders leaned on the back of my seat. He gave my high ponytail a tug. I reached back, swatting at his hand.

"Thanks for coming," Anders said in a quiet voice. "I crashed at JC's last night. We played computer games until way past our bedtime. It was great. But it's really been a suck of a morning."

"Why? What's going on?"

But he'd already cracked the door and climbed out. Gone, just like John. I sipped my still-hot coffee, gathering my stuff. It was all so strange. Despite me delivering him to school, he didn't show in English. I didn't see him again at school that day at all.

chapter
thirty-four

The tap on my window came just before midnight, leaving a smear of blood on the glass. For once, due to the rain, it'd been shut.

"John?" I bolted upright, my book forgotten. An earlier storm had made the wood swell a little and I had to wrestle the window open. "Holy shit!"

"Hey." He swayed in the dim light, the darkness of blood on his face. "Hi, Edie. I, ah..."

"Get in here."

"Right."

I grabbed at his arm, helping him up and in. Actually, dragging his sorry ass inside onto my bed would be a better description. His clothes were soaked through.

"Lie down," I ordered, more than a little freaked out. Split lip, bloody nose, a black eye. Absolute carnage. I pushed up his shirt, inspecting him for scary black marks. Anything that might indicate internal bleeding or something. Where was a medical degree when I needed one?

"I'm okay," he said. "I just, I-I got into a fight."

"You don't say." My voice wavered from the mini heart attack in process. Christ, he'd scared me. I headed for the door. "We need supplies. Stay there. Do not move."

In the bathroom Mom kept a first-aid box with the basics. I grabbed it and a couple of wet face cloths. Thank God she was at work. For her and John to meet under these conditions would not be good.

"I'm not drunk," he said as I climbed back onto the bed and started cleaning up his face. "Only had a few."

"Yeah? Pity. I bet you're in a lot of pain right now."

A grunt.

Once I got the worst of the blood off, things didn't seem quite so bad. He might be a mess, but he'd live. Off came his Converse. I threw his wet T-shirt, socks, and jeans into the washing machine with plenty of detergent. My laundry skills were minimal. In all likelihood, the bloodstains were there to stay. The dirt, however, could probably be dealt with. It gave me something to think about besides the fact that John lay close to naked on my bed.

"Didn't want to go home," he said, his eyes closed. "Sorry."

"It's fine."

Antiseptic cream went on everything, an ice pack over his eye, and a Band-Aid over the cut on his cheek. His split lip had stopped bleeding, so I just left it alone. Next I moved on to his bloody hands.

"What were you fighting about?" I asked, tending carefully to his split knuckles. "Who were you fighting?"

He groaned. "Nothing. Doesn't matter."

"All right. What do you want to talk about?"

"Don't wanna talk," he said, shivering. "Cold."

Since he lay on top of my bedding, I fetched my old spare blanket out of the closet and covered him up to the neck.

"Better?" I asked.

He nodded. "Dillon, we argued. He's the one that messed with my car. Went to talk to him."

"Your brother? Shit. And I take it the visit didn't go so well?"

"No. It didn't." He yawned, groaning in pain. "Business is fucked. He wants me to start selling again."

"What?" I hissed.

"'s all right. I told him no. That's how we got to fighting."

Holy hell, what a bastard.

Soon enough, John's breathing evened out and his body relaxed. I sat there, staring at him, unsure of what to do. God, the swelling on his face looked horrible. Due to my recent adventures in insomnia, I knew Mom had been getting home later recently. More odd behavior from her, though I had enough on my hands to worry about right now. Also, I knew she didn't check on me when she got home. Not if my door had been closed. We both knew me getting some decent sleep happened rarely enough not to risk making a noise. The boy in my bed was safe from maternal drama.

I waited until his clothes were finished in the washer

then transferred them into the dryer. At that point, I'd done about everything I could. No way would I sleep after all this excitement. And with my brain buzzing, concentrating on my book would be equally unlikely. So I lay down beside him, watching his chest rise and fall.

Next thing I knew, morning light blinded my eyes.

"Edie? Hey, wake up."

"Hmm?" Squinting, I slowly woke.

Gentle fingers pushed the hair from my face, dreamy blue eyes gazing down. "Hey."

"'Morning," I said, not quite believing. But it really was. I'd slept. For hours and hours, with no waking up in a panic from freaky nightmares or bad dreams. Wow. I hadn't felt this rested in forever.

"I need my clothes," he said.

"Um. Okay. We'd better be quiet—don't want to wake Mom." I swallowed. "You don't look so good."

"No. Probably not." He half attempted a smile.

I rolled out of bed, needing to put some space between me and the evidence of just how much the morning light adored John's skin. Last night, I'd undressed him. I'd put him in his current state of near nakedness. But last night, I'd been too upset by how hurt he was to appreciate the scenery. To feel the hot thrill of lust running through my veins.

All was quiet. I crept through the house on tippytoes, grabbing his clothes before dashing back to my room. The near-naked boy had started flipping through my current book.

"Be careful," I said, exchanging his clothes for my book. "I don't like the pages getting creased."

"Sorry." He smiled, amused.

Jerk. "Where'd you park your car?"

"I walked here."

"You *what?*" I exclaimed, then slapped a hand over my too-loud mouth. "How long did that take?"

"What?"

I removed the hand and repeated the question.

He just shrugged, dragging his jeans on and doing up the zipper and button. Sweet baby Jesus. Over and over, like some soft-porn GIF, my mind replayed those ten seconds. I couldn't help it. Or didn't want to. Honestly, it was hard to tell exactly which. Forget bacon on pancakes covered in maple syrup; he made me drool.

For shame. There had to be a special level of hell for people who coveted their beat-up best friend. Though, how could I not have a crush on him? That was the question. Best for all involved if he hurried up and put his shirt on. Put me out of my misery.

Head cocked, he asked, "What's that look? What are you thinking about?"

"Canadian bacon."

He blinked. "I'll buy you breakfast."

"Pancakes at Awful Annie's?"

"Whatever you want."

"Okay, give me five to thirty minutes to quickly get ready."

I got busy rifling through my closet. Clean, neutral,

happy thoughts. Not dwelling upon John's pants or what was in them or anything. Not wondering if besides drinking and getting into fights, he'd also used one of his willing naked-fun-time female acquaintances as a distraction from his brother's crap.

Actually, I didn't want to know.

Definitely a ripped black jeans sort of day. Doc sandals, black-and-white-striped tank, underwear, and we were all good. Clothes selected, I turned back to find him checking out my bookshelves.

"I'm not touching anything," he said, holding up his busted hands. "Promise."

"You can touch. Just be gentle."

Another of those secretly amused smiles. Just because he couldn't comprehend my true and enduring love of books. Douche canoe of a boy.

I rushed through a shower, dry-shampooing the crap out of my hair before chucking it up in a bun. Meh, whatever. Given the time constraints, basic makeup would do.

"You'd better go out the window, meet me down the block," I said, shoving the last of my necessary things into a bag. "Be careful. Don't hurt yourself further."

"I'll be fine." He crawled across my bed, careful to keep his still-dirty Converse off the quilt. Once he sat on the windowsill, he stopped, turning back. "Thanks for letting me in last night. For looking after me."

"Of course." Compliments always weirded me out. I couldn't meet his eyes, so I studied my feet. Yep, still ten toes, nails neatly painted black. Amazing. "You'd do it for me."

Because of the split lip, his grin was limited. "See you down the street."

The warmth in my heart lingering after he left, it went well beyond friendship. It felt dangerous.

chapter
thirty-five

The week progressed smoothly until after lunch on Wednesday. If ever a day had been created full of ill will, it would be Wednesday. It's like it just sat there in the middle of the week, taunting me with the two days of school yet to go before we'd reach the weekend.

Bastard.

Despite being unable to avoid my incredibly sexually attractive friend John since he and Anders had taken to sitting with us at lunch every day, things were okay. I'd been able to keep a lid on my feelings. Who knows, maybe denial and repression were good for the soul.

The bell for class rang, the hallways crowded with people. Chatter, laughter, all sorts of loud noises. Happily, none of it set off a panic attack. My freak-outs weren't coming on as often these days. I don't know if it was due to therapy or what, but I liked it a lot.

I stood at my locker, switching books, when someone touched my butt. Not a passing, possibly accidental sort of thing. No way, this was a full-on grab a handful of my flesh and give it a good, bruisingly hard squeeze. Followed by male laughter.

I spun, face no doubt full of surprise. "What the hell?"

"If it's good enough for John, hey?" the Neanderthal said. What he lacked in height he made up for in muscles. I think I recognized him from Chemistry. More laughing from his crew of equally athletic-looking idiot friends.

"Go fuck yourself," I said in my most eloquent voice. My hands balled into fists, I wanted to hit him so badly. It didn't matter that he was packing serious muscle. It no doubt wouldn't end well, but whatever. Pain, hospital, detention, suspension. They were all problems for some remote future. What mattered right now was payback, and replacing that smirk on his face with something a lot uglier.

The sudden thought of Mom intruded on my rush of anger. Her picking me up from the hospital. Again. Her disappointment as she related her conversation with the principal. Again.

My fists stayed by my side, knuckles white.

My fury just made them laugh harder. Hell, there were even some chuckles from others strolling past. Rage roared to life inside of me. If ever I'd had the urge to burn things down, it was then. He did not have the right to do that. To touch me however he wanted. Then to treat touching me, and my outrage at his doing so, like a joke.

No way. Not happening.

Maybe I couldn't break his nose without breaking my mother's heart, but I had other options. I just needed some time to think things through. Revenge would be mine.

As it turned out, I wasn't the only one who wound up in detention that afternoon. (I hadn't meant to almost doze off during Math again, honest.) I'd no sooner pulled out a book and pen when the Neanderthal himself slunk through the door. *Holy shit.* Bloody toilet paper filled both nostrils and his nose looked seriously swollen. Behind him came none other than John.

Coincidence? Not so much.

Ever so calmly, he sat down at the desk beside me, pulling out a textbook.

"You didn't have to do that," I whispered.

"I know."

"I have things under control." A complete lie, though it made me feel better. Capable, even. "And didn't you tell me violence is not the answer?"

"Can't remember."

He hadn't wanted to get dragged into any of my drama at school. He'd definitely said that. And seeing how he'd given up dealing and was putting a real effort into studying, I understood. Besides, I didn't need him to defend me. I might not win every battle, but I was more than willing to fight for myself.

"I mean it, you shouldn't have." I leaned closer to him, talking quietly. "You said you're taking school seriously, cleaning up your act. Not adding to your record because of me, remember?"

"He won't touch you again."

"John."

"Relax," he said, flipping through the pages. "It's fine. You're making too big a deal out of this."

"Bullshit," I hissed. "Why is there one set of rules for you and another for me?"

"Because I never knew a girl I wanted to look after before."

That shut me up.

From the front of the classroom, the teacher watched us with a warning in his eyes. Apparently detention involved less catching up with your friends than I realized. No wonder I used to put more effort into avoiding it.

"We're talking about this later," I said.

One shoulder lifted, all nonchalant. "Sure. Whatever you want, Edie."

He slipped out at the end of detention before we could talk and I didn't get a chance to speak to him for the rest of the school week. He started spending every lunch on the basketball court with Anders, and was the last person to arrive at English and the first to leave. *Jerk.* Guess he didn't like being told what to do any better than I did.

chapter
thirty-six

"If he makes you cry, he's not worth it."

Hang winked at me, setting a pot of rice down on the dining room table. "I don't think he makes her cry, Mom."

"We really are just friends," I said.

"Of course you are." Hang smirked. "He's so unattractive, Mom. Edie couldn't possibly be interested in him. All those yucky muscles and cheekbones like a Rodin sculpture. Disgusting."

"Boys," her mom said, voice full of scorn.

At the other end of the table, her dad kept his head down, ladling a chicken-and-noodle dish called pho into a bowl. There were steamed greens and a spicy dish with fish in it along with the main course. Everything smelled divine and looked amazing. Far superior to the microwave mac and cheese I'd been planning on eating at home.

"This looks delicious," I said.

"Eat," ordered her mother, sounding vaguely pleased with the compliment.

After dinner came a platter of fruit, all while Hang's mom grilled us both on our school grades, social life, and anything else she cared to know about. As long as we avoided the topic of John, I was happy. Meanwhile, her dad barely said a word all evening. I couldn't blame him. With me here and Hang's older brother away at college, the poor man was outnumbered.

"Take these." Mrs. Tran loaded me down with containers of food on our way out. Enough to last for days. Despite my size, she seemed to have serious reservations about how much I had to eat at home. I didn't fight her. Firstly, the food really was delicious; secondly, only a fool would try to say no to the woman. "Home by nine thirty, Hang. It's a school night."

"I will be."

Outside, clouds covered most of the sky. Looked like it would rain later. A pity, but I didn't feel like delaying my mission. "I drove past his place on the way over and the car was out front."

"We're seriously doing this?" asked Hang.

"You don't have to—"

"Oh, no. I have to." She'd been just as outraged by the butt-groping incident. Possibly more. "Keys, please."

I tossed them to her.

"I've never been a getaway driver before," she said, pushing her glasses farther up her nose. It was strange to see her in them; usually she wore contacts.

"I believe in you."

Inside the car, she started the engine and put on her

seat belt before giving the eight cartons of eggs sitting on the backseat a speculative glance. "That's a lot of eggs."

"Justice is about to be served sunny-side up."

Carrie and Sophia had been to a party at the creep's house a few years back. It would be an understatement to say they'd been happy to provide us with the address. Actually, they'd been sad faced about not being included. The more people attending, however, the more likely it was we'd get caught. In and out with a simple two-woman team would work best. At least, it seemed safest. We'd both worn black; no big deal for me of course. Black jeans and T-shirt, my hair braided. Hang had gone for shorts and a top with ruffles down the front, her hair also tied back. Stealth with style.

An upbeat song by The 1975 played on the radio. Not the theme from *Mission Impossible*, but it would do. I'd considered asking John to drive, but he'd already paid his dues with this guy. Plus, this was women's business.

It wasn't far to the house, a nice two-story stucco with a big old willow tree filling the front yard. It was located on a quiet street. Lights were on in the place upstairs and down; people were definitely home. A couple of cars were parked in the wide driveway. Tonight, our target was the black SUV with a bull bar so large it had to be compensating for something.

Dick size, possibly. Manners, definitely. And intellect probably also belonged on the list.

"I'll keep the engine running," said Hang, headlights switched off and the music turned down. She was a natural at this. "Leave the door open on your side. First sign of anyone, run."

I nodded. Though honestly, the thought of getting caught didn't bother me at all. It was even kind of thrilling. Thinking of how the asshole had grabbed me, like it was no big deal, like he had the right because what did I matter anyway...I smiled. "I'm going to enjoy this."

Boxes of eggs cradled in my arms, I crept up the concrete drive. Hopefully there'd be no security lighting. It would be a pity if I were disturbed before my work was finished.

First I went for the windshield. The shells made a gratifying cracking sound as they hit their target. And I might not have been too keen on sports, but pitching eggs came quite naturally to me. Golden yolks slid down the glass; more splattered across the hood. I paid particular attention to the driver's-side door. It got extra-great coverage due to its importance.

Fighting back was exhilarating.

I stood beneath the silver cloud-covered sky, grinning like a loon, circling the SUV, peppering it with eggy goodness. A trail of empty cartons lay strewn behind me. I honestly didn't even hear the yapping of the dog or the voices calling it back. Hang's shouting didn't reach me either, at first. When she lay on the horn, though...I snapped to attention, blinking like I'd just woken from a dream. A happy one. The outside light flicked on, shining bright in my eyes.

"Hey! What the fuck?" yelled a pissed-off male voice

from inside. Keys jangled as he battled with the security lock on the front door. At his feet, the pint-size terror of a dog yapped on. Once the door opened, it was going to go straight on the attack. But there was still time; there had to be.

"Hurry, hurry, hurry!" shouted Hang, revving the engine. "Now!"

Just one second. I tore open the lid of my remaining carton and smashed the contents up against the side of his big SUV.

"Take that, you asshole," I whispered. Then I ran.

Hang took off before I'd even shut the car door, my hatchback surging forward with more force than I'd have thought capable. Heart pounding, breathing hard, I wrestled with the seat belt. Slimy hands were slippery.

"Holy shit," said Hang, looking in the rear mirror.

"We did it."

"No one's following." Her gaze flitted between the mirror and the road, fingers wrapped so tight around the wheel her knuckles stood out. "Except for a small pissed-off dog. Sorry, pup. See you later."

I huffed out a laugh. "Oh, that was so good."

"God. You nearly gave me a heart attack."

"Sorry."

"I was yelling for you to run and you were just standing there, staring at the car." She shook her head, slowing down and turning on the headlights now that we'd covered a suitable distance. "It was like you were in a trance or something."

"Just admiring my work."

"And you just had to use up the last carton, didn't you? Shit, Edie."

"I was so close to finishing."

"He nearly caught us!" She laughed. It sounded more incredulous/hysterical than happy. The whites of her eyes had never seemed so huge. "You're insane. I could kind of kill you right now. Let's not do that again anytime soon, okay?"

Slumped back in the passenger seat, I smiled. "That was awesome, though."

"You got him good."

"*We* got him good."

"Yeah, we did." Reluctantly, she smiled. "Asshole."

chapter
thirty-seven

Anders threw a party Saturday night at his house, which turned out to be not that far from mine. It was his eighteenth birthday.

His dad remained on the scene, playing fantasy basketball with his friends in the den. So long as no major laws or furniture were broken, that's where they'd stay. While his father had been cool with the party, his mom apparently had reservations. As per the usual, there was the keg of beer, though this time it stayed concealed in a small pool house surrounded by a garden. Lots of bikinis and loud music, with people sneaking in and out of the structure holding red Solo cups, ensued.

Still no sign of John.

"And here is a variety of nutritious juices. Lots of vitamins and nutrients," said Anders, giving Hang, Sophia, Carrie, and me a tour of the party. The flashing tiara on his head left little doubt as to in whose honor the event was being held. "Very healthy. You'll be able to dance all night on that natural energy."

"Looks delicious," said Carrie. "And there's the dance floor. See you guys later!"

Soph laughed and off they went, hand in hand.

"Yes, lots of fruit and water. Some sodas, too. But be careful—they have a lot of sugar in them and that's no good for your teeth." Anders carefully pushed aside the sober items to get to the individual bottles of juice-and-vodka mixers below. He popped the lid on one and handed it to Hang, then did the same for me. "Nothing alcoholic, sorry, because Mom is afraid of God smiting us. So, just the good kid stuff tonight."

"What about the keg?"

"You're imagining it, along with that alcoholic beverage in your hand. I wouldn't dare go against my mother's wishes." Anders smiled. "When do I get my birthday kiss?"

Her chin went up. "Who said I was giving you one?"

"Well, what if I just quickly felt you up, then? Over the top of your swimsuit. That would be a nice gift."

"Ha!" Hang headed for the pool. "Dream on."

"What if you felt me up, then? That would be great too. It could be like my gift to you."

"Not happening."

"How about we play spin the bottle, later. Just you and me." He followed behind her like a very large and overeager puppy. "Can't have a party without party games, right?"

Beside a fire pit, John Cole sat surrounded by some of the school's finest. Sports stars, rich ones, and various cool types, all of them laughing and chatting and drinking. Erika had seated herself on a new guy's lap. Not that it mattered. No way would I wander over and say hi to John. He might fit in with those types, but I didn't. I'd stick with my friends and head for the dance floor. Time to burn off some of my pent-up frustration, and other equally unwelcome emotions, with Carrie and Soph.

We took turns fetching drinks. Some were water, some weren't. After an hour or two, I had a nice buzz going, my body drenched in sweat and a broad smile on my face. My friend Marie from Bio had even joined us for a while.

"Pool?" asked Soph, panting.

"Pool," Carrie and I agreed.

They both had bathing suits on under their clothes, but I just toed off my flats. Good enough. In we went, denim shorts and tank top and all, making an almighty splash. Cool water closed over my head and the muted bass of the music thumped on, before I resurfaced to the summertime smell of chlorine. Man, it felt good.

Sophia and Carrie started floating around, kissing. Meanwhile, Anders and Hang appeared to be having a deep and meaningful conversation over by the steps. I was on my own. All good. I climbed out, going in search of first, a towel, and second, food. Turned out John had the first one already covered.

"Hey," he said, wrapping me up in a monster-size towel. Shades of green and yellow decorated his face, the bruises slowly fading. His knuckles seemed a little better too.

"Hi. Thanks."

I wrung out my hair. Only about a gallon of water came out. My wet clothes had the towel saturated in under a minute. This was the problem with going in fully clothed. Oh, well.

"Damn." He smiled. "We need another one just for your hair—come on."

I followed him around the side of the house to another door leading into a laundry room. Guess he'd spent a lot of time here over the years. For certain, he knew his way around. He had two fresh towels out of the closet in no time. One got exchanged for the drenched thing wrapped around me, but the second he kept hold of, using it to gently pat my hair dry.

"I can do that," I said.

"I got it." His voice dropped low, sending a strange thrill down my spine. Given we were platonic, he was certainly being very handsy. No. John was just a friend. Just a...hell, not even I could quite believe that one anymore. "How was the water?"

"Nice. Cooling." And this was strange. Very strange.

Once my clothes reached the point of damp as opposed to dripping, little more could be done. I put the wet towel on top of the washing machine, ready to be hung out once John got done with my hair. Only, work on my head stalled at that point, his gaze flickering from my face to the wet T-shirt competition happening below.

Oh man, my nipples. How pointedly embarrassing.

I crossed my arms over my chest. "So, what have you

been up to? I haven't seen you since detention."

"Yeah." He licked his lips. "I've been busy."

"Avoiding me."

"Possibly."

I laughed. "Definitely. Don't worry, I no longer wish to lecture you on the evils of getting into trouble at school. Especially when it's because of me."

"No?" His expression eased. "Good."

"Though it's totally hypocritical of you to avoid me like that."

He bit back a smile. "Heard someone had their car egged the other day. You know, I think it was that asshole who grabbed you."

"Wow, what a coincidence. And such a shocking attack on private property."

"Mm."

I kept my face blank. Innocent as a lamb. *Baa.*

"You wouldn't know anything about it then?" he asked.

"Absolutely not."

"Uh-huh." Brows scrunched up, he was obviously unconvinced. "Next time, when you're not doing things like that, let me know so I can watch your back. Okay?"

I just smiled.

"I'm serious, Edie."

"I heard you, but my back was covered."

"Anders would have been pissed if you'd gotten Hang into trouble," he said.

"Hang's a big girl; she can make her own choices."

For a moment, he just looked at me. "Can't believe you egged his car."

"I admit to nothing."

He gave me a lopsided smile and it actually made me feel a little light-headed. God, everything this boy did got to me. Either that, or I'd had more to drink than I realized. Whatever. Emergency escape time. I had to get out of here before I did something stupid. "I'm going to head home."

He stopped. "What? You're leaving already?"

"Yeah, I need a change of clothes," I said. "Plus, I've danced, I've drunk, I've swum. Work was actually pretty busy today, so...time for bed."

"How'd you get here?"

"Hang's dad dropped us off. I'll just walk home."

"Okay," he said. "I'll walk with you."

"You don't have to do that."

"You're always telling me what I don't have to do for you." He shook his head, smiling faintly. "I know what's right and wrong, and I know what I want. You're not walking home alone at night, Edie. I'd drive you, but I've had a few drinks myself."

"All right. No need to get feisty."

He just laughed and threw the towel aside. "C'mon, let's go."

I fetched my bag, and as per protocol, texted the girls good-bye. The breeze was chilly. Summer had officially come to an end. John took off the button-down shirt he had on over his T-shirt and handed it to me without a word.

Happily, it also took care of the nipple issue. "Thanks."

"I was watching you dance. You're good."

"Years of playing 'Just Dance' in the family room, and I never did reach the high scores."

"I'm serious."

I groaned. "You're making me self-conscious."

"Don't be."

"Right," I said, laughing a little too loud. "I'll flick off that switch because you said so."

He just smiled and shook his head. Seemed he was doing that a lot tonight.

"Thanks," I eventually mumbled.

"Why can't girls ever take a compliment? They've always got to act embarrassed for some reason."

I harrumphed. "Like you do any better."

"What do I do?" He tipped his chin. "Hmm?"

"You ignore them outright. Just pretend like I never spoke."

A small shake of the head. "No, I don't."

"Yeah, you do."

"Hit me with one," he demanded.

"Um. I don't know." He was the most beautiful thing I'd ever seen, his body a dream. He was sweet and loyal and honest and kind and strong and smart and he made me feel safe, something I didn't think would ever happen again anywhere with anyone. "You're a good driver. Very safe."

"Thank you, Edie."

"You're welcome, John."

"You're damn good at pool. Whipped my ass."

"Thanks," I said.

Up high, clouds covered the sky. No moon to gaze at, no stars to wish upon. Though really, what would I wish for? John was walking beside me and it seemed harsh to burden a distant sun with my desire for world peace. It probably had its own problems.

"When are we playing again?" he asked. "I need a chance to beat you, get back my dignity."

"Can't handle being beaten by a girl?"

The side of his mouth turned up. "No. Just don't like losing in general."

"Fair enough. We can play again whenever you like."

"Good."

He stopped, kicking at a stone on the road. We were at my house already. It really hadn't been far. The porch light was on, the driveway empty. Mom said she had another thing going on with her friends; God knows what time she'd be home. She was out a hell of a lot lately. But since it benefited me, I'd decided not to complain.

"Thanks for walking me," I said, arms crossed over my chest again to hide my nerves. And why I was nervous, I had no idea. "Want to come in?"

The look he gave me, I couldn't read. It was guarded by fences, doors, walls, probably even mines, and a moat.

"Just to hang out," I said. "You know."

"Nah." He looked back the way we'd come. "I, ah, better get back."

"See you later then."

A nod.

"Don't get into any more fights," I said. "Please."

He just smiled. "'Night."

While I unlocked the door, he waited at the curb, watching. He stood with his hands in his pockets, the wind whipping his loose hair about his face. I waved and went inside, locking the door behind me. It felt like a part of me was still out there with him, though. As if I'd been cut in two.

Crazy.

A shower washed the chlorine out of my hair, I'd blow-dried it, and put on my favorite black-and-white polka-dot pajamas. I opened my curtains and pushed up my window, searching the night sky. Only a little of the cloud cover had moved, allowing a couple of stars to shine through.

After a bowl of Cheerios, my stomach was happy. Book in hand, I settled down to read and actually started to get somewhere. Now that the buzz from the drinks had dimmed, it felt good to be home. I'd gone out and socialized with little to no awkwardness. *Go, me.*

The couple in the book wouldn't get their act together. So very annoying.

A voice at the window said my name.

"John?"

Without waiting for an invitation, he climbed right on in. I shuffled back to give him room on my bed. Converse tucked beneath him and hands on his knees, he sat, looking down at me. Studying me. Given my usual patience levels, I could only take about ten seconds of his silence.

"What's wrong?" I asked, setting my book aside.

"Nothing. Nothing's wrong."

"Then why are you looking at me like that?"

He swallowed hard. "I did want to come in and hang out with you earlier, but..."

"But what? Why didn't you then?"

Instead of speaking, he kissed me.

Of course, I kissed him back. Of course I did.

Holy shit. Our mouths moved against each other, his hands cradling my face. This was what I'd needed, what I'd been waiting for without even really knowing. His skin on mine, his breath on my face. I couldn't get close enough, no matter how I tried. Eyes hazy and lips wet, he kissed me slow and sweet. It seemed endless, as necessary to life as breathing.

Then, faces only inches apart, we just stared at each other.

I had nothing. No words at all.

Fingertips slid over my cheek, along my jaw. He swallowed hard. "Hey."

"Hi."

"I was going to head back to Anders's place."

I nodded. "You said."

"Couldn't bring myself to go."

"You've been out there this whole time?"

His expression seemed bewildered and yet amused. Amazed even. The light in his eyes like he was almost laughing. "Must have looked like a goddamn stalker."

"Are you drunk or high?"

"No. I had a few beers earlier, but they've pretty much worn off now."

Huh. "You stared at my house, then climbed in the window and kissed me?"

"Yeah."

"Why?"

His brows rose. "I don't know. 'Cause it was the only thing that made sense. I just, I keep thinking about that night with you at my place."

"You do?"

"It's like I can't get it out of my head."

"I think about it too," I said. "Maybe we both need lobotomies."

"The sex wasn't even that good," he said somewhat bluntly. "'Specially not for you."

"That's not true."

He just gave me a look.

"Well," I hedged. "I mean, I think it was probably as good as it could have been. For me."

"It can be a lot better. I promise," he said. "Anytime you want a do-over, just let me know."

I smiled. "I am glad it was with you."

He smiled too. Then he tucked my hair behind my ear, softly running his thumb over the new scar cutting across my forehead. "Hate how that asshole hurt you."

"You got hurt too. You got shot."

His smile morphed into something altogether more serious. "Yeah. But I should have been able to protect you."

"Don't," I said. "We both got out alive. That's what matters."

"Hmm."

Head tilted, he placed his mouth against mine. It was just that easy, falling back into our kiss. This time he led me down onto the mattress, onto my back. All without our lips separating for more than a moment. Bliss felt like this, his thumb running back and forth along my jawline, fingers resting on my neck. I touched his face and held back his hair. I kissed him deeper, trying to show him how much he meant to me, how much I cared.

Over the top of my tank, his hand stroked down my side, fingers straying close to my breast. *Oh, man.* It all felt so incredibly good. The hot and hard length of his body resting against mine. All sorts of obscene thoughts ran riot through my head. I wanted more and more. I wanted everything. Guess it was a problem with sex. Once you'd gone that far, the expectation would be to go there again. But I didn't know if I was ready. And I really didn't know what doing it with John a second time might mean.

I broke away, breathing hard.

"It's alright," he said, pressing kisses to the side of my face. "We don't have to go any further."

"How did you know?"

"You stiffened up." He tucked his hair behind his ear.

"It's okay. I'm good with just this."

"You are?"

"Yeah."

I frowned, embarrassed. "But you're used to having sex."

"It won't kill me, Edie," he said gently. "Relax."

Timid messed-up maiden, that was me. I slipped my hand beneath the sleeve of his shirt, curving my fingers around his non-injured shoulder. Touching him came naturally, I couldn't have stopped my fingers if I tried. Not that I was interested in trying. "One more uncomfortable question: What does this mean?"

"It means I like being here kissing you."

I let out a long breath. "Okay."

"Is that enough?"

"Yes," I said, because it was. For now. "Next time, don't stand out in the dark. Just come in, okay?"

His gaze softened. "Thanks. Don't know why I did that, why I couldn't just make up my mind. Maybe I really am going crazy."

"You're not crazy."

"Sure about that?" he asked.

"Yes. Well, mostly." Best to be truthful. "I think any-one who went through what we did is bound to come out of it a bit of a mess."

"Yeah." He laughed. "No idea when I slept last. Like, really slept."

"Then lie down." I rolled onto my side, facing him as he lay his head on the pillow next to mine. "Close your eyes."

He did as told for about a second. "Always feel like I'm wired. Like something's about to happen, I just don't know what."

"I get that too," I said. "Sort of like I'm on the edge of a panic attack. Just waiting."

"Weed helps sometimes. Not always."

"Mr. Solomon taught me a breathing technique. Lie on your back," I ordered, doing likewise. "Put one hand on your stomach and one hand on your chest."

"I'd rather put a hand on *your* chest. Probably wouldn't calm me down, though."

"Probably not. One on your stomach and one on your chest. Yours. As in, your own." I waited until he complied, watching him out of the corner of my eye. "Now, breathe in for three seconds through your nose. Then hold it for ten seconds before exhaling through your mouth."

Together, he and I did the breathing. Air rushing in, waiting, then air pushing out.

"Only the hand on your chest is supposed to be moving. Oh, and you're supposed to think 'relax' as you exhale," I said. "Go again."

"This is what your mom pays that shrink a fortune for?"

"Shut up and breathe." I inhaled, holding it in, trying to think peaceful thoughts. Then let it all out.

"How long do we do this for?" he asked, breathing in deeply.

"As long as it takes. Keep going."

I switched off the lamp, watching the outline of him in the dark, waiting for my night vision to kick in. With the required rhythm, his chest rose and fell. Then I realized he still had his shoes on. Not so comfortable. Dealing with the laces made things tricky and he might have laughed at me just a bit for fumbling around in the dark. But whatever.

"Close your eyes and concentrate," I said.

"They're closed." A few minutes later, he yawned, and whispered, "I'll go before your mom gets home."

"Okay." I lay down beside him, listening to his breathing, feeling a cool breeze blow in through the open window. Everything was perfect.

Turned out, we both fell asleep just fine.

chapter
thirty-eight

"Edith Rose Millen!"

"Wha—" I mumbled, doing my best to wake.

Light blinded me, John's long body shifting against my back. There in my doorway stood Mom, cheeks slashed with red and fury blazing in her eyes. And strangely enough, Matt, her old ex-boyfriend, was standing in my room too.

"What the hell is going on here?" yelled Mom, towering over the two of us.

Shit, shit, shit. "Mom. I can—"

"You can what?" Her gaze darted between me and John, finally settling on him. "Oh my God, is that the boy from the Drop Stop? It is."

"Ma'am. I..." John hastily retracted the arm he'd had wrapped around my waist, the leg he'd had thrown over one of mine. I couldn't look at him. Embarrassment swallowed me whole and spat me back out just for fun.

"He's my friend." I sat up, rubbing my eyes.

"He's your friend?" mom parroted, anger filling every word.

"Yes."

Matt stepped forward, putting a hand on Mom's lower back. "Easy."

She threw him a foul look before returning to the problem at hand. Me. "Edie, you have exactly ten seconds to explain this before you're grounded for life. Hell, you're grounded for life anyway."

And I don't know, I just...didn't really care. Not in the way I should have. Now, with my mind mostly awake, the drama didn't seem so soul-crushingly huge.

"He's my friend, Mom, and he's important to me. Very important." Best male friend at any rate. Hang would understand. "I realize this looks bad and I'm not supposed to have people over, let alone have a boy in bed with me. But his pants are on and so are mine. So please calm down."

"Calm down?" Mom echoed me again, disbelief blanking her face.

"She's got a point about the pants," said Matt.

Mom did not reply.

Matt raised his brows at me, mouth grim. Meanwhile, John stealthily searched for his shirt among the bedding. What a clusterfuck. I could feel the rage growing in her, the righteous parenting fury. Of all the nights for her to decide to burst into my bedroom at...God, it was four in the morning. Mom wavered on her feet slightly, arms crossed and face lined. Immediately, Matt moved closer, slipping an arm around her waist and anchoring her to his side. Mom's dress was tight and her heels high. The whole scene made me suspicious. The man had always been my favorite of Mom's few boyfriends, but Mom didn't have men stay over.

"What's going on, anyway?" I said. "Why is Matt here? Not that I'm not happy to see you, Matt."

A nod from him.

"We're not talking about that now," said Mom through gritted teeth. "Are you pregnant?"

"No!" I cried.

"Are you having sex with him?" A polished red fingernail took aim straight at John's heart.

"God, Mom. Nothing happened. We were just lying here together, okay?" Which was basically the truth.

A smirk and low chuckle from Matt. *Jerk.* To think he'd been my favorite, but no longer. Even if he did teach me how to play pool. Meanwhile, the look Mom hurled at him over her shoulder would have nuked a lesser man. Matt just shrugged it off.

"She's seventeen, babe," he said. "Come on. Think about the sort of shit you or I got up to at that age."

"You're not helping."

"I think I should go." John finally found his shirt, pulling it on over his head. "Do you want me to go?"

"I think that would be best," snarled Mom.

"I'll talk to you later." I grimaced. "Sorry about this."

He nodded, picking up his shoes. Mom's laser eyes bore into him as he slipped past, heading out into the hallway. It would be the first time he'd ever actually used our front door, funnily enough. Or not funny at all, as the look on Mom's face indicated.

"Hold up," I said, cocking my head, confused as all hell. "Is that an engagement ring?"

Mom's mouth opened slightly. Matt just kind of smiled.

"What the hell?" I demanded.

"Could you give us a minute?" Mom asked Matt.

"I'll leave you to it," he answered, walking away.

"I love him," said Mom, after he'd gone. "I couldn't say no to him again."

"That's why you barged in here at this hour?"

"We may have had a little champagne to celebrate. I was excited." Her voice firmed. "Also, it's my house. I'll barge in where I like, when I like, thank you very much."

Bewildered, I shook my head. "So, let me see if I've got this right. You got back together with Matt months ago, lied to me about it, and now you're getting married? And what do you mean you couldn't say no to him again? He asked you before?"

Mom sighed, sitting beside me on my bed. Weirdest four-o'clock-in-the-morning family meeting ever.

"He wanted to get married the last time we were seeing each other. But you were so young..."

I scrunched up my face. "I wasn't a baby. I was eleven."

"Yes, and your hormones were raging." She ruffled my hair with one hand. "I needed to be there for you. Plus, you might have liked Matt, but you weren't ready for more. To have someone move in with us and be part of our life, full-time...it's a big deal. If he even dared to try and stay too late, you'd start looking at the clock and glue yourself to my side."

"I don't remember that."

Mom shrugged. "You were a little possessive. But you needed me more than he did. It wasn't a big deal."

"It obviously is if I broke up you and the love of your life." My eyes got itchy despite my best efforts. I was struggling to deal with this revelation and its history in the wake of being busted in bed with John. Guilt, discovery, loss, anger, and compassion bounced around in my mind, turning my insides upside down. "God, I was such a jerk."

"You were a kid who needed her mom and didn't deal with change too well." Her arm slipped around my shoulders, drawing me in against her. "I'd say that's pretty normal."

"You shouldn't have let me just break you up. And you shouldn't have lied to me about seeing him again, either."

"I chose to put you first and I do not regret that."

Crap. A tear slipped over my cheek and I rubbed it away quickly with the palm of my hand. "Well, you should; you deserve a life too. I'm sorry."

"I'm not. And anyway, it all wound up perfectly fine." She pressed a kiss to the top of my head, holding her hand out to let the ring sparkle in the light. "Right up until the part where I found you in bed with the local drug dealer. I put you first all those years ago because I wanted a good life for you. We were both working together for that. But now you're throwing that all away. Even since—"

"That's not who he is," I cut her off. "He doesn't do that anymore. Honest, Mom. He moved in with his uncle and he's really trying hard at school. His uncle has this landscaping business and John works for him all the time. He's a good person, I swear." I sniffed, putting a lid on the weepies.

"No wonder your grades have been plummeting," she said, deaf to my words.

"If anything, he keeps me on track."

Her brow wrinkled in disbelief. "How?"

"Since the shooting, I just can't seem to care about some things. Stuff like grades and schoolwork all seems so...I don't know, irrelevant. But John's not like that. He wants to achieve. He makes me study, helps me with math homework—"

"Climbs into bed with you..."

My lips sealed shut. Deep breaths. "Yes, I obviously like him in that way and he likes me. That's kind of normal for people my age, you know?"

She swore under her breath.

"Come on, I was bound to discover sex and have a boyfriend eventually. It's not like you didn't party and have boyfriends when you were my age. You've told me you did." Which reminded me. "Not that John and I are together. Exactly. Like that."

"You're a booty call for him?"

"No! No, I'm...I don't know. We're working it out."

More muttered swearing. "Christ, kid. Out of all of the people in this town."

"He's the only one who gets me. Who knows what it was like, going through what happened that night," I said. "And he's the only one I know for sure would risk himself to keep me safe. Doesn't that matter to you?"

"Edie, I know he saved your life and I'm grateful to him for that." She stopped to take a breath and I dived right in again.

"Then give him a chance," I said, looking her straight in the eyes. No hesitation. "He really is important to me, Mom. I'm not giving him up."

"You will if I decide you're not allowed to see him."

"No."

Her jaw tightened. "Look, your grandma would just love to have you go live with her."

"I'm not moving to Arizona, either."

"Edie—"

"I'm serious," I ground out, anger and frustration making my blood boil.

"So am I." Mom stopped speaking, exhaling hard.

"You don't understand—he's good for me, Mom. Talking to him, being with him, it's a big part of what's keeping me sane these days," I said, trying to keep my voice even when what I really wanted to do was scream. "Much more than popping pills and seeing a shrink. You should be thanking him."

"Wow, yeah," she said. "Next time I find him in bed with my underage daughter I will definitely do that."

"We weren't even doing anything. Just sleeping, for God's sake."

"Kid, you didn't even tell me you'd been in contact with him, let alone in some intense, possibly co-dependent situation." She rose to her feet, slowly shaking her head. "Christ. I think we both need to calm down... talk about this later."

"Just remember, you lied to me too."

"I'm in my thirties; you're not even eighteen!"

"But I will be soon."

Mom shot me a dark look. "Get some sleep. We'll talk about this later."

Hell yes, we would.

chapter thirty-nine

Monday morning, John was waiting by my locker when I got to school. I'd texted him to say I was still amongst the living, but that I'd explain the terms of my parole in person. Just seeing him again made me feel better. The intensity of my feelings for him actually scared me, to be honest. And overriding all of that was the deeply embarrassing memory of Mom losing it at us yesterday morning.

How many females must he have slept with? Hypothetical question; I didn't really want to know. I highly doubted, however, that he'd ever hung around to get told off by anyone's mom before.

"Hey," he said.

My black Keds were so fascinating. I'd just keep on looking at them. "Hey. Sorry about yesterday, it was—"

"Edie," he said, the frown evident in his voice. "Look at me. What happened?"

I dumped my bag, slumping against the row of lockers. "Well, I'm grounded for all of eternity, of course.

Matt, Mom's fiancé, is going to chaperone me on the nights when Mom is at work."

"Shit."

"Yeah." I shrugged. "I mean, he's not so bad. I know him, I'm comfortable with him being around and everything. But he's not going to let us disappear for drives or anything either. Eventually Mom's going to switch back to just doing day shifts. With Matt living with us, money won't be so tight."

John slumped next to me, keeping his eyes on my face.

"I really am sorry about Mom making a scene," I said.

"Don't worry about it."

"We didn't even really do anything."

Brows raised, he asked, "Regret that now?"

"A little."

An almost smile. "What about weekends, any chance you're allowed out then?"

I hissed through my teeth. "That's the awkward, horrible, and kind of tricky bit."

"Go on."

"You're not going to like it."

"Tell me." His beautiful face remained as cool and calm as ever.

Having a private conversation in a school hallway was difficult business. Some girl walking by called his name. He ignored her. A jock-type dude slapped his back for no apparent reason. Eyes were on us. Of course, together we always warranted attention from the student body. Sad for them to have nothing more interesting going on in their lives. Sometimes the attention bugged me. This morning, though, I just didn't have the energy to care.

We only had about five minutes before class started, but I'd rather blurt it out and be done with it than wait until lunchtime or after school.

"Okay." I took a deep breath. "Mom said I'm only allowed to go out Saturday nights, and my curfew is nine o'clock. She's going to be tracking my phone and randomly calling, because apparently acting like a deranged stalker is cool if you're a parent."

Nothing from him.

"Honestly, it's like I'm twelve instead of seventeen." Amazing, my voice had hardly any whine to it at all. "Might as well tuck me into bed with a teddy bear and turn on the night-light."

"She busted us in your bed." He shrugged. "Kind of expected worse, actually. Surprised she's letting you out at all."

"The negotiations were intense. We argued all yesterday. Things may have been thrown, and not only by me." I winced. "God, this sucks. Maybe I should just move out. Don't suppose you could lend me a few grand?"

"You and your mom are close. You don't want to move out."

"I don't know."

"What about me coming over during the week to study?" he asked. "Is that okay?"

Red alert. I rubbed my damp palms on my jeans. "It's

complicated. Why don't we just study during lunch at school?"

"Complicated? What'd she say?" Lines furrowed his brow. "Edie?"

Shit. "That if we're not serious, there's no need for you to be over during the week."

Silence. So very much silence.

"Look, it's okay. I mean, I'll miss spending time with you. A lot." My words were such a mess. No good answer existed. "John?"

"Okay," he said.

"Okay?"

"We can do that, be serious." His face smoothed, all worries gone. "Right?"

I paused. Not the answer I was expecting.

"That a problem?" he asked, sounding less sure of himself now. He shuffled a little closer. "I mean, guess I should have asked first. But if this is the only way we can keep hanging out..."

"I don't think you understand the depth of my mother's psychosis," I said, trying to ignore the pounding of my heart. "For her to believe we're official, you and your uncle would have to come over for dinner. I'm talking interrogation over pot roast, and she'd probably want to do it every couple of weeks or something. You'd probably be expected to turn up with flowers and candy. Possibly get my name tattooed on your forehead. I don't know exactly. The woman is not sane."

"Pretty sure Levi can fit it in. He likes you, asks me

how you're doing all the time."

"That's nice." I swallowed hard. "It's just, we agreed, Mom and I, not to lie to each other anymore. I'd like to try to stick to that."

His chin dipped. "You think we'd be lying?"

"Wouldn't we be?"

The bell rang, sending people scurrying in all directions.

"We'd better get to class." I spun the dial on my locker at warp speed, picking up my bag and dumping the textbook I wouldn't need until later.

"Edie."

"Let's talk about it at lunch. Mom will kill me if I get detention for again being late." I about-faced and took off down the hall, John following at a more sedate pace. Thing was, official meant something not just to Mom, but to me also. It meant a lot. No matter how much I liked kissing and rolling around with him on my bed, maybe it would be for the best if we cooled things now before my dumbass heart got any more deluded.

Turned out he was busy come lunchtime, off shooting hoops with Anders. Guess there was my answer. John Cole would never be mine. Not in that way.

chapter
forty

S omeone was banging on the front door.

Mom, Matt, and I had just sat down to our first official family dinner. Meat loaf, baked potatoes, corn cobs, and green beans, to be followed by chocolate cake and Cool Whip. Hallelujah. Even my shitty grounded attitude couldn't deny the healing qualities of Cool Whip.

Mom's loved-up smile dimmed for a second as she rose, wiping her hands on a napkin. "Bad timing. Wonder who that could be."

"Want me to get it?" I asked.

"No. It's fine." Her fingers drifted across the back of Matt's neck as she passed. *Gag.* She opened the door, her back snapping straight at the sight of the person standing there. Hostility radiated. "Yes?"

"Whatever I have to do," said a familiar deep voice.

"John?" I stood, surprised.

"However I need to prove myself to you, I'll do it," said John. "I don't mind."

Mom cocked her head. "Is that so?"

"Yes."

Arms crossed, Mom stepped back and to the side, giving us the view of John standing in the doorway. Dark blue jeans and a white button-down shirt with the sleeves rolled up. His hair had been neatly pulled back in a pony-tail and there were two bouquets of bright flowers in his arms. He looked amazingly good. Confident and deter-mined, apart from the careful neutral set of his face, the way his gaze kept moving between me and Mom.

I, on the other hand, broke out in a sweat. My heart beat double time and worse, it ached. Ridiculous, how I could have missed him when I'd only just seen him this morning in English?

Matt simply smiled, the smarmy bastard.

"My daughter is not a toy," announced my mother. "I hope you're aware of that."

"I am, ma'am."

"If I even suspect you're dealing or look like you're getting her into any sort of trouble, I will annihilate you. Is that understood?"

"Yes, ma'am."

"You had points with me for saving her life, but they're gone now as a result of your nighttime visit over the weekend. You get that?"

A nod.

"You're starting from scratch. Impress me."

"Yes, ma'am," said John, handing her one of the bunches of flowers.

"Good start. Go on, take a seat at the table," she ordered, closing the door behind him. Still looking deeply unhappy, she said to his back, "I hope you have children one day so you get what this is like. The fear. The worry. You two have aged me."

John risked the smallest of smiles in my direction.

"But do not have children with my daughter," said Mom. "Or if it is with my daughter, not anytime soon."

"Yes, ma'am." John sat in the seat beside me as I finally put my butt back in my chair. He was here. Holy shit, he was really here. At dinner. He caught my gaze wholly, handing me the second bouquet.

"Thank you," I whispered, holding on tight to the flowers. "You're here?"

"Yeah."

"Why?"

"Because this is where you are," he said, as if it were obvious.

I had nothing.

"Young love," Mom muttered under her breath. She slammed the kitchen cupboard door, rattled the cutlery drawer. All in the process of getting our guest a plate and utensils. He must have felt so welcome.

Dinner went reasonably smoothly, with Matt and John doing most of the talking. I didn't know what to say, and Mom was still in a huff. Happily, Matt dragged her and her hostility out onto the back patio after dessert, leaving John and me to clean up. We huddled near the dishwasher with our backs to the windows.

"Bravely done," I said, keeping my voice down just in

case.

"Your mom's scary. But she's not junkie-with-a-gun scary."

"True."

He smiled, and I had a very small orgasm or something. I'm not sure exactly. But it felt good.

"I have to get going. Anders wants me to train with him tonight," he said. "Walk me out?"

"That should be allowed." I headed over to the sliding screen doors. "I'm just going to see John out."

"Ten minutes," said Mom. "I'm timing you."

I turned away from her and rolled my eyes. "Okay."

Outside, a cold breeze blew. An autumn wind.

"Thanks again for the flowers," I said, trying not to fidget.

"Sure."

"And for coming over."

A questioning look. "You didn't say, this morning. If you wanted to be serious."

"I don't want you to have to do this because of my mom and her new commandant status."

"Been thinking about that." He exhaled, leaning against the side of his car, watching me. All of the black paint and chrome shone in the moonlight.

Across the road, someone slammed a door, cutting off a raised voice. Otherwise, it was quiet.

"And?" I asked.

"I figure we would have wound up there anyway." He stuffed his hands in his pockets. "Being a couple."

The way he said the word, as if he didn't entirely trust it. No wonder I wasn't convinced. I said nothing.

With a quick frown, he pushed off from the car, cradling my face in his hands. His lips met mine and just like that, everything was better. Mouths open, tongues stroking, my arms sliding around his waist. Kissing John was everything. Well, not *everything* everything. I wouldn't die without him. But all of me wanted him, my heart and my head and all of the rest. Without a doubt, he made life better.

"Please don't tell me I'm going to have to get my fucking forehead tattooed before you believe me," he murmured, teeth nipping my ear.

I burst out laughing. "But it would look so pretty."

"No." His body shook with silent laughter. "Not on my forehead, anyway."

"Fine." Tears welled, but I would not cry. I wouldn't. "I lo...umm..."

"Hey?"

Holy hell, what had I been about to say? No way could I just blurt out that I loved him even if I possibly did. *Shit.*

He nuzzled my neck, making my head swim and my body wake right the hell up. This time I ached in the right place.

Just for a moment, I was no longer the remnants of the hostage from the Drop Stop, jumping at shadows and flipping the bird to the future. It was just me and him, together. And that feeling swamped everything else.

"That's enough!" Mom hollered from the front door. Not humiliating at all.

John kissed me quick, keys freed from his pocket and jangling in one hand. "'Bye."

And all of a sudden I hated that word with a passion. Least favorite word ever. "Say 'hi' to Anders for me. See you tomorrow."

The beast's engine revved and he gave me a parting grin, driving off at an extremely safe mom-proof speed. Smart of him, really. Best not to give her anything else to criticize.

"Did you arrange that, him turning up tonight?" she asked, arms crossed yet again. "Because in the future I'd prefer to have some advance warning."

"No, I didn't have a clue."

Eyes narrowed, she studied my face.

I just waited her out.

"Okay." The aggression faded from her face, the line of her mouth relaxing. "You know I just want you safe, right?"

"Yes, but John isn't a threat. And anyway, you can't protect me from the whole world."

She harrumphed.

I turned back to the street, though his car lights were long gone. My boyfriend. Crazy.

"Be smart, honey," she said. "You're young; there's going to be others."

"He came and he said he'd do anything you wanted," I said, staring her straight in the eye. "Mom, you have to give him a chance."

She held her hands up. "I'm giving him a chance. I invited him in for dinner, didn't I?"

"Yes. Thank you."

Stepping forward, she wrapped her arms tightly around me. I hugged her back.

"Next time, though, could we possibly have less cold war across the table?" I asked.

She sighed. "Fine."

chapter forty-one

Boxes of condoms started appearing the very next day. Mom was nothing if not efficient. And she sure as hell couldn't be described as subtle. In my bathroom, my bedside table, my schoolbag—they were pretty much everywhere. By Friday, I'd prepared myself to stage an intervention regarding her prophylactic habit. I'd even get Matt involved if necessary, since he'd proven to be silently supportive of me and John.

When we studied at my place Wednesday night, Matt stayed in Mom's room, working on his laptop. Apart from the bedroom door left open, we'd been given privacy. He didn't even come looking for me for at least half an hour after I walked my boyfriend out.

Just as well.

John had me backed up against his car with his mouth on mine. My hands had been all over him, because touching him just about topped my list of favorite things to do. Luckily the shrubbery blocked the neighbor's view of our soft-porn session.

TRUST

John had talked with Matt about his pool table and a possible game sometime. He complimented Matt on my skills. I'd kind of forgotten how much I liked this one of Mom's boyfriends. Despite the associated drama, it was nice to have him around again.

But back to school. Thursday lunchtime, my week was going well.

"More rubbers?" asked John quietly, sitting beside me.

Not my choice that he knew about them. A box had fallen out of my bag while I was swapping books at my locker the day before. Having already found one box hidden in a pocket of my denim jacket that day, I'd thought I'd been safe. How very wrong.

Happily, John seemed mostly amused.

"Yeah." I closed my bag before anyone else could see. "I forgot to do my morning search while I was still in the car. Insanity. She's the one who needs to have a good, long talk with the therapist."

Around us, the usual noise and chaos of the cafeteria carried on. Thank God. Sophia and Carrie were absent today, off at a school newspaper meeting or something.

"It would take us years to use all of these," I said.

"Not years."

I bumped my knee into his underneath the table. Everything we did stayed out of sight and that suited me fine. Not a problem. "No?"

"No."

"It's nearly Saturday." I took a sip of my water, keep-

305

ing my eyes on him.

"It is." He watched me right back, one of those almost smiles on his lips. "Party out on Old Cemetery Road, if you want to go?"

"You didn't want to go somewhere quieter?"

The way his jaw shifted, his gaze heating, gave me goose bumps.

"Just a thought. I mean, any party will only be starting by the time my curfew kicks in."

"We could go to a movie? You know I'm good for whatever you want to do," he whispered, moving in a little closer. "Not going to pressure you about sex, Edie. I think one of Anders's friends is having a party too, if you don't want to go to the field. Might get going a bit earlier. We've got options."

"Huh? What?" Anders's head shot up from where he'd been huddled with Hang, whispering God knows what in her ear. Given her wide eyes and the way she was biting her lip, I didn't want to know. Seemed to me, they were friends in the same way John and I had been. Friends on the verge of something. Hang denied it, but all the signs were there.

"Throw some hoops?" asked Anders.

"Not yet."

"We're going to run out of time. Again. That's already happened twice this week." Turning to me, Anders scowled, heavy lines on his brow. "Just give him permission to go play already."

I scratched my cheek with my middle finger.

"It's like you have his dick on a leash or something. It's disgusting," Anders ranted, way louder than required. Though to be fair, I doubt he actually had another vocal setting.

"Shh!" I hissed.

John threw his empty soda can at him. "Shut it."

Anders caught the can with ease. "If this is what having a girlfriend is like, then I take it back, Hang. No relationship. Sorry, boo. We'll just have to keep using each other for sex and leave it at that."

"Are you joking?" I asked. When Anders didn't answer, I turned to Hang and asked again, "Is he joking?"

Staying right out of it, Hang bit into an apple.

"And anyway, it's not like that," I began. "John and I are just—"

"Oh, puh-lease," said Anders. "He's my best friend and you're...you. Don't lie to me."

Hang winced. "It is pretty obvious that you're together now."

"If Edie doesn't want people up in her business, that's the way it is." John checked his watch and then stood, picking his bag up off the floor. "Time for class."

Anders swore and stomped off after smacking a surprise kiss on Hang's cheek. The girl barely even bothered to look irritated about his open interest anymore.

"You think I don't want people knowing?" I asked.

John just shrugged. "Not a big deal."

Huh.

"History like mine, can't really blame you," he said,

heading for the door.

"What?"

"Have a think about Saturday night and let me know what you're up for."

"John—"

He kept walking. "We're getting the grade on the paper today, right?"

"Yeah, I think so." I wandered along after him, Hang following close behind. Right on time, the bell rang out, getting everyone moving.

"Is John mad about something?" asked Hang.

"I don't know."

"It's just, he's usually next to you, you know," she said.

I watched his back disappear among the sudden crowd in the hall. "He thinks I don't want us public because of his history."

"And?"

A sudden headache bloomed behind my eyes. I rubbed at my temple, lost, confused, and quite possibly certifiably stupid. "I thought he wanted to keep it on the down low because I'm not one of the cool types or something."

"I repeat," said Hang, "he's usually hovering by your side like you're his delicate, precious little flower who might need protection from the big, bad world at any moment. Or like you might need his help smashing the patriarchy or something. I think when it comes to you, he's pretty much up for anything."

My jaw hung open.

"Does that sound like someone trying to hide the fact you're his girlfriend?"

"Really, he does that?"

She nodded.

Shit. "I'm an idiot."

"We all are sometimes."

Without further thought, I pushed through the crowd, running after him as much as I could. A couple of people swore at me, but never mind. This was urgent. Once he came into sight, I grabbed hold of his arm, pulling him to a halt. People swarmed around us like a mildly pissed-off, inconvenienced, and sweaty horde.

John just gave me a questioning look. Not a happy one.

"We need to talk," I said.

"Later."

Shit. Usually, my emotions were the mess. It had never occurred to me that John might have his own insecurities—at least, not about me. I truly was an idiot, one who needed to pay more attention.

We shuffled into class along with everyone else, taking our usual seats. Mrs. Ryder immediately started giving back the essays on Edgar Allan Poe.

"Much improved," she said, handing mine over.

"Thank you." A-minus. Awesome. A flicker of pride pulled me up straighter in my chair. I'd forgotten what this could feel like. I turned in my seat to show John, the person responsible for getting me to study and actually give a damn again. This was on him.

"...we'll discuss this after class," Mrs. Ryder was saying, shaking the paper in front of his face. "Understood?"

"You think I didn't write this?" asked John, the momentary surprise on his face quickly tightening into anger. "You think I got someone else to do it or something. Because the work's good for a change."

Her mouth skewed.

"I read the book and then I wrote the paper."

"What's going on?" I asked, mystified.

Mrs. Ryder's gaze cut to me, her eyes hard and probing.

"What? You seriously think he didn't do it?" I asked. "That's crazy. We study together, but he does his own work."

"You study together," she repeated, as if that answered everything.

I'd never wanted to kick a teacher so badly in my life. "People aren't allowed to decide to try and do better at school?"

"Edie..." muttered John. "It's all right."

"Do not take that tone with me, young lady." Mrs. Ryder towered over me.

Having to look up at her only pissed me off more. "You're supposed to encourage people to learn."

"We'll discuss this after class, Mr. Cole." She dropped the paper onto his desk, condemning him with barely a glance.

"You're denying him the opportunity of an education," I said, jaw rigid.

Her hand cut through the air. "That's enough. Get out your books."

I went nuclear, heat rushing to my face. "Oh, you can go fu—"

"Test me on it," said John, shooting me a warning look. "If I didn't write the paper then I'm not going to know shit...stuff, about the book. Test me."

My mouth shut tight. He could do it; I knew he could. If she'd just give him the chance.

"Please." John shuffled forward in his seat. "You're right, I've been sleeping through classes for years. But that's not what's going on now, not anymore. Not since..."

Not since the Drop Stop—those were the words unspoken. She must have known it, though.

He blinked, staring down at his desk. "I'm not asking for special treatment. Just a chance."

Mrs. Ryder's eyes narrowed further. I'd be amazed if the woman could see anything, peering out from behind her metal-rimmed glasses. "Meet me here after school. You get one shot with me, Mr. Cole. One. Don't mess it up."

"Thank you, ma'am."

chapter forty-two

"I've been looking for you everywhere."

"Yeah?" John sat on the hood of his car, smoking a cigarette, the lake's dark waters spread out before him. "Why?"

"You didn't answer your phone." I crossed my arms. Not daring to climb up beside him, unsure of my welcome. With good cause. "Anders didn't have a clue where you were, and your uncle—"

"You went to my place?"

"Yes."

His brows descended. "Thought you weren't allowed out on school nights."

"We renegotiated; I have to clean both bathrooms for a month. It was an emergency—I was worried about you."

Bringing the cigarette to his lips, he breathed deep.

"How did it go with Mrs. Ryder?"

"Fine." He tapped the ash off the side of the car at my feet. "I got my B for the paper."

"That's great." I smiled. "Congratulations."

A chin tip.

"I'm sorry I almost told her to go fuck herself," I said, sneaking a little closer. "That was probably unconstructive."

"Not the word that I had in mind. But, yeah, it was."

"Though you shouldn't have to beg to get an education. That's bullshit."

A cool wind blew off the water and I wrapped my arms around myself a little tighter. So racing out of the house in only black flip-flops, ripped jeans, and a tank hadn't been the brightest. Autumn was making its presence known. Still, with the chilly evening, the lakeside was deserted. We were the only two people in sight. Cold weather had some perks.

"But you were wrong about me being ashamed of you," I said, leaning against the side of the car. Always trying to get closer.

With an irritated huff of breath, he climbed off the other side of the hood, stopping to stub out his cigarette on the ground. "You could have seriously screwed me in class today, Edie."

"I know. I'm sorry."

"Insulting her was never going to fix anything." He walked around the car, brow furrowed and mouth a flat line. "You want to go nuts after what happened, I don't blame you. I'm still messed up from it too. But there are consequences to the shit you do; you know this."

I nodded. Even if I could never seem to care about the consequences for myself, at least I could for him.

"Tell me you're going to think first. 'Cause I need that from you."

"I'll think first. I promise."

"And not just about stuff with me, with everything. Because if you get hurt somehow, that fucks me up too."

Damn. My eyes itched. "I'm sorry."

"Don't cry." He moved closer, wrapping me up in his arms. "We'll figure it out."

Breathing his scent in, having him close, it helped. I fisted my hands in his shirt, making sure he couldn't escape. Christ, I was such a train wreck.

"I won't be crazy anymore," I promised.

He laughed quietly. "Nuh, not possible. Pretty sure some of the crazy is just you now. But keep it under the limit for me, hmm?"

"Okay."

"You're so brave sometimes, it scares me."

"I don't feel brave," I said, voice muffled by his shirt.

He scoffed. "Something scares you? I don't believe it."

"I thought I'd lost you."

"That's not going to happen." He rested his cheek on top of my head, holding on a little tighter. "We didn't go through all that shit to let a few misdemeanors mess with us. Or an English paper."

"So why didn't you answer your phone?"

"Not saying I wasn't pissed at you, but we're not breaking up, Edie." His slid his hands into the back pockets of my jeans. "That's not how this works."

"You know how this works?"

"Yeah. We keep trying," he said simply. "If we really want it, then we don't give up. That easy."

I had nothing. Actually, that was a lie. "I could never be ashamed of you. Don't ever think that again."

"Edie, you saw how the teacher was today. What your mom thinks of me. My past isn't going to just disappear."

"That's not you anymore. They'll see."

"You like your privacy, I get that." The wind tossed his loose hair around, blowing it in his face. "Besides, people knowing we're together or not isn't that big a deal. I've already punched one guy and threatened another. No one's going to have the balls to ask you out."

"How very caveman of you."

"Just the way it is." The corner of his mouth curled up. "Offers coming my way have dropped right off ever since you nearly hit Erika."

I smiled.

"See?" he said.

I rested my chin on his chest, looking up into his beautiful face. Since we seemed to be having a bare-our-hearts-all-out honesty session, he might as well know the worst. I took a deep breath and blurted, "Don't freak out or anything, but I love you."

His chin jerked up, eyes widening. "You do?"

"Yes. I love you and I'll try harder not to mess up in future." And he thought nothing scared me—my heart almost beat out of my chest. This ache, the fear of rejection, it felt like broken ribs all over again. It felt like throwing myself off a much higher rock with no idea if

315

water waited below. "Anyway. I just, I thought you should know."

Silence.

"It's not a big deal."

"Yes it fucking is."

His mouth slammed down on mine, stealing my breath. Warm, firm lips, and the thrill of his tongue tracing my teeth before sliding against my own. Kissing had never felt so good. Sure as hell, no half-assed fumbling in the shadows with other boys could compare. John's technique deserved the highest of praise, but the best I could do was moan. My hands slipped beneath his shirt, exploring his skin, laying claim.

In no time at all, he had me backed up against the driver's-side door. His hands roamed, though they stayed on top of my shirt and jeans and remained off the obvious groping areas. Fingers stroked down my arms and slid across my neck. And his kisses kept changing, from sweet and gentle to deep and lingering. I enjoyed them all. Each and every kiss made my head spin and my body light up.

Eventually we paused for breath, pressed up against each other, hearts beating as one. With gentle fingers, John lifted the wide neckline of my T-shirt, setting it back in place over my bra strap.

"You don't have to do that," I said.

"What?"

"I'm not going to break and I'm not going to freak out."

"What do you mean?"

"If I'm allowed to touch you beneath your shirt, you're allowed to do the same to me."

"Edie." He swallowed hard. "We kind of jumped ahead with having sex. But we don't need to rush now."

"This isn't rushing, I'm setting the pace."

"You sure?"

It seemed easier to take action than keep talking. So I took hold of his hand and placed it on my chest. Over the top of my T-shirt and bra, sure. But with the way his hand gently gripped me, taking the weight of one breast, the point had obviously been made.

He licked his lips, gaze a little worried like I might try and take the boob back—change my mind and deny him access or something. Once, twice, he kissed my lips, before moving on to the side of my face, my neck. The hint of stubble on his chin teased my skin, his breath warming me further. Teeth nipped at my flesh. I felt combustible. A fire had been lit and I didn't want it put out.

"You have girls in the back of your car often?" I asked, breathing heavy, my hands gripping his ass. He had such a great ass.

"Shit," he muttered, sliding his spare hand around the nape of my neck. He chuckled. "Why do you ask me things like that?"

I shrugged. "Curious."

"A few times, yeah. But it's not that comfortable."

"Maybe not for actual sex, no. But what about just for fooling around?"

He quickly scanned the area, checking that no one

was near. "Feeling exposed?"

"Cold more than anything. But mostly, I just want to make out with you in the backseat of your car."

"You do?" His thumb rubbed over my hard nipple through the layers of fabric.

A shiver stole through me and I nodded. "I haven't done that before. It'll be another first."

"Then that's what we're doing." He stepped back, reaching for the handle of the rear door. "After you."

I smiled, too nervous to speak. Stupid, really. It wasn't like I hadn't been in his bedroom and on his bed. The backseat of a car shouldn't matter. But it did.

He climbed in after me, shutting the door. I kicked off my flip-flops and pulled my T-shirt off over my head. Not stopping to do stupid self-conscious things like cover my stomach with my hands, because this was John. Also because, I was past that. Or I would be. I'd get there.

"Come here," I said, sliding down a little.

No more hesitation. He knelt on the seat, tearing off his T-shirt, more than ready to meet me for each item of clothing. John was right; it was a little uncomfortable. Even with the Charger's wide backseat, we were really both a bit too tall to fit. The weight of his body on top of mine, however, made everything right. Mouths glued together and his body resting between my spread legs. When I actually spread them, I had no idea. Holy shit did he feel good there.

We were grinding against each other, groaning and panting and muttering about heaven. I never wanted it to end. The tips of my fingers trailed down his back, my short nails digging in just a little. When his tongue traced the edge of my bra, teasing the sensitive skin in my cleavage, I just about lost it completely. And the feel of him. Sweet baby Jesus, the feel of him hard, rubbing against the crotch of my jeans.

"Fucking hell, baby," he whispered into my skin, nibbling at my jawline, making his way back to my mouth.

"Mm?"

"What time do you have to be home?"

"Huh? No. Don't stop."

He swore some more. Then, in a very calm and reasonable voice, said, "Edie, I need to put my hand in your pants."

"Yes."

He paused. "You sure?"

I nodded, stomach and thigh muscles tight, everything low in my belly beyond excited. "Please. John."

John sat back on his heels, hair hanging in his face. God, he looked beautiful, disheveled and half-naked by moonlight. I don't know how I got so lucky. He undid the button and zipper on my jeans, then tugged them down a little.

He lowered himself back over me, taking all of his weight on one arm strategically placed beside my head. Hot, damp lips kissed mine, teeth nipping at my bottom lip. Next he brought his free hand to his mouth and sucked on a couple of fingers, getting them wet.

"Going to get you off quickly, because you got to go

home. You're still grounded, remember?"

"I don't care."

"I do." His hand slid into my panties, fingers brushing over my swollen sex, dipping slightly into the wetness. "Edie. Baby, that feels so fucking good."

The boy had no idea. Tips of his fingers teasing me, skimming over the lips down there. Beyond good and well into great territory. He lifted his hand back to his mouth, licking his thumb, before diving back into my underwear. My body jolted.

"John," I moaned, stretching my neck, turning my head to the side. Might have just been me, but we seemed to be running low on air. Or maybe my lungs weren't quite working. My breasts heaved, mouth open wide. Everything in me centered on what he was doing to me, how incredible he was making me feel.

"I know," he said, voice low and rumbling. "I'll get you there."

First he circled my clit with the pad of his thumb, knuckles brushing lightly across all that sensitive flesh. My breasts ached, belly just about turning inside out. All I could do was clutch at him—his shoulders, his arms, whatever I could grab. Hold him tight and keep him with me, now and always.

"There we go." His lips brushed my earlobe.

The tension inside me built higher and higher, winding me tight and taking me over. One heel dug into the seat, the other pushing against the floor. My whole body pushing into his fingers, needing to get as close as possible.

"Like that?" he asked, the pad of his thumb working me a little harder, faster.

"Yes. Don't stop," I said, voice almost gone, lost.

"No. I won't stop."

"God," I gritted out, bucking against his hand, back arching. "John."

The whole world fell away. There was just me and him and...*fuck*. Every inch of my body floated, stars filling my head. I lay crashed out on the backseat of John's car, flying. No wonder some people were so into sex. With the right person, it could be amazing. Even just a hand job.

I opened my eyes to find him staring down at me, shoulders high, breathing hard. "Well, this is embarrassing."

"What?" I asked. "What's wrong?"

"Nothing. I just..."

"You just?" I asked, heart and lungs slowly returning to normal. The sheen of sweat on me and the fogged-up windows, I could do nothing about.

He frowned at me and I frowned at him. Though my frown no doubt came with a loved-up smile.

He nodded downward. "I'm kind of a mess."

"Oh. *Oh.*"

"Hmm." Moving slowly, carefully, and still with a frown, he sat back on his haunches. "I was watching you and...anyway."

"I think it shows solidarity, commitment to the relationship." I tried not to grin. But I didn't try very hard.

"Really."

"You think me coming in my jeans shows solidarity?"

I just shrugged. "I love you."

"You love..." The edge of his mouth curled upward. Suddenly, he shook it off. "We need to get you home before your mom freaks and decides I'm not allowed inside the door or something."

He started searching around for his T-shirt, finally finding it on the floor. Then he undid his pants and cleaned up. I couldn't see much, but still. Was it wrong that I found the whole process fascinating? If so, I didn't want to be right.

I fiddled with my underwear, yanked my jeans back up, and wriggled into a sitting position. Next, I searched for my T-shirt. "I like the backseat of your car."

"Yeah?" His smile, it slayed me.

"Oh yeah."

He leaned in for a kiss and I gave it to him. Boy did I give it to him. And then some.

Cold air washed over us when he opened the door, stepping back out into the big, wide world. His nipples puckered since he remained without a tee, understandably. I climbed out too, opening the other door wide so the fogged-up windows would clear faster.

John walked me over to my car, his strong hand rubbing my back.

"Drive carefully," he said. "I won't be far behind you."

"You don't need to follow me home. I'll be fine."

"I'll be right behind you."

I shrugged. "Okay. You drive carefully too."

"I will." He didn't move until I was safely buckled into my car. "Edie?"

"Hmm?"

"Me too. On the...you know."

I cocked my head. "You mean the love thing?"

"Yeah. That."

My boyfriend.

Who knew I loved him and who apparently loved me too.

I smiled the whole way home.

chapter forty-three

Hang: Emergency. Send help. I think I have actual feelings for Anders.

Me: Wait. You mean beyond your usual mild annoyance?

Hang: YES

Me: OMG

Hang: It's not my fault. He got in somehow. Like a virus ...a really bad one. What do I do?

Me: Maybe these feelings are like a 24-hour head cold or something and they'll go away.

Hang: No. Don't think so. He's more of a plague than a flu.

Hang: We decided to be sexfriends the night of his birthday. But he keeps hanging around and wanting to do things together and to hold my hand all the damn time. He's even started teaching me how to play basketball. This is all wrong.

Me: Ok. Wow. What do you want to do about it?

Hang: I have the worst feeling I'm going to have to try getting serious with him. Doomed.

Me: He is cute.

Hang: No. Insanity is not cute...well a little maybe.

Me: At least he makes you laugh.

Hang: That's true. How are you doing?

Me: I told John I loved him.

Hang: Yikes.

Me: I know. But screw it, life is short. Why not tell him?

Hang: Now he definitely knows you're not avoiding the whole going public thing.

Me: I hope so.

Hang: And who knows, you could get hunted down by that pack of rabid Pekingese out to get you any day now. Then where would you be if you hadn't told him?

Me: Dying from very small dog bites with regret in my heart.

Hang: Exactly. I think you did the right thing.

Me: Thanks. And I appreciate you taking my doggie doomsday theories seriously.

Hang: No problem. That's what friends are for, right?

Me: Right. ☺

Hang: Mom's yelling at me to go to bed. Let's reconvene on these issues tomorrow. Night. Xx

Me: Night. xx

chapter
forty-four

Erika came up to me outside class, Friday afternoon—exactly what I didn't need spoiling my happy thoughts of the weekend. Saturday night with John was so close and with just a little more work, Mom might give on the nine o'clock curfew. I might wind up cleaning our toilets until the end of the year, but it'd be worth it. Matt's word regarding John and me spending our study dates actually studying had gone a long way toward her calming down. So had evidence of my grades improving.

Though there had been another box of condoms under my pillow when I went to bed last night. With the way she kept throwing them at me, you'd think she wanted to find him in my bed again.

"We need to talk," said Erika, standing in my way.

"Going to have to disagree with you there."

She grabbed my arm, trying to stop me from walking away down the hall. I just gave her hand a look. So tempting to push the bitch back a step, but I'd promised John to

327

take it easy. Still, other students slowed to a halt around us, watching with eager eyes. God save me from drama lovers.

Erika released my arm, but still blocked my path. Obviously nervous, she licked her lips. "John won't talk to me—"

"That's his choice."

"It's about Dillon," she said.

"You still trying to pass on messages from his brother?" I leaned in closer, getting in her face, because why not? "Has it occurred to you that you might be getting used?"

"It's not that." She shuffled her feet, fussing with the strap of her bag. You'd have thought we were doing a deal on some dark street corner with the way the girl was acting.

"Then what?" I asked. "What do you want, Erika?"

"I went over to Dillon's last night and...he's not doing well." Her gaze roamed to the people watching and she frowned. "He was saying all sorts of crazy shit."

"What sort of crazy shit?"

"Just...tell John to be careful."

"What did he say?"

Turning her back on me, she got moving. "Just tell him."

Huh. This, whatever it was, did not feel good. Dillon had managed to scare Erika into sounding like a genuinely concerned human being, instead of a haughty bitch. That was actually kind of frightening.

John had picked me up that morning so we could grab a mom-approved quick breakfast together on our way to school. After the weird chat with Erika, I found him waiting out by the beast, Anders busy spinning a basketball on his finger while Hang watched with an indulgent smile. Nothing going on between them, my ass. They were about as believable as John and I.

"Just had an interesting conversation," I said, leaning my body against his and waiting for my welcome kiss.

He delivered it with a smile. "What?"

"Erika says to be careful of your brother."

His gaze narrowed, lips flattening. "Really?"

"Really." I wandered around to the passenger side and dumped my bag in the car.

"Bestie rides shotgun," pouted Anders. "Everyone knows that."

"Apparently she went over to your old place and he was saying some scary shit. She wouldn't say what. Have you seen him since the fight?" I asked, ignoring the idiot in our midst. Some things were more important. "John?"

He slipped on his sunglasses, looking across the roof of the car at me with a blank face. "He stopped by the other week. Uncle Levi told him he'd sic the cops on him if he saw him near the house again. Nothing since then."

"Ah."

With one finger, he scratched at the side of his nose. "I mean, he's tried calling me a couple of times. But I don't usually answer."

"Usually?" I asked, voice tightening. "He beat you up,

John."

"He's my brother and we beat each other up. Trust me, he didn't come out of it looking too good either."

I don't think I was wearing my happy face.

"You're an only child, Edie. You don't know what it's like," he said. "I can't just turn my back on him."

Brows tight, I fished my own sunglasses out of my bag. The afternoon light was shining blindingly bright. "So he still wants you to deal?"

"It's more complicated than that."

Anders's head swung between us, the basketball still in his hands. "Hang. Boo. Give me a lift home?"

"Sure."

"Talk to you later, loser." He slapped John on the back, then picked up his bag.

"Saturday night?" Hang asked me.

"I don't know. Old Cemetery Road okay with you?"

"You sure?"

"Mom shifted my curfew a little. But I don't mind only catching the start of the party. It'll give John a chance to do some boarding."

"Okay." With a nod, she began unlocking her own car, parked next to the beast. "See you at work tomorrow."

"See you."

"Let's go to your place," said Anders to Hang. "Ask your mom if I can stay for dinner. The food at yours is way better than mine."

"My mom hates you."

"No she doesn't," Anders said, voice incredulous.

"She's just shy."

Hang laughed, slamming her car door shut.

And then we were alone. Or as alone as you can get in a crowded school parking lot. John climbed in and I did likewise, the air hot and stale. Old cracked leather seating warmed the backs of my legs. In a month or two I'd have to get out my tights for winter. Not that Northern California ever got freezing cold, but dresses alone didn't do the job all year round.

"He hurt you," I said.

John revved the engine, setting a hand atop my headrest and turning to check no one was behind us before reversing out. "I know."

We got into the line of cars pouring from the parking lot and into the street. Smiles and laughter carried through the open windows, everyone in a good mood for Friday afternoon. Almost everyone. Memories of the blood and bruises on John's face and body that night kind of made me want to puke.

"Be careful," I said, repeating Erika's warning.

"I will be."

chapter
forty-five

Saturday night, I watched transfixed as John rode his skateboard, doing all sorts of cool moves. Bare chested, which upped the heat content tenfold. I held onto his shirt for him, sniffing it maybe once or twice at most. Certainly no more than say half a dozen times because I wasn't some creepy stalker. Though it should be noted, I wasn't the only one watching, looking at least half in love with the boy. No, I was just the one with no shame when it came to smelling his clothes.

Oh, well. Honestly, I don't think I'd really come down since the first time we kissed.

"Hey." Hang sidled on up to me with a bottle of water in her hands. Despite our drunken antics at her house the night of the bad texting incident, Hang didn't seem to drink very often. "I think Anders has taken up interpretive dancing."

"Your boyfriend scares me," said Carrie, standing on my other side. "I left Sophia to try and keep up with his dancing acrobatics. I'm done."

Hang laughed. Not correcting her about the boy-friend comment, either. "I have no idea where he gets all of the energy."

"How's he doing with your mom?"

She grimaced. "Well, he's certainly committed. But I don't see her accepting him anytime soon."

"Hmm. Your mom is fierce, but my money's on Anders."

"Mine too."

"For certain. The boy doesn't even know how to give up." Carrie chuckled. "It's like the concept doesn't exist in his world."

Hang just grinned. It was good to see her so happy.

Around us, the field was slowly filling with people, the area lit courtesy of the headlights of half a dozen trucks and SUVs. I sipped on my beer while Carrie took sips from a flask. It was just half past eight or so. Early for a Saturday night. But my curfew had only been extended to ten thirty, and John and I had plans that required privacy and the comfort of his bed. Oh, and his Uncle Levi was out until late.

That was critical.

Whatever his uncle's views were on teen sex, the thought of doing anything with someone else in the house was a big no.

John jumped off his board at the top of the half-pipe, landing easy on the flat concrete surface. The boy had to be part acrobat or something. Meanwhile, I could barely touch my toes without falling over. One of the fangirls approached him and he smiled, nodded, and turned away. Then he flipped the board up to his hand with a foot and walked over to us. Another girl stepped up to the edge of the pipe, her board beneath one sneaker. *Whoosh*, she was off.

Maybe one day I should take up a sport besides shopping. Maybe.

"Hey," he said, a line of sweat trickling down the side of his face. I passed him the cup of beer and he gulped some. "Thanks."

"Ever think about going professional with your skateboarding?" I asked, curious.

With a broad smile, he nodded to the girl currently riding. "Watch her."

"All right."

We all did, soon understanding why. The woman had mad skills; the jumps and stunts she did were nothing short of amazing.

"Wow!" said Hang.

Mind blown, I could only nod in agreement.

"That's what pro looks like," John said. "She's heading up to Seattle for a big contest next week. Be surprised if she sticks around here much longer."

"You're still my hero," I told him, leaning in for a kiss. Because kissing John topped my list of favorite things to do.

"I'm sweaty," he said.

"I don't care."

Black nearly swallowed the blue of his eyes. "Ready to

get out of here?"

I nodded, turning immediately to my friends.

"See you later." Carrie saluted me with her flask.

"Later," I said.

"I won't even ask if you have protection," joked Hang.

"You've seen them, huh?" asked John.

"The small mountain of condoms she's trying to hide in the back of her car? Yes."

"It's not a mountain," I said, suppressing a smile. "And don't act like you didn't take some."

"You wanted to share. Who was I to say no?"

John just laughed, handing me the last of the beer and dropping his board so he could put his shirt on. I downed it quickly for the extra courage. With my hand in his, he led me around the crowd.

"Johnny!" a voice yelled, a man cutting through group. "Hey."

Beside me, John swore.

"There you are." The stranger was tall and thin. His face pale and wasted, despite the pleased smile. "Good to see you."

"What are you doing here, Dillon?" asked John, tone of voice less than welcoming. Subtly he moved to stand in front of me.

"We're brothers. Thought it'd be good to catch up."

"Last time we tried catching up it didn't end so well."

Dillon frowned, scratching at the side of his face. "Brothers fight. It's no big deal."

Around us, the party had paused, people watching.

Shit. And John still held my hand, just had it tucked behind his back.

"Who's the girl?" asked Dillon, craning his neck to try and see me.

"No one."

"A blonde, huh?"

"I repeat, she is no one you need to know. Now what do you want?"

His brother laughed. "You always were a randy little bastard. Anyway, we need to talk, so...get rid of her. Let's get away from here."

"This is all the talking we're doing, right here, right now."

"Johnny."

"I'm serious."

Dillon heaved out a sigh. Hard, sunken eyes glared at the nearby onlookers, and some people in the small crowd backed up.

"Come on, don't be like that. We're family, you and me. We need to be looking out for each other, not fighting like this. What do you think our folks would say?"

John hung his head, shaking it. "Christ. I'm quickly losing interest, so what do you want?"

"I need your help."

"Say the word and I'll get you into rehab. I've got the money; we can sort this shit out. I already told you that." John's grip on my fingers tightened, his feet shifting. "Uncle Levi heard of this great place—"

"I don't want fucking rehab!" Dillon bared his teeth,

visibly fighting for control. "But I need the money."

"No."

"Johnny..."

I fished my front door key out of my pocket, ready to start stabbing at the meth-head's eyes if he took so much as a step toward his brother. Christ, this was so much worse than John had described. Or at least, worse than I'd imagined. His brother was all wired and strung out. The same as Chris had been at the Drop Stop. Just the memory made me want to puke or hit something. I gripped the key hard.

"Sell your fucking vehicle, do something, I don't care. But I am not giving you money for drugs, Dillon," said John. "I know you've still got your car—I saw it parked down the street from Uncle Levi's the other day."

"I just wanted to talk. That prick, he's coming between us. Can't you see?"

"No." John shook his head. "All that shit you take, that's what came between us. Uncle Levi had nothing to do with it."

A tall shadow appeared beside me, moving into place beside John.

Dillon smiled, or tried to. The mix of his barely suppressed anger and his thin, haunted face. "Anders. How you doing, man?"

"Shouldn't be here, D."

"You too? Jesus."

Anders said no more.

"Little brother," said Dillon. "It-it shouldn't be like

this. We should be helping each other, you know?"

"You don't want help," said John, stepping to the side and taking me with him. "Come near me again, it's not going to end well."

"You threatening me, you little shit?" Dillon scoffed. His hands were by his sides, but they were curled into fists.

John didn't back down, not even remotely. All of the lean muscle in his arms seemed pumped, ready. "I won't stop next time and I'll break more than your nose. Stay away."

Anders stepped forward, hands stretched out. "All this fucking tension. How about a beer, D? Why don't we just chill out and get a beer, yeah?"

For a moment, Dillon glared past him to John. Then his eyes flickered up to Anders, and around to the crowd watching the pro skater strut her stuff. "Sure," he said, uncurling his fists and pasting the sick smile back onto his face, as if the whole standoff was no big deal. "Okay. Let's do that."

Meanwhile, John moved, taking me with him. Walking fast, we headed back out toward the main parking lot. The lumps and bumps in the dirt path at night kind of sucked.

"John?" I asked.

He didn't slow down. "Let's just get to the car."

Being blessed with grace, I almost tripped on a tree root and landed on my face. Strong hands grabbed me, halting my fall. "Shit."

"You okay?" he asked.

I nodded. "Can we just calm down a little? Please?"

"Yeah. Sorry. Still okay to come to my place?" he asked, fiddling with his car keys. He opened my door, ushering me in. "You don't have to."

"No. I want to."

"Okay." A muscle in his jaw shifted, barely visible in the moonlight. Carefully, he shut the door, jogging around to the driver's side and jumping in. "I'm sorry, Edie. I didn't want him anywhere near you."

"It's not your fault."

He slammed a hand against the wheel, swearing low and furious. Then he started the engine. Not good.

"Are you okay to drive?" I asked.

For a second, his head slumped back against the seat and he glared at the ceiling. Then his shoulders dropped and he exhaled. "I'm sorry. I'll calm down."

"He's in bad shape, your brother."

John rolled his head to the side to meet my eyes. "He's a fucking mess. What am I going to do?"

"You've done all you can," I said. "He won't accept the help he needs. That's not on you."

"I know," he said. "I just...shit."

"Did he throw the first punch that night you fought?"

"Yeah. He started it." He rubbed the back of his neck. "None of this should have touched you."

"It hasn't."

"Yet." His fingers caressed the side of my face, his gaze tortured. "Maybe I should just take you home."

"Maybe we should go to your place like we planned to. Mom and Matt are having a sappy candlelit dinner," I said. "I doubt she's even thinking about what we might be up to just yet."

He gave me a grim smile. "Okay. Let's go."

A couple of cars were coming in the opposite direction on the narrow road. I almost resented them for slowing us down. The sooner we got away from his brother, the better. But also, I wanted to be alone with John, no distractions. I wanted to make him smile properly. Perhaps this was what addiction felt like, the constant need to get close to him, to feel that high. He put my hand on his knee and I fidgeted with a small hole in his jeans the whole way back to his place.

Normalcy started to return. Each mile the car put between us and Dillon let him fade farther into the past.

"My mom loves this song," I said, humming along to Blondie's "Heart of Glass."

"Yeah?" He smiled. "It's a good song."

Up next came "Get It On" by T. Rex. He had to help me out with that one.

When we arrived, the house lay in darkness, only the porch light on. John pulled up in the empty driveway and I hopped out before he could even offer to open the door. Manners were nice, but alone time mattered and the clock was ticking. He turned on only a small lamp sitting on the entryway table. Inside, nothing had changed since the last time I'd been there. Books, potted plants, huge TV, a bit of mess.

"Would you like a drink or anything?" he asked.

"No. Thank you."

"I stink. Let me grab a quick shower," he said, heading for the stairs. "Come on up if you want. Hang out in my room."

I wanted.

Dark gray sheets covered the bed, the same shade as the walls. At least, where they weren't covered with posters. An old Led Zeppelin poster had joined the Ramones. Which made me wonder...

"I don't think that cassette is stuck."

"Huh?" He rifled through a laundry basket full of clothes all neatly folded. First came boxer briefs, followed by a fresh pair of jeans and a faded green T-shirt. Though really, who needed clothes?

"The cassette tape you claimed was stuck in your car stereo," I said, sitting on the edge of his bed. "I don't think it is. I think you just like the music and don't want to admit it for some reason."

Half facing away from me like he was, I almost didn't catch his smile. "Honestly?"

"Always."

"The tape was in there when I bought it," he said, rubbing at his chin with the pad of his thumb. "The car used to belong to this guy who did security, touring with bands back in the day. But he got some disease that messed with his eyesight, so he couldn't drive anymore. That's why he sold it to me."

"How sad."

John nodded. "He gave me the posters, too. I left the tape in as a kind of show of respect. I mean, it's not like I've got another to replace it."

Interesting. "You could hook up your phone, get a system so you can play other music."

"I could." He just watched me.

"Though, honestly?"

"Always."

"I kind of prefer the tape."

"Me too." He smiled.

Not smiling back at him was physically impossible. "You know, I was looking into places that offered those certifications you said you were interested in."

"Oh, yeah?"

"Yeah." I rubbed my hands on his sheets and gripped the edge of the bed, nervous. "There's a place that offers Landscaping near Berkeley."

"Really?" He leaned against a closet door. "That's where you want to go, huh?"

I shrugged, staring at his Chucks. Much less pressure than meeting his eyes. "John, it's...it was just a thought. You know. If you were still interested."

"Let me think about it."

"Of course," I said, pasting on a grin. It wasn't a rejection, it was just a "think about it." And anyway, I had more important things to worry about.

"Right. Shower." He stepped over, kissing me on the forehead. "I won't be long. Read a skating magazine or a textbook or something."

"Thanks." I laughed.

Across the hall, the bathroom door clicked quietly shut. The minute it did, I got busy unlacing my Doc boots. Off went the socks, the whole lot pushed to the side. Then up I stood and off came my denim dress. Nerves hit me and holy hell, old me would have stopped right there and then. But no. Who would wash John's back if I didn't get naked and go in there? Sacrifices must be made. It was time to get brave.

The door creaked ominously as I opened it, the room already filling with steam.

"Edie?" he asked, sounding surprised. Fair enough. My fearlessness kind of impressed me too.

Carefully, I closed the door and locked it. "Hi."

He pulled back the shower curtain, eyes widening, gaze flitting down my body before returning to my face. "You want to come in?"

"Hygiene is important."

"It is."

He moved over, making room for me before drawing me into the small space. Then he kissed me over and over, brushing his lips on the mine, making me crazy with his mouth. Taking it easy and taking his time. The boy made my stomach dip and my head spin. It was out of control, the way he affected me. I slid my hands over his wet skin, up his chest and onto his shoulders. Fingers digging in just a little.

The ugly stress from earlier in the evening was gone at last, replaced by a wholly different feeling.

"Another first," I said. "Showering with a member of the opposite sex."

"I like being part of your firsts."

"Yeah?" I slid my fingers down over his flat belly, getting closer to my target. "I've never actually touched your bare penis. Only through your clothes. Do you realize that?"

"No?"

"No."

Dark, intense eyes stared straight into mine. "Edie, you can touch whatever you want."

I didn't need to be told twice. The skin was so incredibly soft. But the flesh beneath had started hardening, thickening in the loose grip of my fingers. A real live dick. Wow.

"You have this little frown of concentration," he mumbled, lips brushing over my forehead.

"Well, I find this very interesting," I said.

"You make me sound like a science project."

"Do I?"

My fingers strayed lower, discovering the even-softer feel of his sac. Stomach muscles tightening, he widened his feet a little, giving me room to play. Honestly, though, it was his actual penis and getting a good reaction from it that had me really curious. I gripped him more firmly, blinking the water out of my eyes to better see the veins standing out. Over and around, my thumb brushed the smooth crown or the head or whatever the hell it was called. Such a fascinating shape, especially with the little

tuck-in bit interrupting the flare. Guess my fumbling min-
istrations didn't feel too bad, because it wasn't long before
he swore under his breath.

"You okay?" I asked, pushing back my wet hair and
giving his cock a small squeeze. "Is this okay?"

John's breath hitched. "It definitely is."

"I want to make you come."

"Okay. Soap up your hand," he instructed.

I did, then stroked him experimentally, fingers firmer
than before. "Like this?"

"Mind if I show you?"

"No."

"Here." His hand covered mind, gripping tighter,
pulling a little harder. "That's it. That feels damn good."

Together we worked him toward release. He grew
larger, skin hot and flushed by all the blood beneath. The
feel of him in my hand was magnificent. And the way his
whole body hardened, muscles tensing, lungs and heart
pumping so fast. It was intoxicating. Touching John, getting him off, got me all worked up as well.

"Edie," he bit out. "Fuck."

Semen striped my belly, coated our combined hands.
He shook, panting, face tipped up to heaven. Then his
arms slipped around me, pulling me in tight. There wasn't
an inch of space between us. Honestly, it was a little
tough to breathe. But there wouldn't be a word of com-
plaint from me.

"Thank you," he said, the words muffled against my
wet hair.

"Anytime. That was fun."

I couldn't hear him laugh, but his chest vibrated against mine. A minute later he said, "Tell me."

"Hmm? Tell you what?"

His mouth moved to my neck, making everything low in my belly seize up in ecstasy. To be alone with him, skin to skin. Absolute bliss. Also, giving him pleasure turned me on.

"Say it again," he said.

"Oh." *Duh.* "I love you."

And the slow smile that spread across his face, it was everything.

chapter
forty-six

"I can't get the zip up, could you..." I said, walking down the stairs. Still trying to wrestle the stupid thing on the back of my dress into submission. It must have caught on something. "John?"

Everything in the living room was eerie silence and shadows, still only the small lamp on the side table glowing. But this much I could see: John stood close to someone, another male. A horribly familiar one. Face covered in darkness, clothes hanging off his body. Also, the other person, he had something shiny in his hand pointed straight at my boyfriend. A gun.

"Baby, go back upstairs," said John in a voice that was too calm.

I froze.

"Baby," spat the stranger. "Since when do you call your sluts 'baby'?"

Oh, shit. Dillon.

My brain crashed, not wanting to make sense of the scene. "What is this?"

347

"Go back up," John repeated. "Wait for me in my room."

"This isn't even your real home," said Dillon.

"Get upstairs!"

My whole body jolted at the tone of John's voice, the volume. And this...

Shoving his gun under John's chin, Dillon snarled, "She's not going anywhere. Get your ass down here, bitch."

I made my way down the rest of the stairs, one step at a time. Part of me was screaming in panic, making even putting one foot in front of the other a frantic challenge.

But another part of me was quiet, insulated from the fear. Truth was, I knew what was happening downstairs even before I saw the gunmetal glint in Dillon's hand. Danger had a smell. A *taste*. I recognized it in an instant. It was all just as it had been. I was back at the Drop Stop all over again. Beer and blood. Cigarettes and lies.

Except some crazy part of me said that was a lie; that I had never escaped from the Drop Stop. All this time, we had always been here. There had just been me, and John, and a gun with bullets.

I stopped at the bottom of the steps, torn between getting to John's side and getting away from the violence.

"Introduce me properly, little brother."

"This doesn't involve her."

A fist flew, smashing into John's face, once, twice, three times. Then fingers grabbed a handful of his hair, tugging hard. "I'm in charge. You'll both do as you're fucking told."

John's breath hitched in pain. "Dillon, let her go. Just let her go and I'll do whatever the fuck you want. I'll start selling again."

"It's too fucking late for that," said his older brother, still pulling at his hair. "You little shit. This is all your fault, getting out of the business, leaving me on my own."

"I know."

"Get over here," his brother said to me, waving the gun in my general direction.

It wasn't fear that made my hands shake. It was anger. I walked toward him. "You're the asshole who messed with his car and beat him up."

Dillon chuckled, the sick bastard. "I like her. Too fat, but I bet she sucks cock real good. All hungry-like, right?"

John hissed in fury, blood dripping down his chin, onto the ground. My heart stuttered, hurting. The asshole was going to pay for that.

"What do you want, Dillon?" I asked, voice almost calm. "Why are you here?"

"Come to see my little brother." He gave John a shake via the fistful of hair. God, I wanted to kill him. "We've got different business to attend to now. I need your money, all the cash you saved the last few years. I know you've fucking got it."

"You can have it. But she walks out the door unharmed," said John. "Now."

"You're not giving the fucking orders here. How many times do I have to tell you?"

"I won't do shit for you so long as she's here." With the back of his hand, he wiped blood from his mouth.

"Jesus."

"Now, Dillon!"

At this, the man flew into a rage, swinging the gun. It crashed into John's already-battered face as he coldcocked his brother. Bone crunched; I could hear it. John fell to his knees.

"What have you done?" I dropped down at John's side, trying to wipe away the blood, feel for a pulse. Trying to do something.

"Just returning the favor," drawled Dillon. "He broke my nose, so I broke his."

Curled up on the floor, John remained still. I gritted my teeth and tried to calm myself down, tried to find some sign of life. Slowly, his chest moved in and out. *Yes. Thank God.* And there stood Dillon, towering over us, all smiles. So damn happy with himself, the bastard. Brother or not, I'd kill him.

"You did more than break his nose, you asshole," I said. "He's out cold."

Dillon frowned.

"How do you think you're going to get your money now, huh?" I sneered, more pissed off in my life than I could ever remember being. Hadn't we been through enough already? No. This wasn't happening. I would not do this again.

For a moment, the meth-head just looked confused, blinking over and over again. "Well, we wait for him to wake up."

"No," I said simply. "God, you're so fucking stupid. You didn't think this through at all, did you?"

"Don't talk to me like that."

The gun got shoved in my face, barrel staring me down between the eyes. And there I stayed, on my knees, the perfect target. Didn't matter. One mistake, I just needed him to make one mistake so I could bring the asshole down. If I could get the jump on him...

"Smart people put their money in banks, Dillon. What did you think?" I asked. "That he'd have it stashed in his mattress or something?"

"It's drug money. No, there's no way it isn't here somewhere."

"It's in the bank," I singsonged.

"You're lying!"

I *was* lying. It was easy. Just like John with Chris, trying to get through this alive. If Dillon thought the money wasn't here, he'd just have to go. "We did different deposits at different places. I helped him set it up, to make sure it was safe."

Dillon snarled. "Shut up."

"Fact is, he didn't trust you. I mean, come on, you've been practically stalking him, for fuck's sake." My smile was all teeth. "Hello."

"No!"

"Run, Dillon. Leave. Now. There's nothing for you here."

Just like he had with his brother, he grabbed a handful of my wet hair. The gun pressed hard into my forehead. Bet he thought he'd make me cry or piss myself or beg for my life. Not happening.

"It's just past ten," I said, cool as can be. "We've got friends from the field party coming over soon. Anders and Hang and some of the other guys from the basketball team."

Nervous, his gaze darted to the door.

"Yeah, a whole bunch of them are coming over to smoke some weed and drink a few beers."

"You're lying," he repeated. Though not sounding quite so sure of himself now.

"Why do you think we were upstairs having a quickie? It's Saturday night. Party time, duh. We've got things to do."

The gun shook in his hands, his thin lips drawn wide. "No. No one's coming. Uncle Levi—"

"Can't stand you," I finished for him. "But John he just loves. Drives you nuts, doesn't it?"

"You talk too fucking much." He yanked at my hair, tearing some loose. Tears of pain filled my eyes, but I didn't make a noise. I was done playing victim. And still his hand kept jittering, finger caressing the trigger. "Johnny'll wake up soon. Until then, keep your trap shut."

"If you haven't caused him any permanent brain damage. There could be swelling, internal bleeding." I stopped, saying a quick prayer that this really was all lies. "Is that what you wanted for your brother?"

"I didn't hit him that hard."

"Yes you did."

"Well, I didn't mean to!"

"Oh, I think you did," I said. "He needs an ambulance, Dillon. Medical attention."

Gaze torn, agonized, he stared at John still lying so frighteningly quiet on the floor. That's when I made my move, smacking the gun, trying to knock it out of his hand. I grabbed at his wrist, putting my whole body weight behind it, knocking him off balance. He was taller than me but sickly and rake thin. At least I had weight on him. A startled sort of sound left his throat. We wrestled over the weapon, me trying to drag his hand down and pry his fingers open. It went off. The clap of the noise like a shock wave, weapon discharging. Nothing I hadn't heard before. Pain flashed through me, but adrenaline drowned it out.

His hands were slickened with sweat, but it wasn't enough. I wasn't strong enough.

Eventually, Dillon threw me off, kicking me in the stomach for good measure. Blood dampened my side and I sunk to my knees. *Shit.* So this was what it felt like to get shot. It sucked, big time.

He backhanded me.

Still I smiled up at him. "Gunshot," I said, a note of triumph in my voice. "Someone's calling the cops right now."

Nose wrinkled, his gaze was incredulous. "You're fucking crazy."

"And you're not the first dickhead to pull a gun on

me." I managed a shrug.

Poor Dillon. The frown worsened as he looked between me and John. Down the street, a car honked. Dillon jumped.

"Shit," he muttered. "You're that girl. The one who was at the Drop Stop with him, right?"

"Yep." I grinned, blood dribbling from my lip. "And if you think there's anything I wouldn't do to protect your brother, then you're the one that's fucking crazy."

He just looked at me.

The inside of my mouth tasted like blood. Gross, I must have bitten my tongue. I spat onto the ground and made a mental note to apologize to Levi later. If I was still alive. At this rate, who knew? But at least I'd go out fighting. John remained still and silent. My heart felt swollen at the sight. Like it was somehow at two or three times its capacity. Thank God I'd told him I loved him.

If it had to end, at least he knew. To think, Hang and I had joked about it just the other night. *Shit.*

I didn't want to die.

The thought hit me out of nowhere. All of the crazy, risky, wild, dangerous, irrational things I'd been doing, like rushing through my firsts. I'd been wrong, desperate. Just waiting for the end. Waiting for the man with the gun.

Now here he was, and I wanted more time. Not just a bunch of quick thrills. But *time.*

Time with John and time with Mom, too. Time to graduate and move out. Time to travel and grow. I wanted more of everything, but the choice was out of my hands.

I pulled myself to my feet, legs trembling.

The gun barrel was suspended in space, mere inches from my head.

It was shaking. Dillon's hand was shaking. I looked past the gun, fixing my eyes on him. The arm holding the gun was outstretched, the man's weight leaning back away from me, as if the gun was his shield. His confidence had fled.

"Shoot me, and they put you in jail and throw away the key," I said. "You'll be cuffed and locked up in a cell before John even comes to. And you'll be out of his life. Forever."

No matter how this turned out for me, John would live. He would be free. He would have time.

"There's nothing here for you anymore," I said. "And there never will be."

Without a word, Dillon turned and staggered out of the house. The front door banging shut as he disappeared into the darkness.

Gone. Holy shit, he was gone.

Relief swamped me. Hope. I didn't even realize tears were flowing down my face for a while. Panic had held the pain in check. With Dillon gone, the bullet wound in my side sang with agony. I'd been shot. *Holy shit.* Thankfully my brain kicked in. I needed a phone. But moving was out since I suddenly felt like I'd been hit by a truck.

"Think," I ordered myself.

John's back pocket. It was where he kept his cell. I

crawled closer to him, feeling up his ass without any of the usual euphoria associated with the act.

"Edie..." he mumbled.

I held my face close to his, trying to smile but not quite managing. "It's okay—I'm getting help."

"My brother. Where is he?"

"He's gone. Everything's going to be all right." God, I hoped it would be.

The cell's screen was cracked, but it lit up. Blood smeared the screen and I held it to my ear, listening to the ringing. It didn't take long. I squeezed my eyelids shut, gulping as the tears of pain and relief flowed.

"H-hello? We need help..."

epilogue

"We had such a weird beginning, you and me."

John glanced up from his textbook and smiled. "We've had a weird everything."

"True."

Christmas Eve and we were sitting at the dining table at my house, pretending to study. It was basically the only way to make Mom feel safe. After all, we couldn't be getting into gunfights with drug addicts if we were studying. Surely.

It had taken her a while to calm down after the Dillon incident. I couldn't really blame her. Almost having your child killed twice in one year seemed excessive, even to me. She'd tried to ban John from my life. There'd been tears and tantrums, and not only on my side. First she'd threatened me with Arizona, then with returning to my old school. Even Grandma flew out to yell at me, Mom, and anyone else who'd listen. Luckily, Matt put on the charm and calmed her down. Some of the time, at least.

For a month or so, John and I had only been allowed to see each other at school. But we'd waited her out. I had a newfound appreciation for having at least a little patience, and John had been understanding about the whole thing. After all, I had gotten shot. We were both alive, however, and he told me he wasn't going anywhere without me.

There'd been no major internal injuries, thank God. Though there had been surgery to retrieve the bullet. Come summer, the scar wouldn't stop me from wearing a bikini, and John's broken nose gave him a kind of rough look that I liked. If anything, Dillon's attack had only brought us closer. It was us against the world, forever and ever.

The local reporters used the same shitty old photo from last time when they reported on the attack, bless them. I continued to avoid any news or social media. Maybe I'd start new accounts next year, give being normal a chance once all of the crazy calmed down.

School had been a bit hysterical with the news for a while. Hang, Carrie, and Sophia had taken turns at the hospital with me, and then visiting me at home. Bringing me frequent updates and flowers from John. Mom had known better than to confiscate my phone, so he and I had been able to talk whenever we wanted. When I got back to school, he and Anders played bodyguard, making sure nobody jostled me or got in my face.

Eventually everything went back to the way it had been before. People still gave me curious looks in the hallways sometimes, but whatever.

Dillon had disappeared. The cops said it looked like John's parents' place had been cleaned out, abandoned. It might have been tough for John to accept for a while, but I hope his brother stayed gone. His mom had phoned me in tears, apologizing for her eldest son while thanking me for protecting her youngest. Both of his parents had been down while I'd been in the hospital and resting, so I didn't get to meet them in person. We were thinking of maybe taking a road trip to visit them once school finished.

Meanwhile, our study date...

From over on the living room couch, Mom gave us a look. Matt's arm was tight around her shoulders, a bridal magazine open in her lap. I waved and she gave me a small shake of the head before turning back to the Christmas special on TV. At least she didn't glare at John. Maybe the time of year had softened her some, I don't know. I'd turned eighteen a few weeks ago, and it seemed like she'd dialled down on the anger since then. It might have been due to John giving me a friendship ring. The platinum and diamond band had blown my mind and given Mom a mild panic attack. I secretly think John enjoyed that. He'd assured me he still had funds to pay for his landscape certification program and getting set up down in Berkley when the time came.

"How do you think it ends?" I asked, biting the end of a pen.

"How does it end?"

"Yeah."

"You want us to break up?"

"No! Of course not." I grabbed his hand, holding on tight. "I was just wondering."

Heavy sigh. "You're thinking spontaneous combustion or death by random chicken attack, aren't you? That sort of thing?"

"Something like that. Though it would take a lot of chickens." I frowned. "Of course we'll die tragically, each reaching for the other."

"Right."

"While getting pecked to death."

"Sounds fun."

"Well, I don't know about it being a good time. But it would certainly be dramatic."

With a line between his brows, he shook his head. "Think we've had enough drama."

I just smiled. For a while we sat in silence.

"I love you, you know?" he said.

I smiled. "I know. I love you too."

"And it doesn't end, Edie," he answered eventually. "It keeps going. If we want it to."

"I want it to."

He nodded like it was decided.

Because it was.

acknowledgments

This is a book that's been cooking in the back of my brain for a couple of years now. And I have a whole bunch of people to thank for their friendship, support, and assistance in getting it to publication. First and most importantly, my husband, because he's awesome and he too worked damn hard on this book. In no particular order and for a whole bundle of different reasons, many thanks to...Amy Tannenbaum, Tijan, Kristen Callihan, Milasy Mugnolo, Joanna Wylde, Jen Frederick, Jennifer Armentrout, Hang Le, Sali Pow, Lily Reads Books, Joel Naoum, Danielle Sanchez, Kristy Bromberg, Adele Walsh, Danielle Binks, Chelsea M Cameron, Mish, Katy Evans, Kristen Ashley, and Erika Moutaw Wynne. Extra special thanks to the Groupies who are always so supportive.

Find Kylie at:

www.kyliescott.com

Facebook: www.facebook.com/kyliescottwriter

Twitter: @kyliescottbooks

Instagram: kylie_scott_books

Pinterest: @kyliescottbooks

BookBub: www.bookbub.com/authors/kylie-scott

To learn about exclusive content, my upcoming releases and giveaways, join my newsletter:

https://kyliescott.com/subscribe

Also by Kylie Scott

It Seemed Like a Good Idea at the Time

Made in the USA
Middletown, DE
12 October 2018